ANGELS AT THE RITZ

Angels at the Ritz

and Other Stories

WILLIAM TREVOR

THE BODLEY HEAD

LONDON   SYDNEY

TORONTO

ACKNOWLEDGMENTS

These stories first appeared in *Encounter*, the *Irish Press*, the *London Magazine*, the *New Review*, *Nova*, *Transatlantic Review*, *The Eighth Ghost Book*, *Winter's Tales from Ireland*.

© William Trevor 1975
ISBN 0 370 10603 2
Printed in Great Britain for
The Bodley Head Ltd
9 Bow Street, London WC2E 7AL
by Unwin Brothers Ltd, Woking
Set in Monotype Plantin
by Gloucester Typesetting Co. Ltd
First published 1975
Reprinted 1976

CONTENTS

In Isfahan

They met in the most casual way, in the upstairs office of Chaharbagh Tours Inc. In the downstairs office a boy asked Normanton to go upstairs and wait: the tour would start a little later because they were having trouble with the engine of the minibus.

The upstairs office was more like a tiny waiting-room than an office, with chairs lined against two walls. The chairs were rudimentary: metal frames, and red plastic over foam rubber. There was a counter stacked with free guides to Isfahan in French and German, and guides to Shiraz and Persepolis in English as well. The walls had posters on them, issued by the Iranian Tourist Board: Mount Damavand, the Chalus road, native dancers from the Southern tribes, club-swinging, the Apadana Palace at Persepolis, the Theological School in Isfahan. The fees and conditions of Chaharbagh Tours were clearly stated: *Tours by De Lux microbus. Each Person Rls. 375 ($5). Tours in French and English language. Microbus comes to Hotel otherwise you'll come to Office. All Entrance Fees. No Shopping. Chaharbagh Tours Inc. wishes you the best.*

She was writing an air-mail letter with a ballpoint pen, leaning on a brochure which she'd spread out on her hand-bag. It was an awkward arrangement, but she didn't seem to mind. She wrote steadily, not looking up when he entered, not pausing to think about what each sentence might contain. There was no one else in the upstairs office.

He took some leaflets from the racks on the counter. *Isfahan*

était capitale de l'Iran sous les Seldjoukides et les Safavides.
Sous le règne de ces deux dynasties l'art islamique de l'Iran avait
atteint son apogée.

'Are you going on the tour?'

He turned to look at her, surprised that she was English.
She was thin and would probably not be very tall when she
stood up, a woman in her thirties, without a wedding ring.
In a pale face her eyes were hidden behind huge round sunglasses. Her mouth was sensuous, the lips rather thick, her
hair soft and black. She was wearing a pink dress and white
high-heeled sandals. Nothing about her was smart.

In turn she saw a man who seemed to her to be typically
English. He was middle-aged and greying, dressed in a linen
suit and carrying a linen hat that matched it. There were lines
and wrinkles in his face, about the eyes especially, and the
mouth. When he smiled more lines and wrinkles gathered.
His skin was tanned, but with the look of skin that usually
wasn't: he'd been in Persia only a few weeks, she reckoned.

'Yes, I'm going on the tour,' he said. 'They're having
trouble with the minibus.'

'Are we the only two?'

He said he thought not. The minibus would go round the
hotels collecting the people who'd bought tickets for the tour.
He pointed at the notice on the wall.

She took her dark glasses off. Her eyes were her startling
feature: brown, beautiful orbs, with endless depth, mysterious
in her more ordinary face. Without the dark glasses she had
an Indian look: lips, hair and eyes combined to give her that.
But her voice was purely English, made uglier than it might
have been by attempts to disguise a Cockney twang.

'I've been writing to my mother,' she said.

He smiled at her and nodded. She put her dark glasses on
again and licked the edges of the air-mail letter-form.

'Microbus ready,' the boy from downstairs said. He was a

8

smiling youth of about fifteen with black-rimmed spectacles and very white teeth. He wore a white shirt with tidily rolled-up sleeves, and brown cotton trousers. 'Tour commence please,' he said. 'I am Guide Hafiz.'

He led them to the minibus. 'You German two?' he enquired, and when they replied that they were English he said that not many English came to Persia. 'American,' he said. 'French. German people often.'

They got into the minibus. The driver turned his head to nod and smile at them. He spoke in Persian to Hafiz, and laughed.

'He commence a joke,' Hafiz said. 'He wish me the best. This is the first tour I make. Excuse me, please.' He perused leaflets and guide-books, uneasily licking his lips.

'My name's Iris Smith,' she said.

His, he revealed, was Normanton.

They drove through blue Isfahan, past domes and minarets, and tourist shops in the Avenue Chaharbagh, and blue mosaic on surfaces everywhere, and blue taxi-cabs. Trees and grass had a precious look because of the arid earth. The sky was pale with the promise of heat.

The minibus called at the Park Hotel and at the Intercontinental and the Shah Abbas, where Normanton was staying. It didn't call at the Old Atlantic, which Iris Smith had been told at Teheran Airport was cheap and clean. It collected a French party and a German couple who were having trouble with sun-burn, and two wholesome-faced American girls. Hafiz continued to speak in English, explaining that it was the only foreign language he knew. 'Ladies-gentlemen, I am a student from Teheran,' he announced with pride, and then confessed: 'I do not know Isfahan well.'

The leader of the French party, a testy-looking man whom

Normanton put down as a university professor, had already protested at their guide's inability to speak French. He protested again when Hafiz said he didn't know Isfahan well, complaining that he had been considerably deceived.

'No, no,' Hafiz replied. 'That is not my fault, sir, I am poor Persian student, sir. Last night I arrive in Isfahan the first time only. It is impossible my father send me to Isfahan before.' He smiled at the testy Frenchman. 'So listen please, ladies-gentlemen. This morning we commence happy tour, we see many curious scenes.' Again his smile flashed. He read in English from an Iran Air leaflet: '*Isfahan is the showpiece of Islamic Persia, but founded at least two thousand years ago!* Here we are, ladies-gentlemen, at the Chehel Sotun. This is pavilion of lyric beauty, palace of forty columns where Shah Abbas II entertain all royal guests. All please leave microbus.'

Normanton wandered alone among the forty columns of the palace. The American girls took photographs and the German couple did the same. A member of the French party operated a moving camera, although only tourists and their guides were moving. The girl called Iris Smith seemed out of place, Normanton thought, teetering on her high-heeled sandals.

'So now Masjed-e-Shah,' Hafiz cried, clapping his hands to collect his party together. The testy Frenchman continued to expostulate, complaining that time had been wasted in the Chehel Sotun. Hafez smiled at him.

'*Masjed-e-Shah,*' he read from a leaflet as the minibus began again, '*is most outstanding and impressive mosque built by Shah Abbas the Great in early seventeenth century.*'

But when the minibus drew up outside the Masjed-e-Shah it was discovered that the Masjed-e-Shah was closed to tourists because of renovations. So, unfortunately, was the Sheikh Lotfollah.

'So commence to carpet-weaving,' Hafiz said, smiling and shaking his head at the protestations of the French professor.

The cameras moved among the carpet-weavers, women of all ages, producing at speed Isfahan carpets for export. 'Look now at once,' Hafiz commanded, pointing at a carpet that incorporated the features of the late President Kennedy. 'Look please on this skill, ladies-gentlemen.'

In the minibus he announced that the tour was now on its way to the Masjed-e-Jamé, the Friday Mosque. This, he reported after a consultation of his leaflets, displayed Persian architecture of the ninth to the eighteenth century. '*Oldest and largest in Isfahan,*' he read. '*Don't miss it! Many minarets in narrow lanes!* All leave microbus, ladies-gentlemen. All return to microbus in one hour.'

At this there was chatter from the French party. The tour was scheduled to be conducted, points of interest were scheduled to be indicated. The tour was costing three hundred and seventy-five rials.

'O.K., ladies-gentlemen,' Hafiz said. 'Ladies-gentlemen come by me to commence informations. Other ladies-gentlemen come to microbus in one hour.'

An hour was a long time in the Friday Mosque. Normanton wandered away from it, through dusty crowded lanes, into market-places where letter-writers slept on their stools, waiting for illiterates with troubles. In hot, bright sunshine peasants with produce to sell bargained with deft-witted shopkeepers. Crouched on the dust, cobblers made shoes: on a wooden chair a man was shaved beneath a tree. Other men drank sherbet, arguing as vigorously as the heat allowed. Veiled women hurried, pausing to prod entrails at butchers' stalls or to finger rice.

'You're off the tourist track, Mr Normanton.'

Her white high-heeled sandals were covered with dust. She looked tired.

'So are you,' he said.

'I'm glad I ran into you. I wanted to ask how much that dress was.'

She pointed at a limp blue dress hanging on a stall. It was difficult when a woman on her own asked the price of something in this part of the world, she explained. She knew about that from living in Bombay.

He asked the stall-holder how much the dress was, but it turned out to be too expensive, although to Normanton it seemed cheap. The stall-holder followed them along the street offering to reduce the price, saying he had other goods, bags, lengths of cotton, pictures on ivory, all beautiful workmanship, all cheap bargains. Normanton told him to go away.

'Do you live in Bombay?' He wondered if she perhaps was Indian, brought up in London, or half-caste.

'Yes, I live in Bombay. And sometimes in England.'

It was the statement of a woman not at all like Iris Smith: it suggested a grandeur, a certain style, beauty, and some riches.

'I've never been in Bombay,' he said.

'Life can be good enough there. The social life's not bad.'

They had arrived back at the Friday Mosque.

'You've seen all this?' He gestured towards it.

She said she had, but he had the feeling that she hadn't bothered much with the mosque. He couldn't think what had drawn her to Isfahan.

'I love travelling,' she said.

The French party were already established again in the minibus, all except the man with the moving camera. They were talking loudly among themselves, complaining about Hafiz and Chaharbagh Tours. The German couple arrived, their sunburn pinker after their exertions. Hafiz arrived with the two American girls. He was laughing, beginning to flirt with them.

'So,' he said in the minibus, 'we commence the Shaking Minarets. *Two minarets able to shake,*' he read, '*eight kilometres outside the city.* Very famous, ladies-gentlemen, very curious.'

The driver started the bus, but the French party shrilly protested, declaring that the man with the moving camera had been left behind. '*Où est-ce qu'il est?*' a woman in red cried.

'I will tell you a Persian joke,' Hafiz said to the American girls. 'A Persian student commences at a party –'

'*Attention!*' the woman in red cried.

'*Imbecile!*' the professor shouted at Hafiz.

Hafiz smiled at them. He did not understand their trouble, he said, while they continued to shout at him. Slowly he took his spectacles off and wiped a sheen of dust from them. 'So a Persian student commences at a party,' he began again.

'I think you've left someone behind,' Normanton said. 'The man with the moving camera.'

The driver of the minibus laughed and then Hafiz, realising his error, laughed also. He sat down on a seat beside the American girls and laughed unrestrainedly, beating his knees with a fist and flashing his very white teeth. The driver reversed the minibus, with his finger on the horn. 'Bad man!' Hafiz said to the Frenchman when he climbed into the bus, laughing again. 'Heh, heh, heh,' he cried, and the driver and the American girls laughed also.

'*Il est fou!*' one of the French party muttered crossly. '*Incroyable!*'

Normanton glanced across the minibus and discovered that Iris Smith, amused by all this foreign emotion, was already glancing at him. He smiled at her and she smiled back.

Hafiz paid two men to climb into the shaking minarets and shake them. The Frenchman took moving pictures of this motion. Hafiz announced that the mausoleum of a hermit was located near by. He pointed at the view from the roof where they stood. He read slowly from one of his leaflets, informing them that the view was fantastic. 'At the party,' he said to the American girls, 'the student watches an aeroplane on the breast of a beautiful girl. "Why watch you my aeroplane?" the girl commences. "Is it you like my aeroplane?" "It is not the aeroplane which I like," the student commences. "It is the aeroplane's airport which I like." That is a Persian joke.'

It was excessively hot on the roof with the shaking minarets. Normanton had put on his linen hat. Iris Smith tied a black chiffon scarf around her head.

'We commence to offices,' Hafiz said. 'This afternoon we visit Vank Church. Also curious Fire Temple.' He consulted his leaflets. 'An Armenian Museum. *Here you can see a nice collection of old manuscripts and paintings*.'

When the minibus drew up outside the offices of Chaharbagh Tours Hafiz said it was important for everyone to come inside. He led the way, through the downstairs office and up to the upstairs office. Tea was served. Hafiz handed round a basket of sweets, wrapped pieces of candy locally manufactured, very curious taste, he said. Several men in lightweight suits, the principals of Chaharbagh Tours, drank tea also. When the French professor complained that the tour was not satisfactory, the men smiled, denying that they understood either French or English and in no way betraying that they could recognise any difference when the professor changed from one language to the other. It was likely, Normanton guessed, that they were fluent in both.

'Shall you continue after lunch?' he asked Iris Smith. 'The Vank Church, an Armenian museum? There's also the Theological School, which really is the most beautiful of all. No tour is complete without that.'

'You've been on the tour before?'

'I've walked about. I've got to know Isfahan.'

'Then why –'

'It's something to do. Tours are always rewarding. For a start, there are the other people on them.'

'I shall rest this afternoon.'

'The Theological School is easy to find. It's not far from the Shah Abbas Hotel.'

'Are you staying there?'

'Yes.'

She was curious about him. He could see it in her eyes, for she'd taken off her dark glasses. Yet he couldn't believe that he presented as puzzling an exterior as she did herself.

'I've heard it's beautiful,' she said. 'The hotel.'

'Yes, it is.'

'I think everything in Isfahan is beautiful.'

'Are you staying here for long?'

'Until tomorrow morning, the five o'clock bus back to Teheran. I came last night.'

'From London?'

'Yes.'

The tea-party came to an end. The men in the lightweight suits bowed. Hafiz told the American girls that he was looking forward to seeing them in the afternoon, at two o'clock. In the evening, if they were doing nothing else, they might meet again. He smiled at everyone else. They would continue to have a happy tour, he promised, at two o'clock. He would be honoured to give them the informations they desired.

Normanton said goodbye to Iris Smith. He wouldn't, he said, be on the afternoon tour either. The people of a morning tour, he did not add, were never amusing in the afternoon: it wouldn't be funny if the Frenchman with the moving camera got left behind again, the professor's testiness and Hafiz's pidgin English might easily become wearisome as the day wore on.

15

He advised her again not to miss the Theological School. There was a tourist bazaar beside it, with boutiques, where she might find a dress. But prices would be higher there. She shook her head: she liked collecting bargains.

He walked to the Shah Abbas. He forgot about Iris Smith.

She took a mild sleeping-pill and slept on her bed in the Old Atlantic. When she awoke it was a quarter to seven.

The room was almost dark because she'd pulled over the curtains. She'd taken off her pink dress and hung it up. She lay in her petticoat, staring sleepily at a ceiling she couldn't see. For a few moments before she'd slept her eyes had traversed its network of cracks and flaking paint. There'd been enough light then, even though the curtains had been drawn.

She slipped from the bed and crossed to the window. It was twilight outside, a light that seemed more than ordinarily different from the bright sunshine of the afternoon. Last night, at midnight when she'd arrived, it had been sharply different too: as black as pitch, totally silent in Isfahan.

It wasn't silent now. The blue taxis raced their motors as they paused in a traffic-jam outside the Old Atlantic. Tourists chattered in different languages. Bunches of children, returning from afternoon school, called out to one another on the pavements. Policemen blew their traffic whistles.

Neon lights were winking in the twilight, and in the far distance she could see the massive illuminated dome of the Theological School, a fat blue jewel that dominated everything.

She washed herself and dressed, opening a suitcase to find a black and white dress her mother had made her and a black frilled shawl that went with it. She rubbed the dust from her high-heeled sandals with a Kleenex tissue. It would be nicer to wear a different pair of shoes, more suitable for the evening, but that would mean more unpacking and anyway who was there to notice? She took some medicine because for months she'd had a nagging little cough, which usually came on in the evenings. It was always the same: whenever she returned to England she got a cough.

In his room he read that the Shah was in Moscow, negotiating a deal with the Russians. He closed his eyes, letting the newspaper fall on to the carpet.

At seven o'clock he would go downstairs and sit in the bar and watch the tourist parties. They knew him in the bar now. As soon as he entered one of the barmen would raise a finger and nod. A moment later he would receive his vodka lime, with crushed ice. 'You have good day, sir?' the barman would say to him, whichever barman it was.

Since the Chaharbagh tour of the morning he had eaten a chicken sandwich and walked, he estimated, ten miles. Exhausted, he had had a bath, delighting in the flow of warm water over his body, becoming drowsy until the water cooled and began to chill him. He'd stretched himself on his bed and then had slowly dressed, in a different linen suit.

His room in the Shah Abbas Hotel was enormous, with a balcony and blown-up photographs of domes and minarets, and a double bed as big as a nightclub dance-floor. Ever since he'd first seen it he'd kept thinking that his bed was as big as a dance-floor. The room itself was large enough for a quite substantial family to live in.

He went downstairs at seven o'clock, using the staircase because he hated lifts and because, in any case, it was pleasant to walk through the luxurious hotel. In the hall a group of forty or so Swiss had arrived. He stood by a pillar for a moment, watching them. Their leader made arrangements at the desk, porters carried their luggage from the airport bus. Their faces looked happier when the luggage was identified. Swiss archaeologists, Normanton conjectured, a group tour of some Geneva society. And then, instead of going straight to the bar, he walked out of the hotel into the dusk.

They met in the tourist bazaar. She had bought a brooch, a square of coloured cotton, a canvas carrier-bag. When he saw her, he knew at once that he'd gone to the tourist bazaar because she might be there. They walked together, comparing the prices of ivory miniatures, the traditional polo-playing scene, variously interpreted. It was curiosity, nothing else, that made him want to renew their acquaintanceship.

'The Theological School is closed,' she said.

'You can get in.'

He led her from the bazaar and rang a bell outside the school. He gave the porter a few rials. He said they wouldn't be long.

She marvelled at the peace, the silence of the open court-yards, the blue mosaic walls, the blue water, men silently praying. She called it a grotto of heaven. She heard a sound which she said was a nightingale, and he said it might have been, although Shiraz was where the nightingales were. 'Wine and roses and nightingales,' he said because he knew it would please her. Shiraz was beautiful, too, but not as beautiful as Isfahan. The grass in the courtyards of the Theological School was not like ordinary grass, she said. Even the paving stones and the water gained a dimension in all the blueness. Blue was the colour of holiness: you could feel the holiness here.

'It's nicer than the Taj Mahal. It's pure enchantment.'

'Would you like a drink, Miss Smith? I could show you the enchantments of the Shah Abbas Hotel.'

'I'd love a drink.'

She wasn't wearing her dark glasses. The nasal twang of her voice continued to grate on him whenever she spoke, but her eyes seemed even more sumptuous than they'd been in the bright light of day. It was a shame he couldn't say to her that her eyes were just as beautiful as the architecture of the Theological School, but such a remark would naturally be misunderstood.

'What would you like?' he asked in the bar of the hotel. All around them the Swiss party spoke in French. A group of Texan oilmen and their wives, who had been in the bar the night before, were there again, occupying the same corner. The sunburnt German couple of the Chaharbagh tour were there, with other Germans they'd made friends with.

'I'd like some whisky,' she said. 'With soda. It's very kind of you.'

When their drinks came he suggested that he should bring her on a conducted tour of the hotel. They could drink their way around it, he said. 'I shall be Guide Hafiz.'

He enjoyed showing her because all the time she made marvelling noises, catching her breath in marble corridors and fingering the endless mosaic of the walls, sinking her high-heeled sandals into the pile of carpets. Everything made it enchantment, she said: the gleam of gold and mirror-glass among the blues and reds of the mosaic, the beautifully finished furniture, the staircase, the chandeliers.

'This is my room,' he said, turning the key in the lock of a polished mahogany door.

'Gosh!'

'Sit down, Miss Smith.'

They sat and sipped at their drinks. They talked about the room. She walked out on to the balcony and then came and sat down again. It had become quite cold, she remarked, shivering a little. She coughed.

'You've a cold.'

'England always gives me a cold.'

They sat in two dark, tweed-covered armchairs with a glass-topped table between them. A maid had been to turn down the bed. His green pyjamas lay ready for him on the pillow.

They talked about the people on the tour, Hafiz and the testy professor, and the Frenchman with the moving camera. She had seen Hafiz and the American girls in the tourist bazaar, in the teashop. The minibus had broken down that afternoon: he'd seen it outside the Armenian Museum, the driver and Hafiz examining its plugs.

'My mother would love that place,' she said.

'The Theological School?'

'My mother would feel its spirit. And its holiness.'

'Your mother is in England?'

'In Bournemouth.'

'And you yourself –'

'I have been on holiday with her. I came for six weeks and stayed a year. My husband is in Bombay.'

He glanced at her left hand, thinking he'd made a mistake.

'I haven't been wearing my wedding ring. I shall again, in Bombay.'

'Would you like to have dinner?'

She hesitated. She began to shake her head, then changed her mind. 'Are you sure?' she said. 'Here, in the hotel?'

'The food is the least impressive part.'

He'd asked her because, quite suddenly, he didn't like being in this enormous bedroom with her. It was pleasant showing her around, but he didn't want misunderstandings.

'Let's go downstairs,' he said.

In the bar they had another drink. The Swiss party had gone, so had the Germans. The Texans were noisier than they had been. 'Again, please,' he requested the barman, tapping their two glasses.

In Bournemouth she had worked as a shorthand typist for the year. In the past she had been a shorthand typist when she and her mother lived in London, before her marriage. 'My married name is Mrs Azann,' she said.

'When I saw you first I thought you had an Indian look.'

'Perhaps you get that when you marry an Indian.'

'And you're entirely English?'

'I've always felt drawn to the East. It's a spiritual affinity.'

Her conversation was like the conversation in a novelette. There was that and her voice, and her unsuitable shoes, and her cough, and not wearing enough for the chilly evening air: all of it went together, only her eyes remained different. And the more she talked about herself, the more her eyes appeared to belong to another person.

'I admire my husband very much,' she said. 'He's very fine. He's most intelligent. He's twenty-two years older than I am.'

She told the story then, while they were still in the bar. She had, although she did not say it, married for money. And though she clearly spoke the truth when she said she admired her husband, the marriage was not entirely happy. She could not, for one thing, have children, which neither of them had known at the time of the wedding and which displeased her husband when it was established as a fact. She had been displeased herself to discover that her husband was not as rich as he had appeared to be. He owned a furniture business, he'd said in the Regent Palace Hotel, where they'd met by chance when she was waiting for someone else: this was true, but he had omitted to add that the furniture business was doing badly. She had also been displeased to discover on the first night of her marriage that she disliked being touched by him. And there was yet another problem: in their bungalow in Bombay there lived, as well as her husband and herself, his mother and an aunt, his brother and his business manager.

For a girl not used to such communal life, it was difficult in the bungalow in Bombay.

'It sounds more than difficult.'

'Sometimes.'

'He married you because you have an Indian look, while being the opposite of Indian in other ways. Your pale English skin. Your – your English voice.'

'In Bombay I give elocution lessons.'

He blinked, and then smiled to cover the rudeness that might have shown in his face.

'To Indian women,' she said, 'who come to the Club. My husband and I belong to a club. It's the best part of Bombay life, the social side.'

'It's strange to think of you in Bombay.'

'I thought I mightn't return. I thought I'd maybe stay on with my mother. But there's nothing much in England now.'

'I'm fond of England.'

'I thought you might be.' She coughed again, and took her medicine from her handbag and poured a little into her whisky. She drank a mouthful of the mixture, and then apologised, saying she wasn't being very ladylike. Such behaviour would be frowned upon in the Club.

'You should wear a cardigan with that cough.' He gestured at the barman and ordered further drinks.

'I'll be drunk,' she said, giggling.

He felt he'd been right to be curious. Her story was strange. He imagined the Indian women of the Club speaking English with her nasal intonation, twisting their lips to form the distorted sounds, dropping 'h's' because it was the thing to do. He imagined her in the bungalow, with her elderly husband who wasn't rich, and his relations and his business manager. It was a sour little fairy-story, a tale of Cinderella and a prince who wasn't a prince, and the carriage turned into an ice-cold pumpkin. Uneasiness overtook his curiosity, and he wondered again why she had come to Isfahan.

'Let's have dinner now,' he suggested in a slightly hasty voice.

But Mrs Azann, looking at him with her sumptuous eyes, said she couldn't eat a thing.

He would be married, she speculated. There was pain in the lines of his face, even though he smiled a lot and seemed lighthearted. She wondered if he'd once had a serious illness. When he'd brought her into his bedroom she wondered as they sat there if he was going to make a pass at her. But she knew a bit about people making passes, and he didn't seem the type. He was too attractive to have to make a pass. His manners were too elegant; he was too nice.

'I'll watch you having dinner,' she said. 'I don't mind in the least watching you if you're hungry. I couldn't deprive you of your dinner.'

'Well, I am rather hungry.'

His mouth curved when he said things like that, because of his smile. She wondered if he could be an architect. From the moment she'd had the idea of coming to Isfahan she'd known that it wasn't just an idea. She believed in destiny and always had.

They went to the restaurant, which was huge and luxurious like everywhere else in the hotel, dimly lit, with oil lamps on each table. She liked the way he explained to the waiters that she didn't wish to eat anything. For himself, he ordered a chicken kebab and salad.

'You'd like some wine?' he suggested, smiling in the same way. 'Persian wine's very pleasant.'

'I'd love a glass.'

He ordered the wine. She said:

'Do you always travel alone?'

'Yes.'

'But you're married?'

'Yes, I am.'

'And your wife's a home bird?'

'It's a *modus vivendi*.'

She imagined him in a house in a village, near Midhurst possibly, or Sevenoaks. She imagined his wife, a capable woman, good in the garden and on committees. She saw his wife quite clearly, a little on the heavy side but nice, cutting sweet-peas.

'You've told me nothing about yourself,' she said.

'There's very little to tell. I'm afraid I haven't a story like yours.'

'Why are you in Isfahan?'

'On holiday.'

'Is it always on your own?'

'I like being on my own. I like hotels. I like looking at people and walking about.'

'You're like me. You like travel.'

'Yes, I do.'

'I imagine you in a village house, in the Home Counties somewhere.'

'That's clever of you.'

'I can clearly see your wife.' She described the woman she could clearly see, without mentioning about her being on the heavy side. He nodded. She had second sight, he said with his smile.

'People have said I'm a little psychic. I'm glad I met you.'

'It's been a pleasure meeting you. Stories like yours are rare enough.'

'It's all true. Every word.'

'Oh, I know it is.'

'Are you an architect?'

'You're quite remarkable,' he said.

He finished his meal and between them they finished the
wine. They had coffee and then she asked if he would kindly
order more. The Swiss party had left the restaurant,
and so had the German couple and their friends. Other
diners had been and gone. The Texans were leaving just
as Mrs Azann suggested more coffee. No other table was
occupied.

'Of course,' he said.

He wished she'd go now. They had killed an evening together. Not for a long time would he forget either her ugly
voice or her beautiful eyes. Nor would he easily forget the
fairy-story that had gone sour on her. But that was that:
the evening was over now.

The waiter brought their coffee, seeming greatly fatigued
by the chore.

'D'you think,' she said, 'we should have another drink?
D'you think they have cigarettes here?'

He had brandy and she more whisky. The waiter brought
her American cigarettes.

'I don't really want to go back to Bombay,' she said.

'I'm sorry about that.'

'I'd like to stay in Isfahan for ever.'

'You'd be very bored. There's no club. No social life of
any kind for an English person, I should think.'

'I do like a little social life.' She smiled at him, broadening
her sensuous mouth. 'My father was a counter-hand,' she
said. 'In a co-op. You wouldn't think it, would you?'

'Not at all,' he lied.

'It's my little secret. If I told the women in the Club that,
or my husband's mother or his aunt, they'd have a fit. I've

never even told my husband. Only my mother and I share that secret.'

'I see.'

'And now you.'

'Secrets are safe with strangers.'

'Why do you think I told you that secret?'

'Because we are ships that pass in the night.'

'Because you are sympathetic.'

The waiter hovered close and then approached them boldly. The bar was open for as long as they wished it to be. There were lots of other drinks in the bar. Cleverly, he removed the coffee-pot and their cups.

'He's like a magician,' she said. 'Everything in Isfahan is magical.'

'You're glad you came?'

'It's where I met you.'

He rose. He had to stand for a moment because she continued to sit there, her handbag on the table, her black frilled shawl on top of it. She hadn't finished her whisky but he expected that she'd lift the glass to her lips and drink what she wanted of it, or just leave it there. She rose and walked with him from the restaurant, taking her glass with her. Her other hand slipped beneath his arm.

'There's a discotheque downstairs,' she said.

'Oh, I'm afraid that's not really me.'

'Nor me, neither. Let's go back to our bar.'

She handed him her glass, saying she had to pay a visit. She'd love another whisky and soda, she said, even though she hadn't quite finished the one in her glass. Without ice, she said.

The bar was empty except for a single barman. Normanton ordered more brandy for himself and whisky for Mrs Azann. He much preferred her as Iris Smith, in her tatty pink dress and the dark glasses that hid her eyes: she could have been any little typist except that she'd married Mr Azann and had a story to tell.

'It's nice in spite of things,' she explained as she sat down. 'It's nice in spite of him wanting to you-know-what, and the women in the bungalow, and his brother and the business manager. They all disapprove because I'm English, especially his mother and his aunt. He doesn't disapprove because he's mad about me. The business manager doesn't much mind, I suppose. The dogs don't mind. D'you understand? In spite of everything, it's nice to have someone mad about you. And the Club, the social life. Even though we're short of the ready, it's better than England for a woman. There's servants, for a start.'

The whisky was affecting the way she put things. An hour ago she wouldn't have said 'wanting to you-know-what' or 'short of the ready'. It was odd that she had an awareness in this direction and yet could not hear the twang in her voice which instantly gave her away.

'But you don't love your husband.'

'I respect him. It's only that I hate having to you-know-what with him. I really do hate that. I've never actually loved him.'

He regretted saying she didn't love her husband: the remark had slipped out, and it was regrettable because it involved him in the conversation in a way he didn't wish to be.

'Maybe things will work out better when you get back.'

'I know what I'm going back to.' She paused, searching for his eyes with hers. 'I'll never till I die forget Isfahan.'

'It's very beautiful.'

'I'll never forget the Chaharbagh Tours, or Hafiz. I'll never forget that place you brought me to. Or the Shah Abbas Hotel.'

'I think it's time I saw you back to your own hotel.'

'I could sit in this bar for ever.'

'I'm afraid I'm not at all one for night-life.'

'I shall visualise you when I'm back in Bombay. I shall think of you in your village, with your wife, happy in England. I shall think of you working at your architectural plans. I shall often wonder about you travelling alone because your wife doesn't care for it. Your *modus*.'

'I hope it's better in Bombay. Sometimes things are, when you least expect them to be.'

'It's been like a tonic. You've made me very happy.'

'It's kind of you to say that.'

'There's much that's unsaid between us. Will you remember me?'

'Oh yes, of course.'

Reluctantly, she drank the dregs of her whisky. She took her medicine from her handbag and poured a little into the glass and drank that, too. It helped the tickle in her throat, she said. She always had a tickle when the wretched cough came.

'Shall we walk back?'

They left the bar. She clung to him again, walking very slowly between the mosaiced columns. All the way back to the Old Atlantic Hotel she talked about the evening they had spent and how delightful it had been. Not for the world would she have missed Isfahan, she repeated several times.

When they said goodbye she kissed his cheek. Her beautiful eyes swallowed him up, and for a moment he had a feeling that her eyes were the real thing about her, reflecting her as she should be.

He woke at half-past two and could not sleep. Dawn was already beginning to break. He lay there, watching the light increase in the gap he'd left between the curtains so that there'd be fresh air in the room. Another day had passed: he went through it piece by piece, from his early-morning walk to the moment when he'd put his green pyjamas on and got into bed. It was a regular night-time exercise with him. He closed his eyes, remembering in detail.

He turned again into the offices of Chaharbagh Tours and was told by Hafiz to go to the upstairs office. He saw her sitting there writing to her mother, and heard her voice asking him if he was going on the tour. He saw again the sunburnt faces of the German couple and the wholesome faces of the American girls and faces in the French party. He went again on his afternoon walk, and after that there was his bath. She came towards him in the bazaar, with her dark glasses and her small purchases. There was her story as she had told it.

For his part, he had told her nothing. He had agreed with her novelette picture of him, living in a Home Counties village, a well-to-do architect married to a wife who gardened. Architects had become as romantic as doctors, there'd been no reason to disillusion her. She would for ever imagine him travelling to exotic places, on his own because he enjoyed it, because his wife was a home bird.

Why could he not have told her? Why could he not have exchanged one story for another? She had made a mess of things and did not seek to hide it. Life had let her down, she'd let herself down. Ridiculously, she gave elocution lessons to Indian women and did not see it as ridiculous. She had told him her secret, and he knew it was true that he shared it only with her mother and herself.

The hours went by. He should be lying with her in this bed, the size of a dance-floor. In the dawn he should be staring into her sumptuous eyes, in love with the mystery there. He should be telling her and asking for her sympathy, as she had asked for his. He should be telling her that he had walked into a room, not in a Home Counties village, but in harsh, ugly Hampstead, to find his second wife, as once he had found his first, in his bed with another man. He should in humility have asked her why it was that he was naturally a cuckold, why two women of different temperaments and characters had been inspired to have lovers at his expense. He should be telling her, with the warmth of her body warming his, that his second wife had confessed to greater sexual pleasure when she remembered that she was deceiving him.

It was a story no better than hers, certainly as unpleasant. Yet he hadn't had the courage to tell it because it cast him in a certain light. He travelled easily, moving over surfaces and revealing only surfaces himself. He was acceptable as a stranger: in two marriages he had not been forgiven for turning out to be different from what he seemed. To be a cuckold once was the luck of the game, but his double cuckoldry had a whiff of revenge about it. In all humility he might have asked her about that.

At half-past four he stood by the window, looking out at the empty street below. She would be on her way to the bus station, to catch the five o'clock bus to Teheran. He could dress, he could even shave and still be there in time. He could pay, on her behalf, the extra air fare that would accrue. He could tell her his story and they could spend a few days. They could go together to Shiraz, city of wine and roses and nightingales.

He stood by the window, watching nothing happening in the street, knowing that if he stood there for ever he wouldn't find the courage. She had met a sympathetic man, more marvellous to her than all the marvels of Isfahan. She would carry that memory to the bungalow in Bombay, knowing nothing about a pettiness which brought out cruelty in people. And he would remember a woman who possessed, deep beneath her unprepossessing surface, the distinction that her eyes mysteriously claimed for her. In different circumstances, with a less unfortunate story to tell, it would have emerged. But in the early morning there was another truth, too. He was the stuff of fantasy. She had quality, he had none.

The Distant Past

In the town and beyond it they were regarded as harmlessly peculiar. Odd, people said, and in time this reference took on a burnish of affection.

They had always been thin, silent with one another, and similar in appearance: a brother and sister who shared a family face. It was a bony countenance, with pale blue eyes and a sharp, well-shaped nose and high cheek-bones. Their father had had it too, but unlike them their father had been an irresponsible and careless man, with red flecks in his cheeks that they didn't have at all. The Middletons of Carraveagh the family had once been known as, but now the brother and sister were just the Middletons, for Carraveagh didn't count any more, except to them.

They owned four Herefords, a number of hens, and the house itself, three miles outside the town. It was a large house, built in the reign of George II, a monument that reflected in its glory and later decay the fortunes of a family. As the brother and sister aged, its roof increasingly ceased to afford protection, rust ate at its gutters, grass thrived in two thick channels all along its avenue. Their father had mortgaged his inherited estate, so local rumour claimed, in order to keep a Catholic Dublin woman in brandy and jewels. When he died, in 1924, his two children discovered that they possessed only a dozen acres. It was locally said also that this adversity hardened their will and that because of it they came to love the remains of Carraveagh more than they could ever have loved a husband or a wife. They blamed for their ill-fortune the Catholic Dublin woman whom they'd never met and they blamed as well the new national regime, contriving in their eccentric way to relate the two. In the days of the Union Jack such women would have known their place: wasn't it all part and parcel?

Twice a week, on Fridays and Sundays, the Middletons journeyed into the town, first of all in a trap and later in a Ford Anglia car. In the shops and elsewhere they made, quite gently, no secret of their continuing loyalty to the past. They attended on Sundays St Patrick's Protestant Church, a place that matched their mood, for prayers were still said there for the King whose sovereignty their country had denied. The revolutionary regime would not last, they quietly informed the Reverend Packham: what sense was there in green-painted pillar-boxes and a language that nobody understood?

On Fridays, when they took seven or eight dozen eggs to the town, they dressed in pressed tweeds and were accompanied over the years by a series of red setters, the breed there had always been at Carraveagh. They sold the eggs in Keogh's grocery and then had a drink with Mrs Keogh in the part of her shop that was devoted to the consumption of refreshment. Mr Middleton had whiskey and his sister Tio Pepe. They enjoyed the occasion, for they liked Mrs Keogh and were liked by her in return. Afterwards they shopped, chatting to the shopkeepers about whatever news there was, and then they went to Healy's Hotel for a few more drinks before driving home.

Drink was their pleasure and it was through it that they built up, in spite of their loyalty to the past, such convivial relationships with the people of the town. Fat Driscoll, who kept the butcher's shop, used even to joke about the past when he stood with them in Healy's Hotel or stood behind his own counter cutting their slender chops or thinly slicing their liver. 'Will you ever forget it, Mr Middleton? I'd ha' run like a rabbit if you'd lifted a finger at me.' Fat Driscoll would laugh then, rocking back on his heels with a glass of stout in his hand or banging their meat on to his weighing-scales. Mr Middleton would smile. 'There was alarm in your eyes, Mr Driscoll,' Miss Middleton would murmur, smiling also at the memory of the distant occasion.

Fat Driscoll, with a farmer called Maguire and another called Breen, had stood in the hall of Carraveagh, each of them in charge of a shot-gun. The Middletons, children then, had been locked with their mother and father and an aunt into an upstairs room. Nothing else had happened: the expected British soldiers had not, after all, arrived and the men in the hall had eventually relaxed their vigil. 'A massacre they wanted,' the Middletons' father said after they'd gone. 'Damn bloody ruffians.'

The Second World War took place. Two Germans, a man and his wife called Winkelmann who ran a glove factory in the town, were suspected by the Middletons of being spies for the Third Reich. People laughed, for they knew the Winkelmanns well and could lend no credence to the Middletons' latest fantasy: typical of them, they explained to the Winkelmanns, who had been worried. Soon after the War the Reverend Packham died and was replaced by the Reverend Bradshaw, a younger man who laughed also and regarded the Middletons as an anachronism. They protested when prayers were no longer said for the Royal Family in St Patrick's, but the Reverend Bradshaw considered that their protests were as absurd as the prayers themselves had been. Why pray for the monarchy of a neighbouring island when their own island had its chosen President now? The Middletons didn't reply to that argument. In the Reverend Bradshaw's presence they rose to their feet when the BBC played 'God Save the King', and on the day of the coronation of

Queen Elizabeth II they drove into the town with a small Union Jack propped up in the back window of their Ford Anglia. 'Bedad, you're a holy terror, Mr Middleton!' Fat Driscoll laughingly exclaimed, noticing the flag as he lifted a tray of pork-steaks from his display shelf. The Middletons smiled. It was a great day for the Commonwealth of Nations, they replied, a remark which further amused Fat Driscoll and which he later repeated in Phelan's public house. 'Her Britannic Majesty,' guffawed his friend Mr Breen.

Situated in a valley that was noted for its beauty and with convenient access to rich rivers and bogs over which game-birds flew, the town benefited from post-war tourism. Healy's Hotel changed its title and became, overnight, the New Ormonde. Shopkeepers had their shop-fronts painted and Mr Healy organised an annual Salmon Festival. Even Canon Kelly, who had at first commented severely on the habits of the tourists, and in particular on the summertime dress of the women, was in the end obliged to confess that the morals of his flock remained unaffected. 'God and good sense,' he proclaimed, meaning God and his own teaching. In time he even derived pride from the fact that people with other values came briefly to the town and that the values esteemed by his parishioners were in no way diminished.

The town's grocers now stocked foreign cheeses, brie and camembert and Port Salut, and wines were available to go with them. The plush Cocktail Room of the New Ormonde set a standard: the wife of a solicitor, a Mrs O'Brien, began to give six o'clock parties once or twice a year, obliging her husband to mix gin and Martini in glass jugs and herself handing round a selection of nuts and small Japanese crackers. Canon Kelly looked in as a rule and satisfied himself that all was above board. He rejected, though, the mixture in the jugs, retaining his taste for a glass of John Jameson.

From the windows of their convent the Loretto nuns

observed the long, sleek cars with G.B. plates; English and American accents drifted on the breeze to them. Mothers cleaned up their children and sent them to the Golf Club to seek employment as caddies. Sweet shops sold holiday mementoes. The brown, soda and currant breads of Murphy-Flood's bakery were declared to be delicious. Mr Healy doubled the number of local girls who served as waitresses in his dining-room, and in the winter of 1961 he had the builders in again, working on an extension for which the Munster and Leinster Bank had lent him twenty-two thous-and pounds.

But as the town increased its prosperity Carraveagh con-tinued its decline. The Middletons were in their middle-sixties now and were reconciled to a life that became more uncomfortable with every passing year. Together they roved the vast lofts of their house, placing old paint tins and flower-pot saucers beneath the drips from the roof. At night they sat over their thin chops in a dining-room that had once been gracious and which in a way was gracious still, except for the faded appearance of furniture that was dry from lack of polish and of a wallpaper that time had rendered colourless. In the hall their father gazed down at them, framed in ebony and gilt, in the uniform of the Irish Guards. He had conversed with Queen Victoria, and even in their middle-sixties they could still hear him saying that God and Empire and Queen formed a trinity unique in any worthy soldier's heart. In the hall hung the family crest, and on ancient Irish linen the Cross of St George.

The dog that accompanied the Middletons now was called Turloch, an animal whose death they dreaded for they felt they couldn't manage the antics of another pup. Turloch, being thirteen, moved slowly and was blind and a little deaf. He was a reminder to them of their own advancing years and of the effort it had become to tend the Herefords and collect the weekly eggs. More and more they looked forward to Fridays, to the warm companionship of Mrs Keogh and Mr Healy's chatter in the hotel. They stayed longer now with Mrs Keogh and in the hotel, and idled longer in the shops, and drove home more slowly. Dimly, but with no less loyalty, they still recalled the distant past and were listened to without ill-feeling when they spoke of it and of Carraveagh as it had been, and of the Queen whose company their careless father had known.

The visitors who came to the town heard about the Middletons and were impressed. It was a pleasant wonder, more than one of them remarked, that old wounds could heal so completely, that the Middletons continued in their loyalty to the past and that, in spite of it, they were respected in the town. When Miss Middleton had been ill with a form of pneumonia in 1958 Canon Kelly had driven out to Carraveagh twice a week with pullets and young ducks that his housekeeper had dressed. 'An upright couple,' was the Canon's public opinion of the Middletons, and he had been known to add that eccentric views would hurt you less than malice. 'We can disagree without guns in this town,' Mr Healy pronounced in his Cocktail Room, and his visitors usually replied that as far as they could see that was the result of living in a Christian country. That the Middletons bought their meat from a man who had once locked them into an upstairs room and had then waited to shoot soldiers in their hall was a fact that amazed the seasonal visitors. You lived and learned, they remarked to Mr Healy.

The Middletons, privately, often considered that they led a strange life. Alone in their two beds at night they now and again wondered why they hadn't just sold Carraveagh forty-eight years ago when their father had died: why had the tie been so strong and why had they in perversity encouraged it? They didn't fully know, nor did they attempt to discuss the matter in any way. Instinctively they had remained at Carraveagh, instinctively feeling that it would have been cowardly to go. Yet often it seemed to them now to be no more than a game they played, this worship of the distant past. And at other times it seemed as real and as important as the remaining acres of land, and the house itself.

'Isn't that shocking?' Mr Healy said one day in 1967. 'Did you hear about that, Mr Middleton, blowing up them post offices in Belfast?'

Mr Healy, red-faced and short-haired, spoke casually in his Cocktail Room, making midday conversation. He had commented in much the same way at breakfast-time, looking up from the *Irish Independent*. Everyone in the town had said it too: that the blowing up of sub-post offices in Belfast was a shocking matter.

'A bad business,' Fat Driscoll remarked, wrapping the Middletons' meat. 'We don't want that old stuff all over again.'

'We didn't want it in the first place,' Miss Middleton reminded him. He laughed, and she laughed, and so did her brother. Yes, it was a game, she thought: how could any of it be as real or as important as the afflictions and problems of the old butcher himself, his rheumatism and his reluctance to retire? Did her brother, she wondered, privately think so too?

'Come on, old Turloch,' he said, stroking the flank of the red setter with the point of his shoe, and she reflected that you could never tell what he was thinking. Certainly it wasn't the kind of thing you wanted to talk about.

'I've put him in a bit of mince,' Fat Driscoll said, which was something he often did these days, pretending the mince would otherwise be thrown away. There'd been a red setter about the place that night when he waited in the hall for the soldiers: Breen and Maguire had pushed it down into a cellar, frightened of it.

'There's a heart of gold in you, Mr Driscoll,' Miss Middleton murmured, nodding and smiling at him. He was the same age as she was, sixty-six: he should have shut up shop years ago. He would have, he'd once told them, if there'd been a son to leave the business to. As it was, he'd have to sell it and when it came to the point he found it hard to make the necessary arrangements. 'Like us and Carraveagh,' she'd said, even though on the face of it it didn't seem the same at all.

Every evening they sat in the big old kitchen, hearing the news. It was only in Belfast and Derry, the wireless said; outside Belfast and Derry you wouldn't know anything was happening at all. On Fridays they listened to the talk in Mrs Keogh's bar and in the hotel. 'Well, thank God it has nothing to do with the South,' Mr Healy said often, usually repeating the statement.

The first British soldiers landed in the North of Ireland, and soon people didn't so often say that outside Belfast and Derry you wouldn't know anything was happening. There were incidents in Fermanagh and Armagh, in Border villages and towns. One Prime Minister resigned and then another one. The troops were unpopular, the newspapers said; internment became part of the machinery of government. In the town, in St Patrick's Protestant Church and in the Church of the Holy Assumption, prayers for peace were offered, but no peace came.

'We're hit, Mr Middleton,' Mr Healy said one Friday morning. 'If there's a dozen visitors this summer it'll be God's own stroke of luck for us.'

'Luck?'

'Sure, who wants to come to a country with all that malarkey in it?'

'But it's only in the North.'

'Tell that to your tourists, Mr Middleton.'

The town's prosperity ebbed. The Border was more than

sixty miles away, but over that distance had spread some wisps of the fog of war. As anger rose in the town at the loss of fortune so there rose also the kind of talk there had been in the distant past. There was talk of atrocities and counter-atrocities, and of guns and gelignite and the rights of people. There was bitterness suddenly in Mrs Keogh's bar because of the lack of trade, and in the empty hotel there was bitterness also.

On Fridays, only sometimes at first, there was a silence when the Middletons appeared. It was as though, going back nearly twenty years, people remembered the Union Jack in the window of their car and saw it now in a different light. It wasn't something to laugh at any more, nor were certain words that the Middletons had gently spoken, nor were they themselves just an old, peculiar couple. Slowly the change crept about, all around them in the town, until Fat Driscoll didn't wish it to be remembered that he had ever given them mince for their dog. He had stood with a gun in the enemy's house, waiting for soldiers so that soldiers might be killed: it was better that people should remember that.

One day Canon Kelly looked the other way when he saw the Middletons' car coming and they noticed this movement of his head, although he hadn't wished them to. And on another day Mrs O'Brien, who had always been keen to talk to them in the hotel, didn't reply when they addressed her.

The Middletons naturally didn't discuss these rebuffs but they each of them privately knew that there was no conversation they could have at this time with the people of the town. The stand they had taken and kept to for so many years no longer seemed ridiculous in the town. Had they driven with a Union Jack now they would, astoundingly, have been shot.

'It will never cease.' He spoke disconsolately one night, standing by the dresser where the wireless was.

She washed the dishes they'd eaten from, and the cutlery. 'Not in our time,' she said.

'It is worse than before.'

'Yes, it is worse than before.'

They took from the walls of the hall the portrait of their father in the uniform of the Irish Guards because it seemed wrong to them that at this time it should hang there. They took down also the crest of their family and the Cross of St George, and from a vase on the drawing-room mantelpiece they removed the small Union Jack that had been there since the Coronation of Queen Elizabeth II. They did not remove these articles in fear but in mourning for the *modus vivendi* that had existed for so long between them and the people of the town. They had given their custom to a butcher who had planned to shoot down soldiers in their hall and he, in turn, had given them mince for their dog. For fifty years they had experienced, after suspicion had seeped away, a tolerance that never again in the years that were left to them would they know.

One November night their dog died and he said to her after he had buried it that they must not be depressed by all that was happening. They would die themselves and the house would become a ruin because there was no one to inherit it, and the distant past would be set to rest. But she disagreed: the *modus vivendi* had been easy for them, she pointed out, because they hadn't really minded the dwindling of their fortunes while the town prospered. It had given them a life, and a kind of dignity: you could take a pride out of living in peace.

He did not say anything and then, because of the emotion that both of them felt over the death of their dog, he said in a rushing way that they could no longer at their age hope to make a living out of the remains of Carraveagh. They must sell the hens and the four Herefords. As he spoke, he watched

41

her nodding, agreeing with the sense of it. Now and again, he thought, he would drive slowly into the town, to buy groceries and meat with the money they had saved, and to face the silence that would sourly thicken as their own two deaths came closer and death increased in another part of their island. She felt him thinking that and she knew that he was right. Because of the distant past they would die friendless. It was worse than being murdered in their beds.

Angels at the Ritz

The game was played when the party, whichever party it happened to be, had thinned out. Those who stayed on beyond a certain point – beyond, usually, about one o'clock – knew that the game was on the cards and in fact had stayed for that reason. Often, as one o'clock approached, there were marital disagreements about whether or not to go home.

The game of swapping wives and husbands, with chance rather than choice dictating the formations, had been practised in this outer suburb since the mid-1950s. The swinging wives and husbands of that time were now passing into the first years of elderliness, but their party game continued. In the outer suburb it was most popular when the early struggles of marriage were over, after children had been born and were established at school, when there were signs of marital wilting that gin and tonic did not cure.

'I think it's awfully silly,' Polly Dillard pronounced, addressing her husband on the evening of the Ryders' party.

Her husband, whose first name was Gavin, pointed out that they'd known for years that the practice was prevalent at Saturday-night parties in the outer suburb. There'd been, he reminded her, the moment at the Meacocks' when they'd realised they'd stayed too late, when the remaining men threw their car-keys on to the Meacocks' carpet and Sylvia Meacock began to tie scarves over the eyes of the wives.

'I mean, it's silly Sue and Malcolm going in for it. All of a sudden, out of the blue like that.'

'They're just shuffling along with it, I suppose.'

Polly shook her head. Quietly, she said that in the past Sue and Malcolm Ryder hadn't been the kind to shuffle along with things. Sue had sounded like a silly schoolgirl, embarrassed and not looking her in the eye when she told her.

Gavin could see she was upset, but one of the things about Polly since she'd had their two children and had come to live in the outer suburb was that she was able to deal with being upset. She dealt with it now, keeping calm, not raising her voice. She'd have been the same when Sue Ryder averted her eyes and said that she and Malcolm had decided to go in, too, for the outer suburb's most popular party game. Polly would have been astonished and would have said so, and then she'd have attempted to become reconciled to the development. Before this evening came to an end she really would be reconciled, philosophically accepting the development as part of the Ryders' middle age, while denying that it could ever be part of hers.

'I suppose,' Gavin said, 'it's like a schoolgirl deciding to let herself be kissed for the first time. Don't you remember sounding silly then, Polly?'

She said it wasn't at all like that. Imagine, she suggested, finding yourself teamed up with a sweaty creature like Tim Gruffydd. Imagine any schoolgirl in her senses letting Tim Gruffydd within two million miles of her. She still couldn't believe that Sue and Malcolm Ryder were going in for stuff like that. What on earth happened to people? she asked Gavin, and Gavin said he didn't know.

Polly Dillard was thirty-six, her husband two years older. Her short fair hair had streaks of grey in it now. Her thin, rather long face wasn't pretty but did occasionally seem beautiful, the eyes deep blue, the mouth wide, becoming slanted when she smiled. She herself considered that nothing matched properly in her face and that her body was too lanky and her breasts too slight. But after thirty-six years she'd become used to all that, and other women envied her her figure and her looks.

On the evening of the Ryders' party she surveyed the features that did not in her opinion match, applying eye-shadow in her bedroom looking-glass and now and again glancing at the reflection of her husband, who was changing from his Saturday clothes into clothes more suitable for Saturday night at the Ryders': a blue corduroy suit, pink shirt and pinkish tie. Of medium height, fattening on lunches and alcohol, he was dark-haired and still handsome, for his chunky features were only just beginning to trail signs of this telltale plumpness. By profession Gavin Dillard was a direc-tor of promotional films for television, mainly in the soap and detergent field.

The hall-door bell rang as Polly rose from the chair in front of her looking-glass.

'I'll go,' he said, adding that it would be Estrella, their babysitter.

'Estrella couldn't come, I had to ring Problem. Some Irish-sounding girl it'll be.'

'Hannah McCarthy,' a round-faced girl at the door said. 'Are you Mr Dillard, sir?'

He smiled at her and said he was. He closed the door and took her coat. He led her through a white, spacious hall into a sitting-room that was spacious also, with pale blue walls and curtains. One child was already in bed, he told her, the other was still in his bath. Two boys, he explained: Paul and David. His wife would introduce her to them.

'Would you like a drink, Hannah?'

'Well, I wouldn't say no to that, Mr Dillard.' She smiled an extensive smile at him. 'A little sherry if you have it, sir.'

'And how's the old country, Hannah?' He spoke lightly,

trying to be friendly, handing her a glass of sherry. He turned away and poured himself some gin and tonic, adding a sliver of lemon. 'Cheers, Hannah!'

'Cheers, sir! Ireland, d'you mean, sir? Oh, Ireland doesn't change.'

'You go back, do you?'

'Every holidays. I'm in teacher training, Mr Dillard.'

'I was at the Cork Film Festival once. A right old time we had.'

'I don't know Cork, actually. I'm from Listowel myself. Are you in films yourself, sir? You're not an actor, Mr Dillard?'

'Actually I'm a director.'

Polly entered the room. She said she was Mrs Dillard. She smiled, endeavouring to be as friendly as Gavin had been, in case the girl didn't feel at home. She thanked her for coming at such short notice and presumably so far. She was wearing a skirt that Gavin had helped her to buy in Fenwick's only last week, and a white lace blouse she'd had for years, and her jade beads. The skirt, made of velvet, was the same green as the jade. She took the babysitter away to introduce her to the two children.

Gavin stood with his back to the fire, sipping at his gin and tonic. He didn't find it puzzling that Polly should feel so strongly about the fact that Sue and Malcolm Ryder had reached a certain stage in their marriage. The Ryders were their oldest and closest friends. Polly and Sue had known one another since they'd gone together to the Misses Summers' nursery school in Putney. Perhaps it was this depth in the relationship that caused Polly to feel so disturbed by a new development in her friend's life. In his own view, being offered a free hand with an unselected woman in return for agreeing that some man should maul his wife about wasn't an attractive proposition. It surprised him that the Ryders

had decided to go in for this particular party game, and it
surprised him even more that Malcolm Ryder had never
mentioned it to him. But it didn't upset him.

'All right?' Polly enquired from the doorway, with her coat
on. The coat was brown and fur-trimmed and expensive: she
looked beautiful in it, Gavin thought, calm and collected.
Once, a long time ago, she had thrown a milk-jug across a
room at him. At one time she had wept a lot, deploring her
lankiness and her flat breasts. All that seemed strangely out
of character now.

He finished his drink and put the glass down on the mantelpiece. He put the sherry bottle beside the babysitter's glass in
case she should feel like some more, and then changed his
mind and returned the bottle to the cabinet, remembering
that they didn't know the girl: a drunk babysitter – an experience they'd once endured – was a great deal worse than no
babysitter at all.

'She seems very nice,' Polly said in the car. 'She said she'd
read to them for an hour.'

'An hour? The poor girl!'

'She loves children.'

It was dark, half-past eight on a night in November. It was
raining just enough to make it necessary to use the windscreen-
wipers. Automatically, Gavin turned the car radio on: there
was something pleasantly cosy about the glow of a car radio
at night when it was raining, with the background whirr of
the windscreen-wipers and the wave of warmth from the
heater.

'Let's not stay long,' he said.

It pleased her that he said that. She wondered if they were
dull not to wish to stay, but he said that was nonsense.

He drove through the sprawl of their outer suburb, all of it
new, disguised now by the night. Orange street lighting made
the façades of the carefully-designed houses seem different,

changing the colours, but the feeling of space remained, and the uncluttered effect of the unfenced front gardens. Roomy Volvo estate-cars went nicely with the detached houses. So did Vauxhall Victors, and big bus-like Volkswagens. Families were packed into such vehicles on summer Saturday mornings, for journeys to cottages in the Welsh hills or in Hampshire or Herts. The Dillards' cottage was in the New Forest.

Gavin parked the car in Sandiway Crescent, several doors away from the Ryders' house because other cars were already parked closer to it. He'd have much preferred to be going out to dinner in Tonino's with Malcolm and Sue, lasagne and peperonata and a carafe of Chianti Christina, a lazy kind of evening that would remind all of them of other lazy evenings. Ten years ago they'd all four gone regularly to Tonino's trattoria in Greek Street, and the branch that had opened in their outer suburb was very like the original, even down to the framed colour photographs of A.C. Milan.

'Come on *in*!' Sue cried jollily at Number Four Sandiway Crescent. Her face was flushed with party excitement, her large brown eyes flashed adventurously with party spirit. Her eyes were the only outsize thing about her: she was tiny and black-haired, as pretty as a rose-bud.

'Gin?' Malcolm shouted at them from the depths of the crowded hall. 'Sherry, Polly? Burgundy?'

Gavin kissed the dimpled cheek that Sue Ryder pressed up to him. She was in red, a long red dress that suited her, with a red band in her hair and red shoes.

'Yes, wine please, Malcolm,' Polly said, and when she was close enough she slid her face towards his for the same kind of embrace as her husband had given his wife.

'You're looking edible, my love,' he said, a compliment he'd been paying her for seventeen years.

He was an enormous man, made to seem more so by the

smallness of his wife. His features had a mushy look. His head, like a pink sponge, was perched jauntily on shoulders that had once been a force to reckon with in rugby scrums. Although he was exactly the same age as Gavin, his hair had balded away to almost nothing, a rim of fluff not quite encircling the sponge.

'You're looking very smart yourself,' Polly said, a statement that might or might not have been true: she couldn't see him properly because he was so big and she was so close to him, and she hadn't looked when she'd been further away. He was wearing a grey suit of some kind and a blue-striped shirt and the tie of the Harlequins' Rugby Club. Usually he looked smart: he probably did now.

'I'm feeling great,' he said. 'Nice little party we're having, Poll.'

It wasn't really little. Sixty or so people were in the Ryders' house, which was similar to the Dillards' house, well-designed and spacious. Most of the downstairs rooms, and the hall, had coffee-coloured walls, an experiment of Sue's which she believed had been successful. For the party, the bulkier furniture had been taken out of the coffee-coloured sitting-room, and all the rugs had been lifted from the parquet floor. Music came from a tape-recorder, but no one was dancing yet. People stood in small groups, smoking and talking and drinking. No one, so far, appeared to be drunk.

All the usual people were there: the Stubbses, the Burgesses, the Pedlars, the Thompsons, the Stevensons, Sylvia and Jack Meacock, Philip and June Mulally, Oliver and Olive Gramsmith, Tim and Mary-Ann Gruffyd and dozens of others. Not all of them lived in the outer suburb; and some were older, some younger, than the Ryders and the Dillards. But there was otherwise a similarity about the people at the party: they were men who had succeeded or were in the process of succeeding, and women who had kept pace with their husbands' advance. No one looked poor at the Ryders' party.

At ten o'clock there was food, smoked salmon rolled up and speared with cocktail sticks, chicken *vol-au-vent* or beef Stroganoff with rice, salads of different kinds, stilton and brie and Port Salut, and meringues. Wine flowed generously, white burgundy and red. Uncorked bottles were distributed on all convenient surfaces.

The dancing began when the first guests had eaten. To 'Love of the Loved', Polly danced with a man whose name she didn't know, who told her he was an estate agent with an office in Jermyn Street. He held her rather close for a man whose name she didn't know. He was older than Polly, about fifty, she reckoned, and smaller. He had a foxy moustache and foxy hair, and a round stomach, like a ball, which kept making itself felt. So did his knees.

In the room where the food was Gavin sat on the floor with Sylvia and Jack Meacock, and a woman in an orange trouser suit, with orange lips.

'Ralphie wouldn't come,' this woman said, balancing food in the hollow of a fork. 'He got cross with me last night.'

Gavin ate from his fingers a *vol-au-vent* full of chicken and mushrooms that had gone a little cold. Jack Meacock said nothing would hold him back from a party given by the Ryders. Or any party, he added, guffawing, given by anyone. Provided there was refreshment, his wife stipulated. Well naturally, Jack Meacock said.

'He wouldn't come,' the orange woman explained, 'because he thought I misbehaved in Olive Gramsmith's kitchen. A fortnight ago, for God's sake!'

Gavin calculated he'd had four glasses of gin and tonic. He corrected himself, remembering the one he'd had with the babysitter. He drank some wine. He wasn't entirely drunk, he said to himself, he hadn't turned a certain corner, but the corner was the next thing there was.

'If you want to kiss someone you kiss him,' the orange woman said. 'I mean, for God's sake, he'd no damn right to walk into Olive Gramsmith's kitchen. I didn't see you,' she said, looking closely at Gavin. 'You weren't there, were you?'

'We couldn't go.'

'You were there,' she said to the Meacocks. 'All over the place.'

'We certainly were!' Jack Meacock guffawed through his beef Stroganoff, scattering rice on to the coffee-coloured carpet.

'Hullo,' their hostess said, and sat down on the carpet beside Gavin, with a plate of cheese.

'You mean you've been married twelve years?' the estate agent said to Polly. 'You don't look it.'

'I'm thirty-six.'

'What's your better half in? Is here, is he?'

'He directs films. Advertisements for TV. Yes, he's here.'

'That's mine.' He indicated with his head a woman who wasn't dancing, in lime-green. She was going through a bad patch, he said: depressions.

They danced to 'Sunporch Cha-Cha-Cha', Simon and Garfunkel.

'Feeling O.K.?' the estate agent enquired, and Polly said yes, not understanding what he meant. He propelled her towards the mantelpiece and took from it the glass of white burgundy Polly had left there. He offered it to her and when she'd taken a mouthful he drank some from it himself. They danced again. He clutched her more tightly with his arms and flattened a cheek against one of hers, rasping her with his moustache. With dead eyes, the woman in lime-green watched.

At other outer-suburb parties Polly had been through it all

before. She escaped from the estate agent and was caught by Tim Gruffydd, who had already begun to sweat. After that another man whose name she didn't know danced with her, and then Malcom Ryder did.

'You're edible tonight,' he whispered, the warm mush of his lips damping her ear. 'You're really edible, my love.'

'Share my cheese,' Sue offered in the other room, pressing brie on Gavin.

'I need more wine,' the woman in orange said, and Jack Meacock pushed himself up from the carpet. They all needed more wine, he pointed out. The orange woman predicted that the next day she'd have a hangover and Sylvia Meacock, a masculine-looking woman, said she'd never had a hangover in forty-eight years of steady drinking.

'You going to stay a while?' Sue said to Gavin. 'You and Polly going to stay?' She laughed, taking one of his hands because it was near to her. Since they'd known one another for such a long time it was quite in order for her to do that.

'Our babysitter's unknown,' Gavin explained. 'From the bogs of Ireland.'

The orange woman said the Irish were bloody.

'Jack's Irish, actually,' Sylvia Meacock said.

She went on talking about that, about her husband's childhood in County Down, about an uncle of his who used to drink a bottle and a half of whiskey a day – on top of four glasses of stout, with porridge and bread, for his breakfast. If you drank at all you should drink steadily, she said.

Gavin felt uneasy, because all the time Sylvia Meacock was talking about the drinking habits of her husband's uncle in County Down Sue clung on to his hand. She held it lightly, moving her fingers in a caress that seemed to stray outside the realm of their long friendship. He was in love with Polly: he thought that deliberately, arraying the sentiment in his mind as a statement, seeing it suspended there. There was no one he'd

ever known whom he'd been fonder of than Polly, or whom he
respected more, or whom it would upset him more to hurt.
Seventeen years ago he'd met her in the kitchens of the Hotel
Belvedere, Penzance, where they had both gone to work for
the summer. Five years later, having lived with one another
in a flat in the cheaper part of Maida Vale, they'd got married
because Polly wanted to have children. They'd moved to the
outer suburb because the children needed space and fresh air,
and because the Ryders, who'd lived on the floor above theirs
in Maida Vale, had moved there a year before.

'She'll be all right,' Sue said, returning to the subject of
the Irish babysitter. 'She could probably stay the night. She'd
probably be delighted.'

'Oh, I don't think so, Sue.'

He imagined without difficulty the hands of men at the
party unbuttoning Polly's lace blouse, the hands of Jack
Meacock or the sweaty hands of Tim Gruffydd. He imagined
Polly's clothes falling on to a bedroom carpet and then her
thin, lanky nakedness, her small breasts and the faint mark of
her appendix scar. 'Oh, I say!' she said in a way that wasn't
like her when the man, whoever he was, took off his own
clothes. Without difficulty either, Gavin imagined being in a
room himself for the same purpose, with the orange woman
or Sylvia Meacock. He'd walk out again if he found himself
in a room with Sylvia Meacock and he'd rather be in a room
with Sue than with the orange woman. Because he wasn't
quite sober, he had a flash of panic when he thought of what
might be revealed when the orange trouser-suit fell to the
floor: for a brief, disturbing moment he felt it was actually
happening, that in the bonhomie of drunkenness he'd somehow agreed to the situation.

'Why don't we dance?' Sue suggested, and Gavin agreed.

'I think I'd like a drink,' Polly said to Philip Mulally, an
executive with Wolsey Menswear. He was a grey shadow of a

man, not at all the kind to permit himself or his wife to be a party to sexual games. He nodded seriously when Polly interrupted their dance to say she'd like a drink. It was time in any case, he revealed, that he and June were making a move homewards.

'I love you in that lace thing,' Malcolm Ryder whispered boringly as soon as Polly stopped dancing with Philip Mulally. He was standing waiting for her.

'I was saying to Philip I'd like a drink.'

'Of course you must have a drink. Come and quaff a brandy with me, Poll.' He took her by the hand and led her away from the dancers. The brandy was in his den, he said.

She shook her head, following him because she had no option. Above the noise of Cilla Black singing 'Anyone Who Had a Heart' she shouted at him that she'd prefer some more white burgundy, that she was actually feeling thirsty. But he didn't hear her, or didn't wish to. 'Ain't misbehaving,' the foxy estate agent mouthed at her as they passed him, standing on his own in the hall. It was an expression that was often used, without much significance attaching to it, at parties in the outer suburb.

'Evening, all,' Malcolm said in the room he called his den, closing the door behind Polly. The only light in the room was from a desk-lamp. In the shadows, stretched on a mock-leather sofa, a man and a woman were kissing one another. They parted in some embarrassment at their host's jocular greeting, revealing themselves, predictably, as a husband and another husband's wife.

'Carry on, folks,' Malcolm said.

He poured Polly some brandy even though she had again said that what she wanted was a glass of burgundy. The couple on the sofa got up and went away, giggling. The man told Malcolm he was an old bastard.

'Here you are,' Malcolm said, and then to Polly's distaste

he placed his mushy lips on hers and exerted some pressure. The brandy glass was in her right hand, between them: had it not been there, she knew the embrace would have been more intimate. As it was, it was possible for both of them to pretend that what had occurred was purely an expression of Malcolm Ryder's friendship for her, a special little detour to show that for all these years it hadn't been just a case of two wives being friends and the husbands tagging along. Once, in 1965, they'd all gone to the Italian Adriatic together and quite often Malcolm had given her a kiss and a hug while telling her how edible she was. But somehow – perhaps because his lips hadn't been so mushy in the past – it was different now.

'Cheers!' he said, smiling at her in the dimness. For an unpleasant moment she thought he might lock the door. What on earth did you do if an old friend tried to rape you on a sofa in his den?

With every step they made together, the orange woman increased her entwinement of Oliver Gramsmith. The estate agent was dancing with June Mulally, both of them ignoring the gestures of June Mulally's husband, Philip, who was still anxious to move homewards. The Thompsons, the Pedlars, the Stevensons, the Suttons, the Heeresmas and the Fultons were all maritally separated. Tim Gruffydd was clammily tightening his grasp of Olive Gramsmith, Sylvia Meacock's head lolled on the shoulder of a man called Thistlewine.

'Remember the Ritz?' Sue said to Gavin.

He did remember. It was a long time ago, years before they'd all gone together to the Italian Adriatic, when they'd just begun to live in Maida Vale, one flat above the other, none of them married. They'd gone to the Ritz because they couldn't afford it. The excuse had been Polly's birthday.

'March the twenty-fifth,' he said. '1961.' He could feel her breasts, like spikes because of the neat control of her brassière. He'd become too flabby, he thought, since March 25th, 1961.

'What fun it was!' With her dark, petite head on one side, she smiled up at him. 'Remember it all, Gavin?'

'Yes, I remember.'

'I wanted to sing that song and no one would let me. Polly was horrified.'

'Well, it was Polly's birthday.'

'And of course we couldn't have spoiled that.' She was still smiling up at him, her eyes twinkling, the tone of her voice as light as a feather. Yet the words sounded like a criticism, as though she were saying now – fourteen years later – that Polly had been a spoilsport, which at the time hadn't seemed so in the least. Her arms tightened around his waist. Her face disappeared as she sank her head against his chest. All he could see was the red band in her hair and the hair itself. She smelt of some pleasant scent. He liked the sharpness of her breasts. He wanted to stroke her head.

'Sue fancies old Gavin, you know.' Malcolm said in his den.

Polly laughed. He had put a hand on her thigh and the fingers were now slightly massaging the green velvet of her skirt and the flesh beneath it. To have asked him to take his hand away or to have pushed it away herself would have been too positive, too much a reflection of his serious mood rather than her own determinedly casual one. A thickness had crept into his voice. He looked much older than thirty-eight; he'd worn less well than Gavin.

'Let's go back to the party, Malcolm.' She stood up, dislodging his hand as though by accident.

'Let's have another drink.'

He was a solicitor now, with Parker, Hille and Harper. He had been, in fact, a solicitor when they'd all lived in the cheaper part of Maida Vale. He'd still played rugby for the Harlequins then. She and Gavin and Sue used to watch him on Saturday afternoons, in matches against the London clubs, Rosslyn Park and Blackheath, Waterloo, London Welsh, London Irish, and all the others. Malcolm had been a towering wing three-quarter, with a turn of speed that was surprising in so large a man: people repeatedly said, even newspaper commentators, that he should play for England.

Polly was aware that it was a cliché to compare Malcolm as he had been with the blubbery, rather tedious Malcolm beside whom it was unwise to sit on a sofa. Naturally he wasn't the same. It was probably a tedious life being a solicitor with Parker, Hille and Harper day after day. He probably did his best to combat the blubberiness, and no man could help being bald. When he was completely sober, and wasn't at a party, he could still be quite funny and nice, hardly tedious at all.

'I've always fancied you, Poll,' he said. 'You know that.'

'Oh, nonsense, Malcolm!'

She took the brandy glass from him, holding it between them in case he should make another lurch. He began to talk about sex. He asked her if she'd read, a few years ago, about a couple in an aeroplane, total strangers, who had performed the sexual act in full view of the other passengers. He told her a story about Mick Jagger on an aeroplane, at the time when Mick Jagger was making journeys with Marianne Faithfull. He said the springing system of Green Line buses had the same kind of effect on him. Sylvia Meacock was lesbian, he said. Olive Gramsmith was a slapparat. Philip Mulally had once been seen hanging about Shepherd Market, looking at the tarts. He hadn't been faithful to Sue, he said, but Sue knew about it and now they were going to approach all that side of things in a different way. Polly knew about it, too, because Sue had told her: a woman in Parker, Hille and

Harper had wanted Malcolm to divorce Sue, and there'd been, as well, less serious relationships between Malcolm and other women.

'*Since you went away the days grow long*,' sang Nat King Cole in the coffee-coloured sitting-room, '*and soon I'll hear ole winter's song.*' Some guests, in conversation, raised their voices above the voice of Nat King Cole. Others swayed to his rhythm. In the sitting-room and the hall and the room where the food had been laid out there was a fog of cigarette smoke and the warm smell of burgundy. Men sat together on the stairs, talking about the election of Margaret Thatcher as leader of the Conservative party. Women had gathered in the kitchen and seemed quite happy there, with glasses of burgundy in their hands. In a bedroom the couple who had been surprised in Malcolm's den continued their embrace.

'So very good we were,' Sue said on the parquet dance-floor. She broke away from Gavin, seizing him by the hand as she did so. She led him across the room to a teak-faced cabinet that contained gramophone records. On top of it there was a gramophone and the tape-recorder that was relaying the music.

'Don't dare move,' she warned Gavin, releasing his hand in order to poke among the records. She found what she wanted and placed it on the turn-table of the gramophone. The music began just before she turned the tape-recorder off. A cracked female voice sang: '*That certain night, the night we met, there was magic abroad in the air . . .*'

'Listen to it,' Sue said, taking Gavin's hand again and drawing him on to the dancing area.

'*There were angels dining at the Ritz, and a nightingale sang in Berkeley Square.*'

The other dancers, who'd been taken aback by the abrupt change of tempo, slipped into the new rhythm. The two spiky breasts again depressed Gavin's stomach.

'Angels of a kind we were,' Sue said. 'And fallen angels now, Gavin? D'you think we've fallen?'

Once in New York and once in Liverpool he'd made love since his marriage, to other girls. Chance encounters they'd been, irrelevant and unimportant at the time and more so now. He had suffered from guilt immediately afterwards, but the guilt had faded, with both girls' names. He could remember their names if he tried: he once had, when suffering from a bout of indigestion in the night. He had remembered precisely their faces and their naked bodies and what each encounter had been like, but memories that required such effort hadn't seemed quite real. It would, of course, be different with Sue.

'Fancy Sue playing that,' her husband said, pausing outside the den with Polly. 'They've been talking about the Ritz, Poll.'

'Goodness!' With a vividness that was a welcome antidote to Malcolm's disclosure about the sex-life of his guests, the occasion at the Ritz returned to her. Malcolm said:

'It was my idea, you know. Old Gavin and I were boozing in the Hoop and he suddenly said, "It's Polly's birthday next week," and I said ,"For God's sake! Let's all go down to the Ritz."'

'You had oysters, I remember.' She smiled at him, feeling better because they were no longer in the den, and stronger because of the brandy. Malcolm would have realised by now how she felt, he wouldn't pursue the matter.

'We weren't much more than kids.' He seized her hand in a way that might have been purely sentimental, as though he was inspired by the memory.

'My twenty-second birthday. What an extraordinary thing it was to do!'

In fact, it had been more than that. Sitting in the restaurant with people she liked, she'd thought it was the nicest thing that had ever happened to her on her birthday. It was absurd because none of them could afford it. It was absurd to go to the Ritz for a birthday treat: martinis in the Rivoli Bar because Malcolm said it was the thing, the gilt chairs and the ferns. But the absurdity hadn't mattered because in those days nothing much did. It was fun, they enjoyed being together, they had a lot to be happy about. Malcolm might yet play rugby for England. Gavin was about to make his breakthrough into films. Sue was pretty, and Polly that night felt beautiful. They had sat there carelessly laughing, while deferential waiters simulated the gaiety of their mood. They had drunk champagne because Malcolm said they must.

With Malcolm still holding her hand, she crossed the spacious hall of Number Four Sandiway Crescent. People were beginning to leave. Malcolm released his hold of her in order to bid them goodbye.

She stood in the doorway of the sitting-room watching Gavin and Sue dancing. She lifted her brandy glass to her lips and drank from it calmly. Her oldest friend was attempting to seduce her husband, and for the first time in her life she disliked her. Had they still been at the Misses Summers' nursery school she would have run at her and hit her with her fists. Had they still been in Maida Vale or on holiday on the Italian Adriatic she would have shouted and made a fuss. Had they been laughing in the Ritz she'd have got up and walked out.

They saw her standing there, both of them almost in the same moment. Sue smiled at her and called across the coffee-coloured sitting-room, as though nothing untoward were happening, 'D'you think we've fallen, Polly?' Her voice was full of laughter, just like it had been that night. Her eyes still had their party gleam, which probably had been there too.

'Let's dance, Poll,' Malcolm said, putting his arms around her waist from behind.

It made it worse when he did that because she knew by the way he touched her that she was wrong: he didn't realise. He probably thought she'd enjoyed hearing all that stuff about Philip Mulally hanging about after prostitutes and Olive Gramsmith being a slapparat, whatever a slapparat was.

She finished the brandy in her glass and moved with him on to the parquet. What had happened was that the Ryders had had a conversation about all this. They'd said to one another that this was how they wished – since it was the first time – to make a sexual swap. Polly and Gavin were to be of assistance to their friends because a woman in Parker, Hille and Harper had wanted Malcolm to get a divorce and because there'd been other relationships. Malcolm and Sue were approaching all that side of things in a different way now, following the fashion in the outer suburb since the fashion worked wonders with wilting marriages.

'Estrella babysitting, is she?' Malcolm asked. 'All right if you're late, is she? You're not going to buzz off, Poll?'

'Estrella couldn't come. We had to get a girl from Problem.'

He suggested, as though the arrangement were a natural one and had been practised before, that he should drive her home when she wanted to go. He'd drive the babysitter from Problem home also. 'Old Gavin won't want to go,' he pronounced, trying to make it all sound like part of his duties as host. To Polly it sounded preposterous, but she didn't say so. She just smiled as she danced with him.

They'd made these plans quite soberly presumably, over breakfast or when there was nothing to watch on television, or in bed at night. They'd discussed the game that people played with car-keys or playing cards, or by drawing lots in other ways. They'd agreed that neither of them cared for the idea of taking a chance. 'Different,' Malcolm had probably quite casually said, 'if we got the Dillards.' Sue wouldn't have said anything then. She might have laughed, or got up to make tea if they were watching the television, or turned over and gone to sleep. On some other occasion she might have drifted the conversation towards the subject again and Malcolm would have known that she was interested. They would then have worked out a way of interesting their oldest friends. Dancing with Malcolm, Polly watched while Gavin's mouth descended to touch the top of Sue's head. He and Sue were hardly moving on the dance-floor.

'Well, that's fixed up then,' Malcolm said. He didn't want to dance any more. He wanted to know that it was fixed up, that he could return to his party for an hour or so, with something to look forward to. He would drive her home and Gavin would remain. At half-past one or two, when the men threw their car-keys on to the carpet and the blind-folded women each picked one out, Gavin and Sue would simply watch, not taking part. And when everyone went away Gavin and Sue would be alone with all the mess and the empty glasses. And she would be alone with Malcolm.

Polly smiled at him again, hoping he'd take the smile to mean that everything was fixed because she didn't want to go on dancing with him. If one of them had said, that night in the Ritz, that for a couple of hours after dinner they should change partners there'd have been a most unpleasant silence.

Malcolm patted her possessively on the hip. He squeezed her forearm and went away, murmuring that people might be short of drink. A man whom she didn't know, excessively drunk, took her over, informing her that he loved her. As she swayed around the room with him, she wanted to say to Sue and Malcolm and Gavin that yes, they had fallen. Of course Malcolm hadn't done his best to combat his blubberiness, of course he didn't make efforts. Malcolm was awful, and Sue was treacherous. When people asked Gavin if he made films

why didn't he ever reply that the films he made were
television commercials? She must have fallen herself, for it
was clearly in the nature of things, but she couldn't see how.

'It's time we went home, Sue,' Gavin said.

'Of course it isn't, Gavin.'

'Polly – '

'You're nice, Gavin.'

He shook his head. He whispered to her, explaining that
Polly wouldn't ever be a party to what was being suggested.
He said that perhaps they could meet some time, for a drink
or for lunch. He would like to, he said; he wanted to.

She smiled. That night in the Ritz, she murmured, she
hadn't wanted to be a blooming angel. 'I wanted you,' she
murmured.

'That isn't true.' He said it harshly. He pushed her away
from him, wrenching himself free of her arms. It shocked
him that she had gone so far, spoiling the past when there
wasn't any need to. 'You shouldn't have said that, Sue.'

'You're sentimental.'

He looked around for Polly and saw her dancing with a
man who could hardly stand up. Some of the lights in the
room had been switched off and the volume of the tape-
recorder had been turned down. Simon and Garfunkel were
whispering about Mrs Robinson. A woman laughed shrilly,
kicking her shoes across the parquet.

Sue wasn't smiling any more. The face that looked up at
him through the gloom was hard and accusing. Lines that
weren't laughter-lines had developed round the eyes: lines
of tension and probably fury, Gavin reckoned. He could see
her thinking: he had led her on, he had kissed the top of her
head. Now he was suggesting lunch some time, dealing out
the future to her when the present was what mattered. He
felt he'd been rude.

'I'm sorry, Sue.'

They were standing in the other dancers' way. He wanted to dance again himself, to feel the warmth of her small body, to feel her hands, and to smell her hair, and to bend down and touch it again with his lips. He turned away and extricated Polly from the grasp of the drunk who had claimed to love her. 'It's time to go home,' he said angrily.

'You're never going, old Gavin,' Malcolm protested in the hall. 'I'll run Poll home, you know.'

'I'll run her home myself.'

In the car Polly asked what had happened, but he didn't tell her the truth. He said he'd been rude to Sue because Sue had said something appalling about one of her guests and that for some silly reason he'd taken exception to it.

Polly did not believe him. He was making an excuse, but it didn't matter. He had rejected the game the Ryders had wanted to play and he had rejected it for her sake. He had stood by her and shown his respect for her, even though he had wanted to play the game himself. In the car she laid her head against the side of his shoulder. She thanked him, without specifying what she was grateful for.

'I feel terrible about being rude to Sue,' he said.

He stopped the car outside their house. The light was burning in the sitting-room window. The babysitter would be half asleep. Everything was as it should be.

'I'd no right to be rude,' Gavin said, still in the car.

'Sue'll understand.'

'I don't know that she will.'

She let the silence gather, hoping he'd break it by sighing or saying he'd telephone and apologise tomorrow, or simply saying he'd wait in the car for the babysitter. But he didn't sigh and he didn't speak.

'You could go back,' she said calmly, in the end, 'and say you're sorry. When you've driven the babysitter home.'

He didn't reply. He sat gloomily staring at the steering-wheel. She thought he began to shake his head, but she wasn't sure. Then he said:

'Yes, perhaps I should.'

They left the car and walked together on the short paved path that led to their hall-door. She said that what she felt like was a cup of tea, and then thought how dull that sounded.

'Am I dull, Gavin?' she asked, whispering in case the words somehow carried in to the babysitter. Her calmness deserted her for a moment. 'Am I?' she repeated, not whispering any more, not caring about the babysitter.

'Of course you're not dull. Darling, of course you aren't.'

'Not to want to stay? Not to want to go darting into beds with people?'

'Oh, don't be silly, Polly. They're all dull except you, darling. Every single one of them.'

He put his arms around her and kissed her, and she knew that he believed what he was saying. He believed she hadn't fallen as he and the Ryders had, that middle age had dealt no awful blows. In a way that seemed true to Polly, for it had often occurred to her that she, more than the other three, had survived the outer suburb. She was aware of pretences but could not pretend herself. She knew every time they walked into the local Tonino's that the local Tonino's was just an Italian joke, a sham compared with the reality of the original in Greek Street. She knew the party they'd just been to was a squalid little mess. She knew that when Gavin enthused about a fifteen-second commercial for soap his enthusiasm was no cause for celebration. She knew the suburb for what it was, its Volvos and Vauxhalls, its paved paths in unfenced front gardens, its crescents and avenues and immature trees, and the games its people played.

'All right, Polly?' he said, his arms still about her, with tenderness in his voice.

'Yes, of course.' She wanted to thank him again, and to explain that she was thanking him because he had respected her feelings and stood by her. She wanted to ask him not to go back and apologise, but she couldn't bring herself to do that because the request seemed fussy. 'Yes, of course I'm all right,' she said.

In the sitting-room the babysitter woke up and reported that the children had been as good as gold. 'Not a blink out of either of them, Mrs Dillard.'

'I'll run you home,' Gavin said.

'Oh, it's miles and miles.'

'It's our fault for living in such a godforsaken suburb.'

'Well, it's terribly nice of you, sir.'

Polly paid her and asked her again what her name was because she'd forgotten. The girl repeated that it was Hannah McCarthy. She gave Polly her telephone number in case Estrella shouldn't be available on another occasion. She didn't at all mind coming out so far, she said.

When they'd gone Polly made tea in the kitchen. She placed the tea-pot and a cup and saucer on a tray and carried the tray upstairs to their bedroom. She was still the same as she'd always been, they would say to one another, lying there, her husband and her friend. They'd admire her for that, they'd share their guilt and their remorse. But they'd be wrong to say she was the same.

She took her clothes off and got into bed. The outer suburb was what it was, so was the shell of middle age: she didn't complain because it would be silly to complain when you were fed and clothed and comfortable, when your children were cared for and warm, when you were loved and respected. You couldn't forever weep with anger, or loudly deplore yourself and other people. You couldn't hit out with your fists as though you were back at the Misses Summers' nursery school in Putney. You couldn't forever laugh among the waiters at the Ritz just because it was fun to be there.

In bed she poured herself a cup of tea, telling herself that what had happened tonight – and what was probably happening now – was reasonable and even fair. She had rejected what was distasteful to her, he had stood by her and had respected her feelings: his unfaithfulness seemed his due. In her middle-age calmness that was how she felt. She couldn't help it.

It was how she had fallen, she said to herself, but all that sounded silly now.

Mrs Silly

Michael couldn't remember a time when his father had been there. There'd always been the flat where he and his mother lived, poky and cluttered even though his mother tried so. Every Saturday his father came to collect him. He remembered a blue car and then a greenish one. The latest one was white, an Alfa-Romeo.

Saturday with his father was the highlight of the week. Unlike his mother's flat, his father's house was spacious and nicely carpeted. There was Gillian, his father's wife, who never seemed in a hurry, who smiled and didn't waste time. Her smile was cool, which matched the way she dressed. Her voice was quiet and reliable: Michael couldn't imagine it ever becoming shrill or weepy or furious, or in any other way getting out of control. It was a nice voice, as nice as Gillian herself.

His father and Gillian had two little girls, twins of six, two years younger than Michael. They lived near Haslemere, in a half-timbered house in pretty wooded countryside. On Saturday mornings the drive from London took over an hour, but Michael never minded and on the way back he usually fell asleep. There was a room in the house that his father and Gillian had made his own, which the twins weren't allowed to enter in his absence. He had his Triang train circuit there, on a table that had been specially built into the wall for it.

It was in this house, one Saturday afternoon, that Michael's father brought up the subject of Elton Grange. 'You're nearly nine, you know,' his father said. 'It's high time, really, old chap.'

Elton Grange was a preparatory school in Wiltshire, which Michael's father had gone to himself. He'd mentioned it many times before and so had Michael's mother, but in Michael's mind it was a place that belonged to the distant future – with Radley, where his father had gone, also. He certainly knew that he wasn't going to stay at the primary school in Hammersmith for ever, and had always taken it for granted that he would move away from it when the rest of his class moved, at eleven. He felt, without actually being able to recall the relevant conversation, that his mother had quite definitely implied this. But it didn't work out like that. 'You should go in September,' his father said, and that was that.

'Oh, darling,' his mother murmured when the arrangements had all been made. 'Oh, Michael, I'll miss you.'

His father would pay the fees and his father would in future give him pocket money, over and above what his mother gave him. He'd like it at Elton Grange, his father promised. 'Oh yes, you'll like it,' his mother said too.

She was a woman of medium height, five foot four, with a round, plump face and plump arms and legs. There was a soft prettiness about her, about her light-blue eyes and her wide, simple mouth and her fair, rather fluffy hair. Her hands were always warm, as if expressing the warmth of her nature. She wept easily and often said she was silly to weep so. She talked a lot, getting carried away when she didn't watch herself: for this failing, too, she regularly said she was silly. 'Mrs Silly', she used to say when Michael was younger, condemning herself playfully for the two small follies she found it hard to control.

She worked as a secretary for an Indian, a Mr Ashaf, who had an office-stationery business. There was the shop – more of a warehouse, really – with stacks of swivel chairs and filing-cabinets on top of one another and green metal desks, and cartons containing continuation paper and top-copy foolscap and flimsy, and printed invoices. There were other cartons full of envelopes, and packets of paper-clips, drawing-pins and staples. The carbon-paper supplies were kept in the office behind the shop, where Michael's mother sat in front of a typewriter, typing invoices mainly. Mr Ashaf, a small wiry man, was always on his feet, moving between the shop and the office, keeping an eye on Michael's mother and on Dolores Welsh who looked after the retail side. Before she'd married, Michael's mother had been a secretary in the Wedgwood Centre, but returning to work at the time of her divorce she'd found it more convenient to work for Mr Ashaf since his premises were only five minutes away from where she and Michael lived. Mr Ashaf was happy to employ her on the kind of part-time basis that meant she could be at home every afternoon by the time Michael got in from school. During the holidays Mr Ashaf permitted her to take the typewriter to her flat, to come in every morning to collect what work there was and hand over what she'd done the day before. When this arrangement wasn't convenient, due to the nature of the work, Michael accompanied her to Mr Ashaf's premises and sat in the office with her or with Dolores Welsh in the shop. Mr Ashaf used occasionally to give him a sweet.

'Perhaps I'll change my job,' Michael's mother said brightly, a week before he was due to become a boarder at Elton Grange. 'I could maybe go back to the West End. Nice to have a few more pennies.' She was cheering herself up – he could tell by the way she looked at him. She packed his belongings carefully, giving him many instructions about looking after himself, about keeping himself warm and changing any clothes that got wet. 'Oh, darling,' she said at

Paddington on the afternoon of his departure. 'Oh, darling, I'll miss you so!'

He would miss her, too. Although his father and Gillian were in every way more fun than his mother, it was his mother he loved. Although she fussed and was a nuisance sometimes, there was always the warmth, the cosiness of climbing into her bed on Sunday mornings or watching Magic Roundabout together. He was too big for Magic Roundabout now, or so he considered, and he rather thought he was too big to go on climbing into her bed. But the memories of all this cosiness had become part of his relationship with her.

She wept as they stood together on the platform. She held him close to her, pressing his head against her breast. 'Oh, darling!' she said. 'Oh, my darling.'

Her tears damped his face. She sniffed and sobbed, whispering that she didn't know what she'd do. 'Poor thing!' someone passing said. She blew her nose. She apologised to Michael, trying to smile. 'Remember where your envelopes are,' she said. She'd addressed and stamped a dozen envelopes for him so that he could write to her. She wanted him to write at once, just to say he'd arrived safely.

'And don't be homesick now,' she said, her own voice trembling again. 'Big boy, Michael.'

The train left her behind. He waved from the corridor window, and she gestured at him, indicating that he shouldn't lean out. But because of the distances between them he couldn't understand what the gesture meant. When the train stopped at Reading he found his writing-paper and envelopes in his overnight bag and began to write to her.

At Elton Grange he was in the lowest form, Miss Brooks's form. Miss Brooks, grey-haired at sixty, was the only woman on the teaching staff. She did not share the men's common-room but sat instead in the matrons' room, where she smoked Senior Service cigarettes between lessons. There was pale tobacco-tinged hair on her face and on Tuesday and Friday afternoons she wore jodhpurs, being in charge of the school's riding. Brookie she was known as.

The other women at Elton Grange were Sister, and the undermatron Miss Trenchard, the headmaster's wife Mrs Lyng, the lady cook Miss Arland, and the maids. Mrs Lyng was a stout woman, known among the boys as Outsize Dorothy, and Sister was thin and brisk. Miss Trenchard and Miss Arland were both under twenty-three, Miss Arland was pretty and Miss Trenchard wasn't. Miss Arland went about a lot with the history and geography master, Cocky Marshall, and Miss Trenchard was occasionally seen with the P.T. instructor, a Welshman, who was also in charge of the carpentry shop. Among the older boys Miss Trenchard was sometimes known as Tampax.

Twice a week Michael wrote to his mother, and on Sundays he wrote to his father as well. He told them that the headmaster was known to everyone as A.J.L. and he told them about the rules, how no boy in the three lower forms was permitted to be seen with his hands in his pockets and how no boy was permitted to run through A.J.L.'s garden. He said the food was awful because that was what everyone else said, although he quite liked it really.

At half-term his father and Gillian came. They stayed in the Grand, and Michael had lunch and tea there on the Saturday and on the Sunday, and just lunch on the Monday because they had to leave in the afternoon. He told them about his friends, Carson and Tichbourne, and his father suggested that next half-term Carson and Tichbourne might like to have lunch or tea at the Grand. 'Or maybe Swagger Thompson,' Michael said. Thompson's people lived in Kenya and his grandmother, with whom he spent the holidays, wasn't always able to come at half-term. 'Hard up,' Michael said.

Tichbourne and Carson were in Michael's dormitory, and one other boy, called Andrews: they were all aged eight. At night, after lights out, they talked about most things: about their families and the houses they lived in and the other schools they'd been at. Carson told about the time he'd put stink-bombs under the chair-legs when people were coming to play bridge, and Andrews about the time he'd been caught, by a policeman, stealing strawberries.

'What's it like?' Andrews asked in the dormitory one night. 'What's it like, a divorce?'

'D'you see your mother?' Tichbourne asked, and Michael explained that it was his mother he lived with, not his father.

'Often wondered what it's like for the kids,' Andrews said. 'There's a woman in our village who's divorced. She ran off with another bloke, only the next thing was he ran off with someone else.'

'Who'd your mum run off with?' Carson asked.

'No one.'

'Your dad run off then?'

'Yes.'

His mother had told him that his father left her because they didn't get on any more. He hadn't left her because he knew Gillian. He hadn't met Gillian for years after that.

'D'you like her?' Andrews asked. 'Gillian?'

'She's all right. They've got twins now, my dad and Gillian. Girls.'

'I'd hate it if my mum and dad got divorced,' Tichbourne said.

'Mine quarrelled all last holidays,' Carson said, 'about having a room decorated.'

'Can't stand it when they quarrel,' Andrews said.

73

Intrigued by a situation that was strange to them, the other boys often asked after that about the divorce. How badly did people have to quarrel before they decided on one? Was Gillian different from Michael's mother? Did Michael's mother hate her? Did she hate his father?

'They never see one another,' Michael said. 'She's not like Gillian at all.'

At the end of the term the staff put on a show called Staff Laughs. Cocky Marshall was incarcerated all during one sketch in a wooden container that was meant to be a steam bath. Something had gone wrong with it. The steam was too hot and the catch had become jammed. Cocky Marshall was red in the face and nobody knew if he was putting it on or not until the end of the sketch, when he stepped out of the container in his underclothes. Mr Waydelin had to wear a kilt in another sketch and Miss Arland and Miss Trenchard were dressed up in rugby togs, with Cocky Marshall's and Mr Brine's scrum caps. The Reverend Green – mathematics and divinity – was enthusiastically applauded in his Mrs Wagstaffe sketch. A.J.L. did his magic, and as a grand finale the whole staff, including Miss Brooks, sang together, arm-in-arm, on the small stage. 'We're going home,' they sang. 'We're going home. We're on the way that leads to home. We've seen the good things and the bad and now we're absolutely mad. We're g-o-i-n-g home.' All the boys joined in the chorus, and that night in Michael's dormitory they ate Crunchie, Galaxy and Mars Bars and didn't wash their teeth afterwards. At half-past twelve the next day Michael's mother was waiting for him at Paddington.

At home, nothing was different. On Saturdays his father came and drove him away to the house near Haslemere. His mother talked about Dolores Welsh and Mr Ashaf. She hadn't returned to work in the West End. It was quite nice really, she said, at Mr Ashaf's.

Christmas came and went. His father gave him a new Triang locomotive and Gillian gave him a pogo-stick and the twins a magnet and a set of felt-pens. His mother decorated the flat and put fairy-lights on a small Christmas tree. She filled his stocking on Christmas Eve when he was asleep and the next day, after they'd had their Christmas dinner, she gave him a football and a glove puppet and a jigsaw of Windsor Castle. He gave her a brooch he'd bought in Woolworth's. On January 14th he returned to Elton Grange.

Nothing was different at Elton Grange either, except that Cocky Marshall had left. Nobody had known he was going to leave, and some boys said he had been sacked. But others denied that, claiming that he'd gone of his own accord, without giving the required term's notice. They said A.J.L. was livid.

Three weeks passed and then one morning Michael received a letter from his father saying that neither he nor Gillian would be able to come at half-term because he had to go to Tunisia on business and wanted to take Gillian with him. He sent some money to make up for the disappointment.

In a letter to his mother, not knowing what to say because nothing much was happening, Michael revealed that his father wouldn't be there at half-term. *Then I shall come*, his mother wrote back.

She stayed, not in the Grand, but in a boarding-house called Sans Souci, which had coloured gnomes fishing in a pond in the front garden, and a black gate with one hinge broken. They weren't able to have lunch there on the Saturday because the woman who ran it, Mrs Malone, didn't do lunches. They had lunch in the Copper Kettle, and since Mrs Malone didn't do teas either they had tea in the Copper Kettle as well. They walked around the town between lunch and tea, and after tea they sat together in his mother's bedroom until it was time to catch the bus back to school.

The next day she said she'd like to see over the school, so he brought her into the chapel, which once had been the gate-lodge, and into the classrooms and the gymnasium and the art-room and the changing-rooms. In the carpentry shop the P.T. instructor was making a cupboard. 'Who's that boy?' his mother whispered, unfortunately just loud enough for the P.T. instructor to hear. He smiled. Swagger Thompson, who was standing about doing nothing, giggled.

'But how could he be a boy?' Michael asked dismally, leading the way on the cinder path that ran around the cricket pitch. 'Boys at Elton only go up to thirteen and a half.'

'Oh dear, of course,' his mother said. She began to talk of other things. She spoke quickly. Dolores Welsh, she thought, was going to get married, Mr Ashaf had wrenched his arm. She'd spoken to the landlord about the damp that kept coming in the bathroom, but the landlord had said that to cure it would mean a major upheaval for them.

All the time she was speaking, while they walked slowly on the cinder path, he kept thinking about the P.T. instructor, unable to understand how his mother could ever have mistaken him for a boy. It was a cold morning and rather damp, not raining heavily, not even drizzling, but misty in a particularly wetting kind of way. He wondered where they were going to go for lunch, since the woman in the Copper Kettle had said yesterday that the café didn't open on Sundays.

'Perhaps we could go and look at the dormitories?' his mother suggested when they came to the end of the cinder path.

He didn't want to, but for some reason he felt shy about saying so. If he said he didn't want to show her the dormitories, she'd ask him why and he wouldn't know what to say because he didn't know himself.

'All right,' he said.

They walked through the dank mist, back to the school buildings, which were mostly of red brick, some with a straggle of Virginia creeper on them. The new classrooms, presented a year ago by the father of a boy who had left, were of pinker brick than the rest. The old classrooms had been nicer, Michael's father said: they'd once been the stables.

There were several entrances to the house itself. The main one, approached from the cricket pitch by crossing A.J.L.'s lawns and then crossing a large, almost circular gravel expanse, was grandiose in the early Victorian style. Stone pillars supported a wide gothic arch through which, in a sizeable vestibule, further pillars framed a heavy oak front door. There were croquet mallets and hoops in a wooden box in this vestibule, and deck-chairs and two coloured golfing umbrellas. There was an elaborate wrought-iron scraper and a revolving brush for taking the mud from shoes and boots. On either side of the large hall-door there was a round window, composed of circular, lead-encased panes. 'Well, at least they haven't got rid of those,' Michael's father had said, for these circular windows were a feature that boys who had been to Elton Grange often recalled with affection.

The other entrances to the house were at the back and it was through one of these, leading her in from the quadrangle and the squat new classrooms, past the kitchens and the staff lavatory, that Michael directed his mother on their way to the dormitories. All the other places they'd visited had been outside the house itself – the gymnasium and the changing-rooms were converted outbuildings, the carpentry shop was a wooden shed tucked neatly out of the way beside the garages, the art-room was an old conservatory, and the class-room block stood on its own, forming two sides of the quad-rangle.

'What a nice smell!' Michael's mother whispered as they passed the kitchens, as Michael pressed himself against the wall to let Miss Brooks, in her jodhpurs, go by. Miss Brooks was carrying a riding stick and had a cigarette going. She didn't smile at Michael, nor at Michael's mother.

They went up the back stairs and Michael hoped they wouldn't meet anyone else. All the boys, except the ones like Swagger Thompson whose people lived abroad, were out with their parents and usually the staff went away at half-term, if they possibly could. But A.J.L. and Outsize Dorothy never went away, nor did Sister, and Miss Trenchard had been there at prayers.

'How ever do you find your way through all these passages?' his mother whispered as he led her expertly towards his dormitory. He explained, in a low voice also, that you got used to the passages.

'Here it is,' he said, relieved to find that neither Sister nor Miss Trenchard was laying out clean towels. He closed the door behind them. 'That's my bed there,' he said.

He stood against the door with his ear cocked while she went to the bed and looked at it. She turned and smiled at him, her head a little on one side. She opened a locker and looked inside, but he explained that the locker she was look-ing in was Carson's. 'Where'd that nice rug come from?' she asked, and he said that he'd written to Gillian to say he'd been cold once or twice at night, and she'd sent him the rug immediately. 'Oh,' his mother said dispiritedly. 'Well, that was nice of Gillian,' she added.

She crossed to one of the windows and looked down over A.J.L.'s lawns to the chestnut trees that surrounded the playing-fields. It really was a beautiful place, she said.

She smiled at him again and he thought, what he'd never thought before, that her clothes were cheap-looking. Gillian's clothes were clothes you somehow didn't notice: it didn't occur to you to think they were cheap-looking or expensive. The women of Elton Grange all dressed differently, Outsize Dorothy in woollen things, Miss Brooks in suits, with a tie, and Sister and Miss Trenchard and Miss Arland always had white coats. The maids wore blue overalls most of the time but sometimes you saw them going home in the evenings in their ordinary clothes, which you never really thought about and certainly you never thought were cheap-looking.

'Really beautiful,' she said, still smiling, still at the window. She was wearing a headscarf and a maroon coat and another scarf at her neck. Her handbag was maroon also, but it was old, with something broken on one of the buckles: it was the handbag, he said to himself, that made you think she was cheaply dressed.

He left the door and went to her, taking her arm. He felt ashamed that he'd thought her clothes were cheap-looking. She'd been upset when he'd told her that the rug had been sent by Gillian. She'd been upset and he hadn't bothered.

'Oh, Mummy,' he said.

She hugged him to her, and when he looked up into her face he saw the mark of a tear on one of her cheeks. Her fluffy hair was sticking out a bit beneath the headscarf, her round, plump face was forcing itself to smile.

'I'm sorry,' he said.

'Sorry? Darling, there's no need.'

'I'm sorry you're left all alone there, Mummy.'

'Oh, but I'm not at all. I've got the office every day, and one of these days I really will see about going back to the West End. We've been awfully busy at the office, actually, masses to do.'

The sympathy he'd showed caused her to talk. Up to now –

ever since they'd met the day before – she'd quite deliberately held herself back in this respect, knowing that to chatter on wouldn't be the thing at all. Yesterday she'd waited until she'd returned to Sans Souci before relaxing. She'd had a nice long chat with Mrs Malone on the landing, which unfortunately had been spoiled by a man in one of Mrs Malone's upper rooms poking his head out and asking for a bit of peace. 'Sorry about that,' she'd heard Mrs Malone saying to him later. 'Couldn't really stop her.' – a statement that had spoiled things even more. 'I'm ever so sorry,' she'd said quietly to Mrs Malone at breakfast.

'Let's go down now,' Michael said.

But his mother didn't hear this remark, engaged as she was upon making a series of remarks herself. She was no longer discreetly whispering, but chattering on with more abandon than she had even displayed on Mrs Malone's stairs the night before. A flush had spread over her cheeks and around her mouth and on the portion of her neck which could be seen above her scarf. Michael could see she was happy.

'We'll have to go to Dolores' wedding,' she said. 'On the eighth. The eighth of May, a Thursday I think it is. They're coming round actually, Dolores and her young chap, Brian Haskins he's called. Mr Ashaf says he wouldn't trust him, but actually Dolores is no fool.'

'Let's go down now, Mum.'

She said she'd like to see the other dormitories. She'd like to see the senior dormitories, into one of which Michael would eventually be moving. She began to talk about Dolores Welsh and Brian Haskins again and then about Mrs Malone, and then about a woman Michael had never heard of before, a person called Peggy Urch.

He pointed out that the dormitories were called after imperial heroes. His was Drake, others were Raleigh, Nelson, Wellington, Marlborough and Clive. 'I think I'll be moving to Nelson,' Michael said. 'Or Marlborough. Depends.' But he knew she wasn't listening, he knew she hadn't taken in the fact that the dormitories were named nke that. She was talking about Peggy Urch when he led her into Marlborough. Outsize Dorothy was there with Miss Trenchard, taking stuff out of Verschoyle's locker because Verschoyle had just gone to the sanatorium.

'Very nice person,' Michael's mother was saying. 'She's taken on the Redmans' flat – the one above us, you know.'

It seemed to Michael that his mother didn't see Outsize Dorothy and Miss Trenchard. It seemed to him for a moment that his mother didn't quite know where she was.

'Looking for me?' Outsize Dorothy said. She smiled and waddled towards them. She looked at Michael, waiting for him to explain who this visitor was. Miss Trenchard looked, too.

'It's my mother,' he said, aware that these words were inept and inelegant.

'I'm Mrs Lyng,' Outsize Dorothy said. She held out her hand and Michael's mother took it.

'The Matron,' she said. 'I've heard of you, Mrs Lyng.'

'Well actually,' Outsize Dorothy contradicted with a laugh, 'I'm the headmaster's wife.' All the flesh on her body wobbled when she laughed. Tichbourne said he knew for a fact she was twenty stone.

'What a lovely place you have, Mrs Lyng. I was just saying to Michael. What a view from the windows!'

Outsize Dorothy told Miss Trenchard to go on getting Verschoyle's things together, in a voice that implied that Miss Trenchard wasn't paid to stand about doing nothing in the dormitories. All the women staff – the maids and Sister and Miss Arland and Miss Trenchard – hated Outsize Dorothy because she'd expect them, even Sister, to go on rooting in a locker while she talked to a parent. She wouldn't in a million years say: 'This is Miss Trenchard, the undermatron.'

'Oh, I'm afraid we don't have much time for views at Elton,' Outsize Dorothy said. She was looking puzzled, and Michael imagined she was thinking that his mother was surely another woman, a thinner, smarter, quieter person. But then Outsize Dorothy wasn't clever, as she often lightheartedly said herself, and was probably saying to herself that she must be confusing one boy's mother with another.

'Dorothy!' a voice called out, a voice which Michael instantly and to his horror recognised as A.J.L.'s.

'We had such a view at home!' Michael's mother said. 'Such a gorgeous view!' She was referring to her own home, a rectory in Somerset somewhere. She'd often told Michael about the rectory and the view, and her parents, both dead now. Her father had received the call to the Church late in life: he'd been in the Customs and Excise before that.

'Here, dear,' Outsize Dorothy called out. 'In Marlborough.'

Michael knew he'd gone red in the face. His stomach felt hot also, the palms of his hands were clammy. He could hear the clatter of the headmaster's footsteps on the uncarpeted back stairs. He began to pray, asking for something to happen, anything at all, anything God could think of.

His mother was more animated than before. More fluffy hair had slipped out from beneath her headscarf, the flush had spread over a greater area of her face. She was talking about the lack of view from the flat where she and Michael lived in Hammersmith, and about Peggy Urch who'd come to live in the flat directly above them and whose view was better because she could see over the poplars.

'Hullo,' A.J.L. said, a stringy, sandy man, the opposite of Outsize Dorothy and in many ways the perfect cömplement. Tichbourne said he often imagined them naked in bed, A.J.L. winding his stringiness around her explosive bulk.

Hands were shaken again. 'Having a look round?' A.J.L. said. 'Staying at the Grand?'

Michael's mother said she wasn't staying at the Grand but at Sans Souci, did he know it? They'd been talking about views, she said, it was lovely to have a room with a view, she hoped Michael wasn't giving trouble, her husband of course – well, ex-husband now – had been to this school in his time, before going on to Radley. Michael would probably go to Radley too.

'Well, we hope so,' A.J.L. said, seizing the back of Michael's neck. 'Shown her the new classrooms, eh?'

'Yes, sir.'

'Shown her where we're going to have our swimming-pool?'

'Not yet, sir.'

'Well, then.'

His mother spoke of various diseases Michael had had, measles and whooping cough and chicken-pox, and of diseases he hadn't had, mumps in particular. Miss Trenchard was like a ghost, all in white, still sorting out the junk in Verschoyle's locker, not daring to say a word. She was crouched there, with her head inside the locker, listening to everything.

'Well, we mustn't keep you,' A.J.L. said, shaking hands again with Michael's mother. 'Always feel free to come.'

There was such finality about these statements, more in the headmaster's tone than in the words themselves, that Michael's mother was immediately silent. The statements had a physical effect on her, as though quite violently they had struck her across the face. When she spoke again it was in the whisper she had earlier employed.

'I'm sorry,' she said. 'I'm ever so sorry for going on so.'

A.J.L. and Outsize Dorothy laughed, pretending not to understand what she meant. Miss Trenchard would tell Miss Arland. Sister would hear and so would Brookie, and the P.T. Instructor would say that this same woman had imagined him to be one of the boys. Mr Waydelin would hear, and Square-jaw Simpson – Cocky Marshall's successor – and Mr Brine and the Reverend Green.

'I have enjoyed it,' Michael's mother whispered. 'So nice to meet you.'

He went before her down the back stairs. His face was still red. They passed by the staff lavatory and the kitchens, out on to the concrete quadrangle. It was still misty and cold.

'I bought things for lunch,' she said, and for an awful moment he thought that she'd want to eat them somewhere in the school or in the grounds – in the art-room or the cricket pavilion. 'We could have a picnic in my room,' she said.

They walked down the short drive, past the chapel that once had been the gate-lodge. They caught a bus after a wait of half an hour, during which she began to talk again, telling him more about Peggy Urch, who reminded her of another friend she'd had once, a Margy Bassett. In her room in Sans Souci she went on talking, spreading out on the bed triangles of cheese and tomatoes and rolls and biscuits and oranges. They sat in her room when they'd finished, eating Rollo. At six o'clock they caught a bus back to Elton Grange. She wept a little when she said goodbye.

Michael's mother did not, as it happened, ever arrive at Elton Grange at half-term again. There was no need for her to do so because his father and Gillian were always able to come themselves. For several terms he felt embarrassed in the presence of A.J.L. and Outsize Dorothy and Miss Trenchard, but no one at school mentioned the unfortunate visit, not even Swagger Thompson, who had so delightedly overheard her assuming the P.T. Instructor to be one of the boys. School continued as before and so did the holidays, Saturdays in Haslemere and the rest of the week in Hammersmith, news of Mr Ashaf and Dolores Welsh, now Dolores Haskins. Peggy

Urch, the woman in the flat upstairs, often came down for a chat.

Often, too, Michael and his mother would sit together in the evenings on the sofa in front of the electric fire. She'd tell him about the rectory in Somerset and her father who had received the call to the Church late in his life, who'd been in the Customs and Excise. She'd tell him about her own childhood, and even about the early days of her marriage. Sometimes she wept a little, hardly at all, and he would take her arm on the sofa and she would smile and laugh. When they sat together on the sofa or went out together, to the cinema, or for a walk by the river or to the teashop called the Maids of Honour near Kew Gardens, Michael felt that he would never want to marry because he'd prefer to be with his mother. Even when she chatted on to some stranger in the Maids of Honour he felt he loved her: everything was different from the time she'd come to Elton Grange because away from Elton Grange things didn't matter in the same way.

Then something unpleasant threatened. During his last term at Elton Grange Michael was to be confirmed. 'Oh, but of course I must come,' his mother said.

It promised to be worse than the previous occasion. After the service you were meant to bring your parents in to tea in the Great Hall and see that they had a cup of tea and sandwiches and cakes. You had to introduce them to the Bishop of Bath and Wells. Michael imagined all that. In bed at night he imagined his father and Gillian looking very smart, his father chatting easily to Mr Brine, Gillian smiling at Outsize Dorothy, and his mother's hair fluffing out from beneath her headscarf. He imagined his mother and his father and Gillian having to sit together in a pew in chapel, as naturally they'd be expected to, being members of the same party.

'There's no need to,' he said in the flat in Hammersmith. 'There's really no need to, Mum.'

She didn't mention his father and Gillian, although he'd repeatedly said that they'd be there. It was as if she didn't want to think about them, as if she was deliberately pretending that they'd decided not to attend. She'd stay in Sans Souci again, she said. They'd have a picnic in her room, since the newly confirmed were to be excused school tea on the evening of the service. 'Dinner at the Grand, old chap,' his father said. 'Bring Tichbourne if you want to.'

Michael returned to Elton Grange at the end of the Easter holidays, leaving his mother in a state of high excitement at Paddington Station because she'd be seeing him again within five weeks. He thought he might invent an illness a day or two before the confirmation, or say at the last moment that he had doubts. In fact, he did hint to the Reverend Green that he wasn't certain about being quite ready for the occasion, but the Reverend Green sharply told him not to be silly. Every time he went down on his knees at the end of a session with the Reverend Green he prayed that God might come to his rescue. But God did not, and all during the night before the confirmation service he lay awake. It wasn't just because she was weepy and embarrassing, he thought: it was because she dressed in that cheap way, it was because she was common, with a common voice that wasn't at all like Gillian's or Mrs Tichbourne's or Mrs Carson's or even Outsize Dorothy's. He couldn't prevent these thoughts from occurring. Why couldn't she do something about her fluffy hair? Why did she have to gabble like that? 'I think I have a temperature,' he said in the morning, but when Sister took it it was only 98.

Before the service the other candidates waited outside the chapel to greet their parents and godparents, but Michael went into the chapel early and took up a devout position. Through his fingers he saw the Reverend Green lighting the candles and preparing the altar. Occasionally, the Reverend Green glanced at Michael, somewhat suspiciously.

'Defend, O Lord, this Thy child,' said the Bishop of Bath and Wells, and when Michael walked back to his seat he kept his head down, not wanting to see his parents and Gillian. They sang Hymn 459. 'My God, accept,' sang Michael, 'my heart this day.'

He walked with Swagger Thompson down the aisle, still with his eyes down. 'Fantastic,' said Swagger Thompson outside the chapel, for want of anything better to say. 'Bloody fantastic.' They waited for the congregation to come out.

Michael had godparents, but his father had said that they wouldn't be able to attend. His godmother had sent him a prayer-book.

'Well done,' his father said. 'Well done, Mike.'

'What lovely singing!' Gillian murmured. She was wearing a white dress with a collar that was slightly turned up, and a white wide-rimmed hat. On the gravel outside the chapel she put on dark glasses against the afternoon sun.

'Your mother's here somewhere,' his father said. 'You'd better see to her, Mike.' He spoke quietly, with a hand resting for a moment on Michael's shoulder. 'We'll be all right,' he added.

Michael turned. She was standing alone, as he knew she would be. Unable to prevent himself, he wished she wouldn't always wear headscarves. 'Oh, darling,' she said.

She took his hands and pulled him towards her. She kissed him, apologising for the embrace but saying that it was a special occasion. She wished her father were alive, she said.

'Tea in the Great Hall,' A.J.L. was booming, and Outsize Dorothy was waddling about in flowered yellow, smiling at the faces of parents and godparents. 'Do come and have tea,' she gushed.

'Oh, I'd love a cup of tea,' Michael's mother whispered.

The crowd was moving through the sunshine, suited men,

the Reverend Green in his cassock, the Bishop in crimson, women in their garden-party finery. They walked up the short drive from the chapel. They passed through the wide gothic arch that heralded the front door, through the vestibule where the croquet set was tidily in place and the deck-chairs neat against a wall. They entered what A.J.L. had years ago christened the Great Hall, where buttered buns and sandwiches and cakes and sausage-rolls were laid out on trestle tables. Miss Trenchard and Miss Arland were in charge of two silver-plated tea-urns.

'I'll get you something to eat,' Michael said to his mother, leaving her although he knew she didn't want to be left. 'Seems no time since I was getting done myself,' he heard his father saying to A.J.L.

Miss Arland poured a cup of tea for his mother and told him to offer her something to eat. He chose a plate of sausage-rolls. She smiled at him. 'Don't go away again,' she whispered.

But he had to go away again because he couldn't stand there holding the sausage-rolls. He darted back to the table and left the plate there, taking one for himself. When he returned to his mother she'd been joined by the Reverend Green and the Bishop.

The Bishop shook Michael's hand and said it had been a very great pleasure to confirm him.

'My father was in the Church,' Michael's mother said, and Michael knew that she wasn't going to stop now. He watched her struggling to hold the words back, crumbling the pastry of her sausage-roll beneath her fingers. The flush had come into her cheeks, there was a brightness in her eyes. The Bishop's face was kind: she couldn't help herself, when kindness like that was there.

'We really must be moving,' the Reverend Green said, but the Bishop only smiled, and on and on she went about her father and the call he'd received so late in life. 'I'm sure you knew him, my lord,' was one suggestion she made, and the Bishop kindly agreed that he probably had.

'Mrs Grainer would like to meet the Bishop,' Outsize Dorothy murmured to the Reverend Green. She looked at Michael's mother and Michael could see her remembering her and not caring for her.

'Well, if you'll excuse us,' the Reverend Green said, seizing the Bishop's arm.

'Oh Michael dear, isn't that a coincidence!'

There was happiness all over her face, bursting from her eyes, in her smile and her flushed cheeks and her fluffy hair. She turned to Mr and Mrs Tichbourne, who were talking to Mrs Carson, and said the Bishop had known her father, apparently quite well. She hadn't even been aware that it was to be this particular bishop today, it hadn't even occurred to her while she'd been at the confirmation service that such a coincidence could be possible. Her father had passed away fifteen years ago, he'd have been a contemporary of the Bishop's. 'He was in the Customs and Excise,' she said, 'before he received the call.'

They didn't turn away from her. They listened, putting in a word or two, about coincidences and the niceness of the Bishop. Tichbourne and Carson stood eating sandwiches, offering them to one another. Michael's face felt like a bonfire.

'We'll probably see you later,' Mr Tichbourne said, eventually edging his wife away. 'We're staying at the Grand.'

'Oh no, I'm at Sans Souci. Couldn't ever afford the Grand!' She laughed.

'Don't think we know the Sans Souci,' Mrs Tichbourne said.

'Darling, I'd love another cup of tea,' his mother said to Michael, and he went away to get her one, leaving her with Mrs Carson. When he returned she was referring to Peggy Urch.

It was then, while talking to Mrs Carson, that Michael's mother fell. Afterwards she said that she'd felt something slimy under one of her heels and had moved to rid herself of it. The next thing she knew she was lying on her back on the floor, soaked in tea.

Mrs Carson helped her to her feet. A.J.L. hovered solicitously. Outsize Dorothy picked up the cup and saucer.

'I'm quite all right,' Michael's mother kept repeating. 'there was something slippy on the floor, I'm quite all right.'

She was led to a chair by A.J.L. 'I think we'd best call on Sister,' he said. 'Just to be sure.'

But she insisted that she was all right, that there was no need to go bothering Sister. She was as white as a sheet.

Michael's father and Gillian came up to her and said they were sorry. Michael could see Tichbourne and Carson nudging one another, giggling. For a moment he thought of running away, hiding in the attics or something. Half a buttered bun had got stuck to the sleeve of his mother's maroon coat when she'd fallen. Her left leg was saturated with tea.

'We'll drive you into town,' his father said. 'Horrible thing to happen.'

'It's just my elbow,' his mother whispered. 'I came down on my elbow.'

Carson and Tichbourne would imitate it because Carson and Tichbourne imitated everything. They'd stand there, pretending to be holding a cup of tea, and suddenly they'd be lying flat on their backs. 'I think we'd best call on Sister,' Carson would say, imitating A.J.L.

His father and Gillian said goodbye to Outsize Dorothy and to A.J.L. His mother, reduced to humble silence again, seemed only to want to get away. In the car she didn't say anything at all and when they reached Sans Souci she didn't seem to expect Michael to go in with her. She left the car, whispering her thanks, a little colour gathering in her face again.

That evening Michael had dinner with Gillian and his father in the Grand. Tichbourne was there also, and Carson, and several other boys, all with their parents. 'I can drive a few of them back,' his father said, 'save everyone getting a car out.' He crossed the dining-room floor and spoke to Mr Tichbourne and Mr Carson and the father of a boy called Mallabedeely. Michael ate minestrone soup and chicken with peas and roast potatoes. Gillian told him what the twins had been up to and said his father was going to have a swimming-pool put in. His father returned to the table and announced that he'd arranged to drive everyone back at nine o'clock.

Eating his chicken, he imagined his mother in Sans Souci, sitting on the edge of the bed, probably having a cry. He imagined her bringing back to London the stuff she'd bought for a picnic in her room. She'd never refer to any of that, she'd never upbraid him for going to the Grand for dinner when she'd wanted him to be with her. She'd consider it just that she should be punished.

As they got into the car, his father said he'd drive round by Sans Souci so that Michael could run in for a minute. 'We're meant to be back by a quarter past,' Michael said quickly. 'I've said goodbye to her,' he added, which wasn't quite true.

It would perhaps have been different if Tichbourne and Carson hadn't been in the car. He'd have gone in and paused with her for a minute because he felt pity for her. But the unattractive façade of Sans Souci, the broken gate of the small front garden and the fishermen gnomes would have caused further nudging and giggling in his father's white Alfa-Romeo.

'You're sure now?' his father said. 'I'll get you there by a quarter past.'

'No, it's all right.'

She wouldn't be expecting him. She wouldn't even have unpacked the picnic she'd brought.

'Hey, was that your godmother?' Tichbourne asked in the dormitory. 'The one who copped it on the floor?'

He began to shake his head and then he paused and went on shaking it. An aunt, he said, some kind of aunt, he wasn't sure what the relationship was. He hadn't thought of saying that before, yet it seemed so simple, and so right and so natural, that a distant aunt should come to a confirmation service and not stay, like everyone else, in the Grand. 'God, it was funny,' Carson said, and Tichbourne did his imitation, and Michael laughed with his friends. He was grateful to them for assuming that such a person could not be his mother. A.J.L. and Outsize Dorothy and Miss Trenchard knew she was his mother, and so did the Reverend Green, but for the remainder of his time at Elton Grange none of these people would have cause to refer to the fact in public. And if by chance A.J.L. did happen to say in class tomorrow that he hoped his mother was all right after her fall, Michael would say afterwards that A.J.L. had got it all wrong.

In the dark, he whispered to her in his mind. He said he was sorry, he said he loved her better than anyone.

The Tennis Court

Old Mrs Ashburton used to drive about the lanes in a governess cart drawn by a donkey she called Trot. We often met
her as we cycled home from school, when my brother and my
sister were at the Grammar School and I was still at Miss
Pritchard's Primary. Of the three of us I was Mrs Ashburton's
favourite, and I don't know why that was except that I was
the youngest. 'Hullo, my Matilda,' Mrs Ashburton would
whisper in her throaty, crazy-sounding way. 'Matilda,' she'd
repeat, lingering over the name I so disliked, drawing each
syllable away from the next. 'Dear Matilda.' She was excessively thin, rather tall, and frail-looking. We made allowances
for her because she was eighty-one.

Usually when we met her she was looking for wild flowers,
or if it was winter or autumn just sitting in her governess cart
in some farmer's gateway, letting the donkey graze the farmer's grass. In spring she used to root out plants from the
hedges with a little trowel. Most of them were weeds, my
brother said; and looking back on it now, I realise that it
wasn't for wild flowers, or weeds, or grazing for her donkey
that she drove about the lanes. It was in order to meet us
cycling back from school.

'There's a tennis court at Challacombe Manor,' she said
one day in May, 1939. 'Any time you ever wanted to play,
Dick.' She stared at my brother with piercing black eyes that
were the colour of quality coal. She was eccentric, standing
there in a long, very old and bald fur coat, stroking the ears

93

of her donkey while he nibbled a hedge. Her hat was attached to her grey hair by a number of brass hat-pins. The hat was of faded green felt, the hat-pins had quite large knobs at the ends of them, inlaid with pieces of green glass. Green, Mrs Ashburton often remarked, was her favourite colour, and she used to remove these hat-pins to show us the glass additions, emphasising that they were valueless. Her bald fur coat was valueless also, she assured us, and not even in its heyday would it have fetched more than five pounds. In the same manner she remarked upon her summer hats and dresses, and her shoes, and the governess cart, and the donkey.

'I mean, Dick,' she said that day in 1939, 'it's not much of a tennis court, but it was once, of course. And there's a net stacked away in one of the out-houses. And a roller, and a marker. There's a lawnmower, too, because naturally you'll need that.'

'You mean, we could play on your court, Mrs Ashburton?' my sister Betty said.

'Of course I mean that, my dear. That's just what I mean. You know, before the War we really did have marvellous tennis parties at Challacombe. Everyone came.'

'Oh, how lovely!' Betty was fourteen and Dick was a year older, and I was seven. Betty was fair-haired like the rest of us, but much prettier than me. She had very blue eyes and a wide smiling mouth that boys at the Grammar School were always trying to kiss, and a small nose, and freckles. Her hair was smooth and long, the colour of hay. It looked quite start-ling sometimes, shining in the sunlight. I used to feel proud of Betty and Dick when they came to collect me every afternoon at the Primary School. Dick was to leave the Grammar School in July, and on the afternoons of that warm May, as Betty and I cycled home with him, we felt sorry that he wouldn't be there next term. But Dick said he was glad. He was big, as tall as my father, and very shy. He'd begun to

smoke, a habit not approved of by my father. On the way
home from school we had to stop and go into a ruined cottage
so that he could have a Woodbine. He was going to work on
the farm; one day the farm would be his.

'It would be lovely to play tennis,' Betty said.

'Then you must, my dear. But if you want to play this
summer you'll have to get the court into trim.' Mrs Ashburton smiled at Betty in a way that made her thin, elderly
face seem beautiful. Then she smiled at Dick. 'I was passing
the tennis court the other day, Dick, and I suddenly thought
of it. Now why shouldn't those children get it into trim? I
thought. Why shouldn't they come and play, and bring their
friends?'

'Yes,' Dick said.

'Why ever don't you come over to Challacombe on Saturday? Matilda, too, of course. Come for tea, all three of you.'

Mrs Ashburton smiled at each of us in turn. She nodded
at us and climbed into the governess cart. 'Saturday,' she
repeated.

'Honestly, Betty!' Dick glared crossly at my sister, as
though she were responsible for the invitation. 'I'm not going,
you know.'

He cycled off, along the narrow, dusty lane, big and red-
faced and muttering. We followed him more slowly, talking
about Mrs Ashburton. 'Poor old thing!' Betty said, which
was what people round about often said when Mrs Ashburton
was mentioned, or when she was seen in her governess cart.

The first thing I remember in all my life was my father breaking a fountain-pen. It was a large black and white pen, like
tortoiseshell or marble. That was the fashion for fountain-
pens then: two or three colours marbled together, green and
black, blue and white, red and black-and-white. Conway

Stewart, Waterman's, Blackbird. Propelling pencils were called Eversharp.

The day my father broke his pen I didn't know all that: I learnt it afterwards at Miss Pritchard's Primary. I was three the day he broke the pen. 'It's just a waste of blooming money!' he shouted. He smashed the pen across his knee while my mother anxiously watched. Waste of money or not, she said, it wouldn't help matters to break the thing. She fetched him the ink and a dip-pen from a drawer of the dresser. He was still angry, but after a minute or two he began to laugh. He kissed my mother, pulling her down on to the knee he'd broken the pen over. Dick, who must have been eleven then, didn't even look up from his homework. Betty was there too, but I can't remember what she was doing.

The kitchen hasn't changed much. The big light-oak dresser is still there, with the same brass handles on its doors and drawers, and the same Wedgwood-blue dinner-set on its shelves, and the same blue cups and jugs hanging on hooks. The ceiling is low, the kitchen itself large and rect-angular, with the back stairs rising from the far end of it, and a door at the bottom of them. There are doors to the pantry and the scullery, and to the passage that leads to the rest of the house, and to the yard. There's a long narrow light-oak table, with brass handles on its drawers, like the dresser ones, and oak chairs that aren't as light as all the other oak because chairs darken with use. The table itself, even now, is scrubbed once a week. I do it myself: I live alone in the farm-house now.

I remember the kitchen with oil-lamps, and the time, the day after my fifth birthday, when the men came to wire the house for electricity. The same range is still there. My mother used to talk about an Aga, and often when she took us shopping with her she'd bring us to Archers', the builders' merchants, to look at big cream-coloured Agas. After a time,

Mr Gray of the Aga department didn't even bother to bustle up to her when he saw her coming. She'd stand there, plump and pink-cheeked, her reddish hair neat beneath the brim of her hat, touching the display models, opening the oven doors and lifting up the two big hot-plate covers. When we returned to the farm-house my father would tease her, knowing she'd been to Archers' again. She'd blush, cutting ham at tea-time or offering round salad. My father would then forget about it. 'Well, I'm damned,' he'd say, and he'd read out an item from the weekly paper, about some neighbouring farmer or new County Council plans. My mother would listen and then both of them would nod. They were very good friends, even though my father teased her. She blushed like a rose, he said: he teased her to see it.

Once, before the electricity came, I had a nightmare. It was probably only a few months before, because when I came crying down to the kitchen my father kept comforting me with the reminder that it would soon be my fifth birthday. 'You'll never cry then, Matilda,' he whispered to me, cuddling me to him. 'Big girls of five don't cry.' I fell asleep, but it's not that that I remember now, not the fear from the nightmare going away, or the tears stopping, or my father's caressing: it's the image of my parents in the kitchen as I stumbled down the back stairs. There were two oil-lamps lit and the fire in the range was glowing red-hot behind its curved bars, and the heavy black kettle wasn't quite singing. My father was asleep with last Saturday's weekly paper on his knees, my mother was reading one of the books from the bookcase in the dining-room we never used, probably *The Garden of Allah*, which was her favourite. The two sheepdogs were asleep under the table, and when I opened the door at the top of the stairs they both barked because they knew that at that particular time no one should be opening that door. 'Oh, now, now,' my mother said, coming to me, listening to me when I said that there were cows on my bedroom wall. I remember the image of the two of them because they looked so happy sitting there, even though my mother hadn't got her Aga, even though my father was sometimes worried about the farm.

Looking back on it now, there was a lot of happiness, although perhaps not more than many families experience. Everything seems either dismal or happy in retrospect, and the happiness in the farm-house is what I think of first whenever I think now of that particular past. I remember my mother baking in the kitchen, flour all over her plump arms, and tiny beads of sweat on her forehead, because the kitchen was always hot. I remember my father's leathery skin and his smile, and the way he used to shout at the sheepdogs, and the men, Joe and Arthur, sitting on yellow stubble, drinking tea out of a bottle, on a day hay had been cut.

Our farm had once been the home-farm of Challacombe Manor, even though our farm-house was two miles away from the Manor house. There'd been servants and gardeners at Challacombe Manor then, and horses in the stables, and carriages coming and going. But the estate had fallen into rack and ruin after the First World War because Mr Ashburton hadn't been able to keep it going and in the end, in 1924, he'd taken out various mortgages. When he died, in 1929, the extent of his debts was so great that Mrs Ashburton had been obliged to let Lloyd's Bank foreclose on the mortgages, which is how it came about that my father bought Challacombe Farm. It was a tragedy, people round about used to say, and the real tragedy was that Mr Ashburton had come back from the War in such a strange state that he hadn't minded about everywhere falling into rack and ruin. According to my father, Lloyd's Bank owned Challacombe Manor itself and had granted Mrs Ashburton permission to live there in her lifetime. It wouldn't surprise him, my father said, if it turned out that Lloyd's Bank owned Mrs Ashburton as well. 'He drank himself to death,' people used to say about Mr Ashburton. 'She watched him and didn't have the heart to stop him.' Yet before the First World War Mr Ashburton had been a different kind of man, energetic and sharp. The Challacombe estate had been a showpiece.

To me in particular Mrs Ashburton talked about her husband. She was lucky that he'd come back from the War, even if he hadn't been able to manage very well. His mind had been affected, she explained, but that was better than being dead. She told me about the men who'd died, gardeners at Challacombe Manor, and farm workers on the estate, and men she and her husband had known in the town. 'I thanked God,' Mrs Ashburton said, 'when he came safely back here all in one piece. Everything fell to bits around us, but it didn't matter because at least he was still alive. You understand, Matilda?'

I always nodded, although I didn't really understand. And then she'd go on about the estate as it had been, and then about her husband and the conversations they used to have. Sometimes she didn't address me directly. She smiled and just talked, always returning to the men who had been killed and how lucky she was that her husband had at least come back. She'd prayed, she said, that he'd come back, and every time another man from the estate or from the neighbourhood had been reported dead she'd felt that there was a better chance that her husband wouldn't die also. 'By the law of averages,' she explained, 'some had to come back. Some men have always come back from wars, you convince yourself.'

At this point I would always nod again, and Mrs Ashburton would say that looking back on it now she felt ashamed that she had ever applied the law of averages to the survival or death of men. Doing so was as horrible as war itself: the women who were left at home became cruel in their fear and their selfishness. Cruelty was natural in war, Mrs Ashburton said.

At the time she'd hated the Germans, and she was ashamed of that too, because the Germans were just people like other people. But when she talked about them the remains of the hatred was still in her voice, and I imagined the Germans from what she told me about them: people who ate black bread and didn't laugh much, who ate raw bacon, who were dour, grey and steely. She described the helmets they wore in wartime. She told me what a bayonet was, and I used to feel sick when I thought of one going into a man's stomach and being twisted in there to make sure the man would die. She told me about poison gas, and the trenches, and soldiers being buried alive. The way she spoke I knew she was repeating, word for word, the things her husband had told her, things that had maybe been the cause of his affected mind. Even her voice sounded unusual when she talked about the War, as though she was trying to imitate her husband's voice, and the terror that had been in it. He used to cry, she said, as he walked about the gardens, unable to stop the tears once they'd begun.

Dick didn't say anything while we rode the two miles over to Challacombe Manor that Saturday. He didn't even say anything when he suddenly dismounted and leaned his bicycle against a black gate, and climbed over the gate to have a smoke behind the hedge. If my father had come by he'd have known what was happening because he would have seen Betty and myself waiting in the lane, surrounded by the cloud of smoke that Dick always managed to make with his Woodbine. Our job was to warn him if we saw my father coming, but my father didn't come that afternoon and when Dick had finished we continued on our way.

We'd often been to tea at Challacombe Manor before. Mrs Ashburton said we were the only visitors she had because most of her friends were dead, which was something that happened, she explained, if you were eighty-one. We always had tea in the kitchen, a huge room that smelt of oil, with armchairs in it and a wireless, and an oil-stove on which Mrs Ashburton cooked, not wishing to have to keep the range going. There were oatcakes for tea, and buttered white and brown bread, and pots of jam that Mrs Ashburton bought in the town, and a cake she bought also, usually a fruitcake. Afterwards we'd walk through the house with her, while she pointed out the places where the roof had given way, and the dry rot, and windows that were broken. She hadn't lived in most of the house since the War, and had lived in even less of it since her husband had died in 1929. We knew these details by heart because she'd told us so many times. In one of the out-houses there was an old motor-car with flat tyres, and the gardens were now all overgrown with grass and weeds. Rhododendrons were choked, and buddleia and kerria and hydrangeas.

The house was grey and square with two small wings, a stone Georgian house with wide stone steps leading to a front door that had pillars on either side of it and a fan-light above it. The gravel expanse in front of it was grassy now, and slippery in wet weather because of moss that had accumulated. French windows opened on to it on either side of the hall-door, from the rooms that had been the drawing-room and the dining-room. Lawns stretched around the house, with grass like a meadow on them now. The tennis court, which we'd never known about until Mrs Ashburton mentioned it, was hidden away, beyond the jungle of a shrubbery.

'You see?' she said. 'You see, Dick?' She was wearing a long, old-fashioned dress and a wide-brimmed white hat, and sunglasses because the afternoon was fiercely bright.

The grass on the tennis court was a yard high, as high as the rusty iron posts that were there to support the net. 'Look,' Mrs Ashburton said.

She led us to the stable-yard, past the out-house where the motor-car was, and into a smaller out-house. There was a lawnmower there, as rusty as the tennis posts, and a marker in the same condition, and an iron roller. Tucked into the beams above our heads was a rolled-up tennis net. 'He adored tennis,' she said. 'He really loved it.'

She turned and we followed her across the stable-yard, into the kitchen by the back door. She talked about her husband while she made tea.

We ate the bought fruitcake, listening to her. We'd heard it all before, but we always considered it was worth it because of the cake and the biscuits and the buttered bread and the pots of jam. And always before we left she gave us ginger beer and pieces of chocolate broken up on a saucer. She told us about the child which had been born to her husband and herself, six months after the beginning of the War, but which had not survived. 'Everything went wrong,' she said. She told us about the parties there'd been at Challacombe Manor. Champagne and strawberries and cream, and parties with games that she described, and fancy dress.

'No reason at all,' she said, 'why we shouldn't have a tennis party.'

Dick made a sighing sound, a soft, slight noise that Mrs Ashburton didn't hear.

'Tennis party?' Betty murmured.

'No reason, dear.'

That morning Dick and Betty had had an argument. Betty had said that of course he must go to tea with Mrs Ashburton, since he'd always gone in the past. And Dick had said that Mrs Ashburton had been cunning: all these years, he said, she'd been inviting us to tea so that when the time was ripe she could get us to clean up her old tennis court. 'Oh, don't be silly!' Betty had cried, and then had said that it would be the cruellest thing that Dick had ever done if he didn't go to tea with an old woman just because she'd mentioned her tennis court. I'd been cross with Dick myself, and none of us felt very happy because the matter of the tennis court had unattractively brought into the open the motive behind our putting up with Mrs Ashburton. I didn't like it when she called me her Matilda and put her arms around me, and said she was sure her child would have been a little girl, and that she was almost as sure that she'd have called her Matilda. I didn't like it when she went on and on about the War and her husband coming back a wreck, or about the champagne and the strawberries and cream. 'Poor Mrs Ashburton!' we'd always said, but it wasn't because she was poor Mrs Ashburton that we'd filled the emptiness of Saturday afternoons by cycling over to Challacombe Manor.

'Shall we go and have another look at it?' she said when we'd eaten all the food that was on the table. She smiled in her frail, almost beautiful way, and for a moment I wondered if Dick wasn't perhaps right about her cunning. She led the way back to the overgrown tennis court and we all four stood looking at it.

'It's quite all right to smoke, Dick,' Mrs Ashburton said, 'if you want to.'

Dick laughed because he didn't know how else to react. He'd gone as red as a sunset. He kicked at the rusty iron tennis-post, and then as casually as he could he took a packet of squashed Woodbines from his pocket and began to fiddle with a box of matches. Betty poked him with her elbow, suggesting that he should offer Mrs Ashburton a cigarette.

'Would you like one, Mrs Ashburton?' Dick said, proffering the squashed packet.

'Well, you know, I think I would, Dick.' She laughed and took the cigarette, saying she hadn't smoked a cigarette since 1915. Dick lit it for her. Some of the matches fell from the matchbox on to the long grass. He picked them up and replaced them, his own cigarette cocked out of the corner of his mouth. They looked rather funny, the two of them, Mrs Ashburton in her big white hat and sunglasses.

'You'd need a scythe,' Dick said.

That was the beginning of the tennis party. When Dick walked over the next Saturday with a scythe, Mrs Ashburton had a packet of twenty Craven A waiting for him. He scythed the grass and got the old hand-mower going. The stubble was coarse and by the time he'd cut it short there were quite large patches of naked earth, but Betty and Mrs Ashburton said they didn't matter. The court would do as it was for this summer, but in the spring Dick said he'd put down fresh grass-seed. It rained heavily a fortnight later, which was fortunate, because Dick was able to even out some of the bumps with the roller. Betty helped him, and later on she helped him mark the court out. Mrs Ashburton and I watched, Mrs Ashburton holding my hand and often seeming to imagine that I was the child which hadn't been born to her.

We took to going to Challacombe Manor on Sunday mornings as well as Saturdays. There were always packets of Craven A, and ginger beer and pieces of chocolate. 'Of course, it's not her property,' my father said whenever anyone mentioned the tennis court, or the net that Mrs Ashburton had found rolled up in an out-house. At dinnertime on Sundays, when we all sat around the long table in the kitchen, my father would ask Dick how he'd got on with the court. He'd then point out that the tennis court and everything that went with it was the property of Lloyd's Bank. Every Sunday dinnertime we had the same: roast beef and roast potatoes and Yorkshire pudding, and carrots or brussels sprouts according to the seasonal variation, and apple-pie and cream.

Dick didn't ever say much when my father asked him about the tennis court. 'You want to be careful, lad,' my father used to say, squashing roast potatoes into gravy. 'Lloyd's is strict, you know.' My father would go on for ages, talking about Lloyd's Bank or the Aga cooker my mother wanted, and you never quite knew whether he was being serious or not. He would sit there with his jacket on the back of his chair, not smiling as he ate and talked. Farmers were like that, my mother once told Betty when Betty was upset by him. Farmers were cautious and watchful and canny. He didn't at all disapprove of what Betty and Dick and Mrs Ashburton were doing with the tennis court, my mother explained, rather the opposite; but he was right when he reminded them that everything, including the house itself, was the property of Lloyd's Bank.

Mrs Ashburton found six tennis racquets in presses, which were doubtless the property of Lloyd's Bank also. Dick examined them and said they weren't too bad. They had an antiquated look, and the varnish had worn off the frames, but only two of them had broken strings. Even those two, so Dick said, could be played with. He and Mrs Ashburton handed the racquets to one another, blowing at the dust that had accumulated on the presses and the strings. They lit up Craven A cigarettes, and Mrs Ashburton insisted on giving Dick ten shillings to buy tennis balls with.

I sat with Mrs Ashburton watching Dick and Betty playing their first game on the court. The balls bounced in a peculiar way because in spite of all the rolling there were still hollows and bumps on the surface. The grass wasn't green. It was a brownish yellow, except for the bare patches, which were ochre-coloured. Mrs Ashburton clapped every time there was a rally, and when Dick had beaten Betty 6–1, 6–4, he taught me how to hit the ball over the net, and how to volley it and keep it going. 'Marvellous, Matilda!' Mrs Ashburton cried, in her throaty voice, applauding again. 'Marvellous!'

We played all that summer, every Saturday and Sunday until the end of term, and almost every evening when the holidays came. We had to play in the evenings because at the end of term Dick began to work on the farm. 'Smoke your cigarettes if you want to,' my father said the first morning of the holidays, at breakfast. 'No point in hiding it, boy.' Friends of Dick's and Betty's used to come to Challacombe Manor to play also, because that was what Mrs Ashburton wanted: Colin Gregg and Barbara Hosell and Peggy Goss and Simon Turner and Willie Beach.

Sometimes friends of mine came, and I'd show them how to do it, standing close to the net, holding the racquet handle in the middle of the shaft. Thursday, August 31st, was the day Mrs Ashburton set for the tennis party: Thursday because it was half-day in the town.

Looking back on it now, it really does seem that for years and years she'd been working towards her tennis party. She'd hung about the lanes in her governess cart waiting for us because we were the children from the farm, the nearest children to Challacombe Manor. And when Dick looked big and strong enough and Betty of an age to be interested, she'd made her bid, easing matters along with fruitcake and Craven A. I can imagine her now, on her own in that ruin of a house, watching the grass grow on her tennis court and watching Dick and Betty growing up, and dreaming of one more tennis party at Challacombe, a party like there used to be before her husband was affected in the head by the Kaiser's War.

'August 31st,' Betty reminded my parents one Sunday at dinnertime. 'You'll both come,' she said fiercely, blushing when they laughed at her.

'I hear Lloyd's is on the rampage,' my father said laboriously. 'Short of funds. Calling everything in.'

Dick and Betty didn't say anything. They ate their roast beef, pretending to concentrate on it.

'Course they're not,' my mother said.

'They'll sell Challacombe to some building fellow, now that it's all improved with tennis courts.'

'Daddy, don't be silly,' Betty said, blushing even more. All three of us used to blush. We got it from my mother. If my father blushed you wouldn't notice.

'True as I'm sitting here, my dear. Nothing like tennis courts for adding a bit of style to a place.'

Neither my mother nor my father had ever seen the tennis court. My father wouldn't have considered it the thing, to go walking over to Challacombe Manor to examine a tennis court. My mother was always busy, cooking and polishing brass. Neither my father nor my mother knew the rules of tennis. When we first began to play Betty used to draw a tennis court on a piece of paper and explain.

'Of course we'll come to the tennis party,' my mother said quietly. 'Of course, Betty.'

In the middle of the tennis party, my father persisted, a man in a hard black hat from Lloyd's Bank would walk on to the tennis court and tell everyone to go home.

'Oh, Giles, don't be silly now,' my mother said quite sharply, and added that there was such a thing as going on too much. My father laughed and winked at her.

Mrs Ashburton asked everyone she could think of to the tennis party, people from the farms round about and shop-keepers from the town. Dick and Betty asked their friends and their friends' parents, and I asked Belle Frye and the Gorrys and the Seatons. My mother and Betty made meringues and brandy-snaps and fruitcakes and Victoria sponge cakes and scones and buns and shortbread. They made sardine sandwiches and tomato sandwiches and egg sandwiches and ham sandwiches. I buttered the bread and whipped up cream and wrapped the plates of sandwiches in damp teacloths. Dick cleared a place in the shrubbery beside the tennis court and built a fire to boil kettles on. Milk was poured into bottles and left to keep cool in the larder. August 31st was a fine, hot day.

At dinnertime my father pretended that the truck which was to convey all the food, and all of us too, to the tennis court had a broken carburettor. He and Joe had been working on it all morning, he said, but utterly without success. No one took any notice of him.

I remember, most of all, what they looked like. Mrs Ashburton thin as a rake in a long white dress and her wide-brimmed white hat and her sunglasses. My father in his Sunday clothes, a dark blue suit, his hair combed and his leathery brown face shining because he had shaved it and washed it specially. My mother had powder on her cheeks and her nose, and a touch of lipstick on her lips, although she didn't usually wear lipstick and must have borrowed Betty's. She was wearing a pale blue dress speckled with tiny white flowers. She'd spent a fortnight making it herself, for the occasion. Her reddish hair was soft and a little unruly, being freshly washed. My father was awkward in his Sunday suit, as he always was in it. His freckled hands lolled uneasily by his sides, or awkwardly held tea things, cup and saucer and plate. My mother blushed beneath her powder, and sometimes stammered, which she did when she was nervous.

Betty was beautiful that afternoon, in a white tennis dress that my mother had made her. Dick wore long white flannels that he'd been given by old Mr Bowe, a solicitor in the town who'd been to other tennis parties at Challacombe Manor but had no further use for white flannel trousers, being seventy-two now and too large for the trousers he'd kept for more than fifty years. My mother had made me a tennis dress, too, but I felt shy that day and didn't want to do anything except hand round plates of meringues and cake. I certainly didn't want to play, for the tennis was serious: mixed doubles, Betty and Colin Gregg against Dick and Peggy Goss, and Simon Turner and Edie Turner against Barbara Hosell and Willie Beach.

People were there whom my father said he hadn't seen for years, people who had no intention of playing tennis, any more than he had. Between them, Dick and Betty and Mrs Ashburton had cast a wide net, and my father's protests at the mounds of food that had been prepared met with their answer as car after car drew up, and dog-carts and pony-and-traps. Belle Frye and I passed around the plates of meringues, and people broke off in their conversations to ask us who we were. Mrs Ashburton had spread rugs on the grass around the court, and four white ornamental seats had been re-painted by Dick the week before. 'Just like the old days,' a man called Mr Race said, a corn merchant from the town. My mother nervously fidgeted, and I could feel her thinking that perhaps my father's laborious joke would come true, that any moment now the man from Lloyd's Bank would arrive and ask people what on earth they thought they were doing, playing tennis without the Bank's permission.

But that didn't happen. The balls zipped to and fro across the net, pinging off the strings, throwing up dust towards the end of the afternoon. Voices called out in exasperation at missed shots, laughter came and went. The sun continued to shine warmly, the tennis players wiped their foreheads with increasing regularity, the rugs on the grass were in the shade. Belle Frye and I collected the balls and threw them back to the servers. Mr Bowe said that Dick had the makings of a fine player.

Mrs Ashburton walked among the guests with a packet of Craven A in her hand, talking to everyone. She kept going up to my mother and thanking her for everything she'd done.

Whenever she saw me she kissed me on the hair. Mr Race said she shook hands like a duchess. The rector, Mr Throat-away, laughed jollily.

At six o'clock, just as people were thinking of going, my father surprised everyone by announcing that he had a barrel of beer and a barrel of cider in the truck. I went with him and there they were, two barrels keeping cool beneath a tarpaulin, and two wooden butter-boxes full of glasses that he'd borrowed from the Heart of Oak. He drove the truck out from beneath the shade of the trees and backed it close to the tennis court. He and Dick set the barrels up and other men handed round the beer and cider, whichever anyone wanted. 'Just like him,' I heard a woman called Mrs Garland saying. 'Now, that's just like him.'

It was a quarter to ten that evening before they stopped playing tennis. You could hardly see the ball as it swayed about from racquet to racquet, looping over the net, driven out of court. My father and Mr Race went on drinking beer, and Joe and Arthur, who'd arrived after milking, stood some distance away from them, drinking beer also. Mrs Garland and my mother and Miss Sweet and Mrs Tissard made more tea, and the remains of the sandwiches and cakes were passed around by Belle Frye and myself. Joe said he reckoned it was the greatest day in Mrs Ashburton's life. 'Don't go drinking that cider now,' Joe said to Belle Frye and myself.

We all sat around in the end, smacking at midges and finishing the sandwiches and cakes. Betty and Colin Gregg had cider, and you could see from the way Colin Gregg kept looking at Betty that he was in love with her. He was holding her left hand as they sat there, thinking that no one could see because of the gloom, but Belle Frye and I saw, all right. Just before we all went home, Belle Frye and I were playing at being ghosts round at the front of the house and we came across Betty and Colin Gregg kissing behind a rhododendron bush. They were lying on the grass with their arms tightly encircling one another, kissing and kissing as though they were never going to stop. They didn't even know Belle Frye and I were there. 'Oh, Colin!' Betty kept saying. 'Oh, Colin, Colin!'

We wanted to say goodbye to Mrs Ashburton, but we couldn't find her. We ran around looking everywhere, and then Belle Frye suggested that she was probably in the house.

'Mrs Ashburton!' I called, opening the door that led from the stable-yard to the kitchen. 'Mrs Ashburton!'

It was darker in the kitchen than it was outside, almost pitch-dark it was because the windows were so dirty that even in daytime it was gloomy.

'Matilda,' Mrs Ashburton said. She was sitting in an arm-chair by the oil stove. I knew she was because that was where her voice came from. We couldn't see her.

'We came to say goodbye, Mrs Ashburton.'

She told us to wait. She had a saucer of chocolate for us, she said, and we heard her rooting about on the table beside her. We heard the glass being removed from a lamp and then she struck a match. She lit the wick and put the glass back. In the glow of lamplight she looked exhausted. Her eyes seemed to have receded, the thinness of her face was almost sinister.

We ate our chocolate in the kitchen that smelt of oil, and Mrs Ashburton didn't speak. We said goodbye again, but she didn't say anything. She didn't even nod or shake her head. She didn't kiss me like she usually did, so I went and kissed her instead. The skin of her face felt like crinkled paper.

'I've had a very happy day,' she said when Belle Frye and I had reached the kitchen door. 'I've had a lovely day,' she said, not seeming to be talking to us but to herself. She was crying, and she smiled in the lamplight, looking straight ahead of her. 'It's all over,' she said. 'Yet again.'

We didn't know what she was talking about and presumed she meant the tennis party. 'Yet again,' Belle Frye repeated as we crossed the stable-yard. She spoke in a soppy voice because she was given to soppiness. 'Poor Mrs Ashburton!' she said, beginning to cry herself, or pretending to. 'Imagine being eighty-one,' she said. 'Imagine sitting in a kitchen and remembering all the other tennis parties, knowing you'd have to die soon. Race you,' Belle Frye said, forgetting to be soppy any more.

Going home, Joe and Arthur sat in the back of the truck with Dick and Betty. Colin Gregg had ridden off on his bicycle, and Mr Bowe had driven away with Mrs Tissard beside him and Mr Tissard and Miss Sweet in the dickey of his Morris Cowley. My mother, my father and myself were all squashed into the front of the truck, and there was so little room that my father couldn't change gear and had to drive all the way to the farm in first. In the back of the truck Joe and Arthur and Dick were singing, but Betty wasn't, and I could imagine Betty just sitting there, staring, thinking about Colin Gregg. In Betty's bedroom there were photographs of Clark Gable and Ronald Coleman, and Claudette Colbert and the little Princesses. Betty was going to marry Colin, I kept saying to myself in the truck. There'd be other tennis parties and Betty would be older and would know her own mind, and Colin Gregg would ask her and she'd say yes. It was very beautiful, I thought, as the truck shuddered over the uneven back avenue of Challacombe Manor. It was as beautiful as the tennis party itself, the white dresses and Betty's long hair, and everyone sitting and watching in the sunshine, and evening slowly descending. 'Well, that's the end of that,' my father said, and he didn't seem to be talking about the tennis party because his voice was too serious for that. He repeated a conversation he'd had with Mr Bowe and one he'd had with Mr Race, but I didn't listen because his voice was so lugubrious, not at all like it had been at the tennis party. I was huddled on my mother's knees, falling asleep. I imagined my father was talking about Lloyd's Bank again, and I could hear my mother agreeing with him.

I woke up when my mother was taking off my dress in my bedroom.

'What is it?' I said. 'Is it because the tennis party's over? Why's everyone so sad?'

My mother shook her head, but I kept asking her because she was looking sorrowful herself and I wasn't sleepy any more. In the end she sat on the edge of my bed and said that people thought there was going to be another war against the Germans.

'Germans?' I said, thinking of the grey, steely people that Mrs Ashburton had so often told me about, the people who ate black bread.

It would be all right, my mother said, trying to smile. She told me that we'd have to make special curtains for the windows so that the German aeroplanes wouldn't see the lights at night. She told me there'd probably be sugar rationing.

I lay there listening to her, knowing now why Mrs Ashburton had said that yet again it was all over, and knowing what would happen next. I didn't want to think about it, but I couldn't help thinking about it: my father would go away, and Dick would go also, and Joe and Arthur and Betty's Colin Gregg. I would continue to attend Miss Pritchard's Primary and then I'd go on to the Grammar, and my father would be killed. A soldier would rush at my father with a bayonet and twist the bayonet in my father's stomach, and Dick would do the same to another soldier, and Joe and Arthur would be missing in the trenches, and Colin Gregg would be shot.

My mother kissed me and told me to say my prayers before I went to sleep. She told me to pray for the peace to continue, as she intended to do herself. There was just a chance, she said, that it might.

She went away and I lay awake, beginning to hate the Germans and not feeling ashamed of it, like Mrs Ashburton was. No German would ever have played tennis that day, I thought, no German would have stood around having tea and sandwiches and meringues, smacking away the midges when night came. No German would ever have tried to re-capture the past, or would have helped an old woman to do so, like my mother and my father had done, and Mr Race and Mr Bowe and Mr Throataway and Mrs Garland and Betty and Dick and Colin Gregg. The Germans weren't like that. The Germans wouldn't see the joke when my father said that for all he knew Lloyd's Bank owned Mrs Ashburton.

I didn't pray for the peace to continue, but prayed instead that my father and Dick might come back when the war was over. I didn't pray that Joe and Arthur and Colin Gregg should come back since that would be asking too much, because some men had to be killed, according to Mrs Ash-burton's law of averages. I hadn't understood her when Mrs Ashburton had said that cruelty was natural in wartime, but I understood now. I understood her law of averages and her sitting alone in her dark kitchen, crying over the past. I cried myself, thinking of the grass growing on her tennis court, and the cruelty that was natural.

A Complicated Nature

At a party once Attridge overheard a woman saying he gave her the shivers. 'Vicious-tongued,' this woman, a Mrs de Paul, had said. 'Forked like a serpent's.'

It was true, and he admitted it to himself without apology, though 'sharp' was how he preferred to describe the quality the woman had referred to. He couldn't help it if his quick eye had a way of rooting out other people's defects and didn't particularly bother to search for virtues.

Sharp about other people, he was sharp about himself as well: confessing his own defects, he found his virtues tedious. He was kind and generous to the people he chose as his friends, and took it for granted that he should be. He was a tidy man, but took no credit for that since being tidy was part of his nature. He was meticulous about his dress, and he was cultured, being particularly keen on opera – especially the operas of Wagner – and on Velasquez. He had developed his own good taste, and was proud of the job he had made of it.

A man of fifty, with hair that had greyed and spectacles with fine, colourless rims, he was given to slimming, for the weight he had gained in middle age rounded his face and made it pinker than he cared for: vanity was a weakness in him.

Attridge had once been married. In 1952 his parents had died, his father in February and his mother in November. Attridge had been their only child and had always lived with them. Disliking – or so he then considered – the solitude their death left him in, he married in 1953 a girl called Bernice Golder, but this most unfortunate conjunction had lasted only three months. 'Nasty dry old thing,' his ex-wife had screamed at him on their honeymoon in Siena, and he had enraged her further by pointing out that nasty and dry he might be but old he wasn't. 'You were never young,' she had replied more calmly than before. 'Even as a child you must have been like dust.' That wasn't so, he tried to explain; the truth was that he had a complicated nature. But she didn't listen to him.

Attridge lived alone now, existing comfortably on profits from the shares his parents had left him. He occupied a flat in a block, doing all his own cooking and taking pride in the small dinner parties he gave. His flat was just as his good taste wished it to be. The bathroom was tiled with blue Italian tiles, his bedroom severe and male, the hall warmly rust. His sitting-room, he privately judged, reflected a part of himself that did not come into the open, a mysterious element that even he knew little about and could only guess at. He'd saved up for the Egyptian rugs, scarlet and black and brown, on the waxed oak boards. He'd bought the first one in 1959 and each year subsequently had contrived to put aside his January and February Anglo-American Telegraph dividends until the floor was covered. He'd bought the last one a year ago.

On the walls of the room there was pale blue hessian, a background for his four tiny Velasquez drawings, and for the Toulouse Lautrec drawing and the Degas, and the two brown charcoal studies, school of Michelangelo. There was a sofa and a sofa-table, authenticated Sheraton, and a Regency table in marble and gold that he had almost made up his mind to get rid of, and some Staffordshire figures. There was drama in the decoration and arrangement of the room, a quite flam-boyant drama that Attridge felt was related to the latent element in himself, part of his complicated nature.

'I'm hopeless in an emergency,' he said in this room one afternoon, speaking with off-putting asperity into his ivory-coloured telephone. A woman called Mrs Matara, who lived in the flat above his, appeared not to hear him. 'Something has gone wrong, you see,' she explained in an upset voice, adding that she'd have to come down. She then abruptly replaced the receiver.

It was an afternoon in late November. It was raining, and already – at half-past three – twilight had settled in. From a window of his sitting-room Attridge had been gazing at all this when his telephone rang. He'd been looking at the rain dismally falling and lights going on in other windows and at a man, five storeys down, sweeping sodden leaves from the concrete forecourt of the block of flats. When the phone rang he'd thought it might be his friend, old Mrs Harcourt-Egan. He and Mrs Harcourt-Egan were to go together to Persepolis in a fortnight's time and there were still some minor arrangements to be made, although the essential booking had naturally been completed long since. It had been a considerable surprise to hear himself addressed by name in a voice he had been quite unable to place. He'd greeted Mrs Matara once or twice in the lift and that was all: she and her husband had moved into the flats only a year ago.

'I do so apologise,' Mrs Matara said when he opened the door to her. Against his will he welcomed her into the hall and she, knowing the geography of the flat since it was the same as her own, made for the sitting-room. 'It's really terrible of me,' she said, 'only I honestly don't know where to turn.' She spoke in a rushed and agitated manner, and he sighed as he followed her, resolving to point out when she revealed what her trouble was that Chamberlain, the janitor, was employed to deal with tenants' difficulties. She was just the kind of woman to make a nuisance of herself with a neighbour, you could tell that by looking at her. It irritated him that he hadn't sized her up better when he'd met her in the lift.

She was a woman of about the same age as himself, he guessed, small and thin and black-haired, though the hair, he also guessed, was almost certainly dyed. He wondered if she might be Jewish, which would account for her emotional condition: she had a Jewish look, and the name was presumably foreign. Her husband, whom he had also only met in the lift, had a look about the eyes which Attridge now said to himself might well have been developed in the clothing business. Of Austrian origin, he hazarded, or possibly even Polish. Mrs Matara had an accent of some kind, although her English appeared otherwise to be perfect. She was not out of the top drawer, but then people of the Jewish race rarely were. His own ex-wife, Jewish also, had most certainly not been.

Mrs Matara sat on the edge of a chair he had bought for ninety guineas fifteen years ago. It was also certainly Sheraton, a high-back chair with slim arms in inlaid walnut. He'd had it resprung and upholstered and covered in striped pink, four different shades.

'A really ghastly thing,' Mrs Matara said, 'a terrible thing has happened in my flat, Mr Attridge.'

She'd fused the whole place. She couldn't turn a tap off. The garbage disposal unit had failed. His ex-wife had made a ridiculous fuss when, because of her own stupidity, she'd broken her electric hair-curling apparatus on their honeymoon. Grotesque she'd looked with the plastic objects in her hair; he'd been relieved that they didn't work.

'I really can't mend anything,' he said. 'Chamberlain is there for that, you know.'

She shook her head. She was like a small bird sitting there, a wren or an undersized sparrow. A Jewish sparrow, he said to himself, pleased with this analogy. She had a handkerchief between her fingers, a small piece of material, which she now raised to her face. She touched her eyes with it, one after the other. When she spoke again she said that a man had died in her flat.

'Good heavens!'

'It's terrible!' Mrs Matara cried. 'Oh, my God!'

He poured brandy from a Georgian decanter that Mrs Harcourt-Egan had given him three Christmases ago, after their trip to Sicily. She'd given him a pair, in appreciation of what she called his kindness on that holiday. The gesture had been far too generous: the decanters were family heirlooms, and he'd done so little for her in Sicily apart from reading *Northanger Abbey* aloud when she'd had her stomach upset.

The man, he guessed, was not Mr Matara. No woman would say that a man had died, meaning her husband. Attridge imagined that a window-cleaner had fallen off a step-ladder. Quite clearly, he saw in his mind's eye a step-ladder standing at a window and the body of a man in white overalls huddled on the ground. He even saw Mrs Matara bending over the body, attempting to establish its condition.

'Drink it all,' he said, placing the brandy glass in Mrs Matara's right hand, hoping as he did so that she wasn't going to drop it.

She didn't drop it. She drank the brandy and then, to Attridge's surprise, held out the glass in a clear request for more.

'Oh, if only you would,' she said as he poured it, and he realised that while he'd been pouring the first glass, while his mind had been wandering back to the occasion in Sicily and the gift of the decanters, his guest had made some demand of him.

'You could say he was a friend,' Mrs Matara said.

She went on talking. The man who had died had died of a heart attack. The presence of his body in her flat was an embarrassment. She told a story of a love affair that had begun six years ago. She went into details: she had met the man at a party given by people called Morton, the man had been married, what point was there in hurting a dead man's wife? what point was there in upsetting her own husband, when he need never know? She rose and crossed the room to the brandy decanter. The man, she said, had died in the bed that was her husband's as well as hers.

'I wouldn't have come here – oh God, I wouldn't have come here if I hadn't been desperate.' Her voice was shrill. She was nearly hysterical. The brandy had brought out two patches of brightness in her cheeks. Her eyes were watering again, but she did not now touch them with the handkerchief. The water ran, over the bright patches, trailing mascara and other make-up with it.

'I sat for hours,' she cried. 'Well, it seemed like hours. I sat there looking at him. We were both without a stitch, Mr Attridge.'

'Good heavens!'

'I didn't feel anything at all. I didn't love him, you know. All I felt was, Oh God, what a thing to happen!'

Attridge poured himself some brandy, feeling the need for it. She reminded him quite strongly of his ex-wife, not just because of the Jewish thing or the nuisance she was making of herself but because of the way she had so casually said they'd been without a stitch. In Siena on their honeymoon his ex-wife had constantly been flaunting her nakedness, striding about their bedroom. 'The trouble with you,' she'd said, 'you like your nudes on canvas.'

'You could say he was a friend,' Mrs Matara said again. She wanted him to come with her to her flat. She wanted him to help her dress the man. In the name of humanity, she was suggesting, they should falsify the location of death.

He shook his head, outraged and considerably repelled. The images in his mind were most unpleasant. There was the naked male body, dead on a bed. There was Mrs Matara and himself pulling the man's clothes on to his body, struggling because *rigor mortis* was setting in.

'Oh God, what can I do?' cried Mrs Marata.

'I think you should telephone a doctor, Mrs Matara.'

'Oh, what use is a doctor, for God's sake? The man's dead.'

'It's usual – '

'Look, one minute we're having lunch – an omelette, just as usual, and salad and Pouilly Fuissé – and the next minute the poor man's dead.'

'I thought you said – '

'Oh, you know what I mean. "Lovely, oh darling, lovely," he said, and then he collapsed. Well, I didn't know he'd collapsed. I mean, I didn't know he was dead. He collapsed just like he always collapses. Post-coital – '

'I'd rather not hear – '

'Oh, for Jesus' sake!' She was shouting. She was on her feet, again approaching the decanter. Her hair had fallen out of the pins that held it and was now dishevelled. Her lipstick was blurred, some of it even smeared her chin. She looked most unattractive, he considered.

'I cannot help you in this matter, Mrs Matara,' he said as firmly as he could. 'I can telephone a doctor – '

'Will you for God's sake stop about a doctor!'

'I cannot assist you with your friend, Mrs Matara.'

'All I want you to do is to help me put his clothes back on. He's too heavy, I can't do it myself – '

'I'm very sorry, Mrs Matara.'

'And slip him down here. The lift is only a few yards – '

'That's quite impossible.'

She went close to him, with her glass considerably replenished. She pushed her face at his in a way that he considered predatory. He was aware of the smell of her scent, and of another smell that he couldn't prevent himself from thinking must be the smell of sexual intercourse: he had read of this odour in a book by Ernest Hemingway.

'My husband and I are a contentedly married couple,' she said, with her lips so near to his that they almost touched. 'That man upstairs has a wife who doesn't know a thing, an innocent woman. Don't you understand such things, Mr Attridge? Don't you see what will happen if the dead body of my lover is discovered in my husband's bed? Can't you visualise the pain it'll cause?'

He moved away. It was a long time since he had felt so angry and yet he was determined to control his anger. The woman knew nothing of civilised behaviour or she wouldn't have come bursting into the privacy of a stranger like this, with preposterous and unlawful suggestions. The woman, for all he knew, was unbalanced.

'I'm sorry,' he said in what he hoped was an icy voice. 'I'm sorry, but for a start I do not see how you and your husband could possibly be a contentedly married couple.'

'I'm telling you we are. I'm telling you my lover was contentedly married also. Listen, Mr Attridge.' She approached him again, closing in on him like an animal. 'Listen, Mr Attridge; we met for physical reasons, once a week at lunchtime. For five years ever since the Mortons' party, we've been meeting once a week, for an omelette and Pouilly Fuissé, and sex. It had nothing to do with our two marriages. But it will now: that woman will see her marriage as a failure now. She'll mourn it for the rest of her days, when she should be mourning her husband. I'll be divorced.'

'You should have thought of that – '

She hit him with her left hand. She hit him on the face, the palm of her hand stinging the pink, plump flesh.

'Mrs Matara!'

He had meant to shout her name, but instead his protest came from him in a shrill whisper. Since his honeymoon no one had struck him, and he recalled the fear he'd felt when he'd been struck then, in the bedroom in Siena. 'I could kill you,' his ex-wife had shouted at him. 'I'd kill you if you weren't dead already.'

'I must ask you to go, Mrs Matara,' he said in the same shrill whisper. He cleared his throat. 'At once,' he said, in a more successful voice.

She shook her head. She said he had no right to tell her what she should have thought of. She was upset as few women can ever be upset: in all decency and humanity it wasn't fair to say she should have thought of that. She cried out noisily in his sitting-room and he felt that he was in a nightmare. It had all the horror and absurdity and violence of a nightmare: the woman standing in front of him with water coming out of her eyes, drinking his brandy and hitting him.

She spoke softly then, not in her violent way. She placed the brandy glass on the marble surface of the Regency table and stood there with her head down. He knew she was still weeping even though he couldn't see her face and couldn't hear any noise coming from her. She whispered that she was sorry.

'Please forgive me, Mr Attridge. I'm very sorry.'

He nodded, implying that he accepted this apology. It was all very nasty, but for the woman it was naturally an upsetting thing to happen. He imagined, when a little time had passed, telling the story to Mrs Harcourt-Egan and to others, relating how a woman, to all intents and purposes a stranger to him, had telephoned him to say she was in need of assistance and then had come down from her flat with this awful tragedy to relate. He imagined himself describing Mrs Matara, how at first she'd seemed quite smart and then had become dishevelled, how she'd helped herself to his brandy and had suddenly struck him. He imagined Mrs Harcourt-Egan and others gasping when he said that. He seemed to see his own slight smile as he went on to say that the woman could not be blamed. He heard himself saying that the end of the matter was that Mrs Matara just went away.

But in fact Mrs Matara did not go away. Mrs Matara continued to stand, weeping quietly.

'I'm sorry too,' he said, feeling that the words, with the finality he'd slipped into them, would cause her to move to the door of the sitting-room.

'If you'd just help me,' she said, with her head still bent. 'Just to get his clothes on.'

He began to reply. He made a noise in his throat.

'I can't manage,' she said, 'on my own.'

She raised her head and looked across the room at him. Her face was blotched all over now, with make-up and tears. Her hair had fallen down a little more, and from where he stood Attridge thought he could see quite large areas of grey beneath the black. A rash of some kind, or it might have been flushing, had appeared on her neck.

'I wouldn't bother you,' she said, 'if I could manage on my own.' She would have telephoned a friend, she said, except there wouldn't be time for a friend to get to the block of flats. 'There's very little time, you see,' she said.

It was then, while she spoke those words, that Attridge felt the first hint of excitement. It was the same kind of excitement that he experienced just before the final curtain of *Tannhäuser*, or whenever, in the Uffizi, he looked upon Credi's Annunciation. Mrs Matara was a wretched, unattractive creature who had been conducting a typical hole-in-corner affair and had received her just rewards. It was hard to feel sorry for her, and yet for some reason it was harder not to. The man who had died had got off scot-free, leaving her to face the music miserably on her own. 'You're inhuman,' his ex-wife had said in Siena. 'You're incapable of love. Or sympathy, or anything else.' She'd stood there in her underclothes, taunting him.

'I'll manage,' Mrs Matara said, moving towards the door.

He did not move himself. She'd been so impatient, all the time in Siena. She didn't even want to sit in the square and watch the people. She'd been lethargic in the cathedral. All she'd ever wanted was to try again in bed. 'You don't like women,' she'd said, sitting up with a glass of Brolio in her hand, smoking a cigarette.

He followed Mrs Matara into the hall, and an image entered his mind of the dead man's wife. He saw her as Mrs Matara had described her, as an innocent woman who believed herself faithfully loved. He saw her as a woman with fair hair, in a garden, simply dressed. She had borne the children of the man who now lay obscenely dead, she had made a home for him and had entertained his tedious business friends, and now she was destined to suffer. It was a lie to say he didn't like women, it was absurd to say he was incapable of sympathy.

Once more he felt a hint of excitement. It was a confused feeling now, belonging as much in his body as in his mind. In a dim kind of way he seemed again to be telling the story to Mrs Harcourt-Egan or to someone else. Telling it, his voice was quiet. It spoke of the compassion he had suddenly felt for the small unattractive Jewish woman and for another woman, a total stranger whom he'd never even seen. 'A moment of truth,' his voice explained to Mrs Harcourt-Egan and others. 'I could not pass these women by.'

He knew it was true. The excitement he felt had to do with sympathy, and the compassion that had been engendered in it. His complicated nature worked in that way: there had to be drama, like the drama of a man dead in a bed, and the beauty of being unable to pass the women by, as real as the beauty of the Madonna of the Meadow. With her cigarette and her Brolio, his ex-wife wouldn't have understood that in a million years. In their bedroom in Siena she had expected something ordinary to take place, an act that rats performed.

Never in his entire life had Attridge felt as he felt now. It was the most extraordinary, and for all he knew the most important, occasion in his life. As though watching a play, he saw himself assisting the dead, naked man into his clothes. It would be enough to put his clothes on, no need to move the body from one flat to another, enough to move it from the bedroom. 'We put it in the lift and left it there,' his voice said, still telling the story. ' "No need," I said to her, "to involve my flat at all." She agreed; she had no option. The man became a man who'd had a heart attack in a lift. A travelling salesman, God knows who he was.'

The story was beautiful. It was extravagant and flamboyant, incredible almost, like all good art. Who really believed in the Madonna of the Meadow, until jolted by the genius of Bellini? *The Magic Flute* was an impossible occasion, until Mozart's music charged you like an electric current.

'Yes, Mr Attridge?'

He moved towards her, fearing to speak lest his voice emerged from him in the shrill whisper that had possessed it before. He nodded at Mrs Matara, agreeing in this way to assist her.

Hurrying through the hall and hurrying up the stairs because one flight of stairs was quicker than the lift, he felt the excitement continuing in his body. Actually it would be many months before he could tell Mrs Harcourt-Egan or anyone else about any of it. It seemed, for the moment at least, to be entirely private.

'What was he?' he asked on the stairs in a whisper.

'Was?'

'Professionally.' He was impatient, more urgent now than she. 'Salesman or something, was he?'

She shook her head. Her friend had been a dealer in antiques, she said.

Another Jew, he thought. But he was pleased because the man could have been on his way to see him, since dealers in antiques did sometimes visit him. Mrs Matara might have said to the man, at another party given by the Mortons or anywhere else you liked, that Mr Attridge, a collector of pictures and Staffordshire china, lived in the flat below hers. She could have said to Attridge that she knew a man who might have stuff that would interest him and then the man might have telephoned him, and he'd have said come round one afternoon. And in the lift the man collapsed and died.

She had her latchkey in her hand, about to insert it into the lock of her flat door. Her hand was shaking. Surprising himself, he gripped her arm, preventing her from completing the action with the key.

'Will you promise me,' he said, 'to move away from these flats? As soon as you conveniently can?'

'Of course, of course! How could I stay?'

'I'd find it awkward, meeting you about the place, Mrs Matara. Is that a bargain?'

'Yes, yes.'

She turned the key in the lock. They entered a hall that was of the exact proportions of Attridge's but different in other ways. It was a most unpleasant hall, he considered, with bell chimes in it, and two oil paintings that appeared to be the work of some emergent African, one being of negro children playing on crimson sand, the other of a negro girl with a baby at her breast.

'Oh, God!' Mrs Matara cried, turning suddenly, unable to proceed. She pushed herself at him, her sharp head embedding itself in his chest, her hands grasping the jacket of his grey suit.

'Don't worry,' he said, dragging his eyes away from the painting of the children on the crimson sand. One of her hands had ceased to grasp his jacket and had fallen into one of his. It was cold and had a fleshless feel.

'We have to do it,' he said, and for a second he saw himself again as he would see himself in retrospect: standing with the Jewish woman in her hall, holding her hand to comfort her.

While they still stood there, just as he was about to propel her forward, there was a noise.

'My God!' whispered Mrs Matara.

He knew she was thinking that her husband had returned, and he thought the same himself. Her husband had come back sooner than he usually did. He had found a corpse and was about to find his wife holding hands with a neighbour in the hall.

'Hey!' a voice said.

'Oh no!' cried Mrs Matara, rushing forward into the room that Attridge knew was her sitting-room.

There was the mumble of another voice, and then the sound of Mrs Matara's tears. It was a man's voice, but the man was not her husband: the atmosphere which came from the scene wasn't right for that.

'There now,' the other voice was saying in the sitting-room. 'There now, there now.'

The noise of Mrs Matara's weeping continued, and the man appeared at the door of the sitting-room. He was fully dressed, a sallow man, tall and black-haired, with a beard. He'd guessed what had happened, he said, as soon as he heard voices in the hall: he'd guessed that Mrs Matara had gone to get help. In an extremely casual way he said he was really quite all right, just a little groggy due to the silly blackout he'd had. Mrs Matara was a customer of his, he explained, he was in the antique business. 'I just passed out,' he said. He smiled at Attridge. He'd had a few silly blackouts recently and despite what his doctor said about there being nothing to worry about he'd have to be more careful. Really embarrassing, it was, plopping out in a client's sitting-room.

Mrs Matara appeared in the sitting-room doorway. She leaned against it, as though requiring its support. She giggled through her tears and the man spoke sharply to her, forgetting she was meant to be his client. He warned her against becoming hysterical.

'My God, you'd be hysterical,' Mrs Matara cried, 'if you'd been through all that kerfuffle.'

'Now, now – '

'For Christ's sake, I thought you were a goner. Didn't I?' she cried, addressing Attridge without looking at him and not waiting for him to reply. 'I rushed downstairs to this man here. I was in a frightful state. Wasn't I?'

'Yes.'

'We were going to put your clothes on and dump you in his flat.'

Attridge shook his head, endeavouring to imply that that was not accurate, that he'd never have agreed to the use of his flat for this purpose. But neither of them was paying any attention to him. The man was looking embarrassed, Mrs Matara was grim.

'You should damn well have told me if you were having blackouts.'

'I'm sorry,' the man said. 'I'm sorry you were troubled,' he said to Attridge. 'Please forgive Mrs Matara.'

'Forgive *you*, you mean!' she cried. 'Forgive you for being such a damn fool!'

'Do try to pull yourself together, Miriam.'

'I tell you, I thought you were dead.'

'Well, I'm not. I had a little blackout – '

'Oh, for Christ's sake, stop about your wretched blackout!'

The way she said that reminded Attridge very much of his

ex-wife. He'd had a headache once, he remembered, and she'd protested in just the same impatient tone of voice, employing almost the same words. She'd married again, of course – a man called Saunders in ICI.

'At least be civil,' the man said to Mrs Matara.

They were two of the most unpleasant people Attridge had ever come across. It was a pity the man hadn't died. He'd run to fat and was oily, there was a shower of dandruff on his jacket. You could see his stomach straining his shirt, one of the shirt-buttons had actually given way.

'Well, thank you,' Mrs Matara said, approaching Attridge with her right hand held out. She said it gracelessly, as a duty. The same hand had struck him on the face and later had slipped for comfort into one of his. It was hard and cold when he shook it, with the same fleshless feel as before. 'We still have a secret,' Mrs Matara said. She smiled at him in her dutiful way, without displaying interest in him.

The man had opened the hall-door of the flat. He stood by it, smiling also, anxious for Attridge to go.

'This afternoon's a secret,' Mrs Matara murmured, dropping her eyes in a girlish pretence. 'All this,' she said, indicating her friend. 'I'm sorry I hit you.'

'Hit him?'

'When we were upset. Downstairs. I hit him.' She giggled, apparently unable to help herself.

'Great God!' The man giggled also.

'It doesn't matter,' Attridge said.

But it did matter. The secret she spoke of wasn't worth having because it was sordid and nothing else. It was hardly the kind of thing he'd wish to mull over in private, and certainly not the kind he'd wish to tell Mrs Harcourt-Egan or anyone else. Yet the other story might even have reached his ex-wife, it was not impossible. He imagined her hearing it, and her amazement that a man whom she'd once likened to

dust had in the cause of compassion falsified the circumstances of a death. He couldn't imagine the man his ex-wife
had married doing such a thing, or Mrs Matara's husband,
or the dandruffy man who now stood by the door of the flat.
Such men would have been frightened out of their wits.

'Goodbye,' she said.

'Goodbye,' the man said, smiling at the door.

Attridge wanted to say something. He wanted to linger for
a moment longer and to mention his ex-wife. He wanted to
tell them what he had never told another soul, that his ex-
wife had done terrible things to him. He disliked all Jewish
people, he wanted to say, because of his ex-wife and her lack
of understanding. Marriage repelled him because of her. It
was she who had made him vicious-tongued. It was she who
had embittered him.

He looked from one face to the other. They would not
understand and they would not be capable of making an
effort, as he had when faced with the woman's predicament.
He had always been a little on the cold side, he knew that
well. But his ex-wife might have drawn on the other aspects
of his nature and dispelled the coldness. Instead of displaying
all that impatience, she might have cosseted him and accepted
his complications. The love she sought would have come in
its own good time, as sympathy and compassion had eventually come that afternoon. Warmth was buried deep in some
people, he wanted to say to the two faces in the hall, but he
knew that, like his ex-wife, the faces would not understand.

As he went he heard the click of the door behind him and
imagined a hushed giggling in the hall. He would be feeling
like a prince if the man had really died.

Teresa's Wedding

The remains of the wedding-cake was on top of the piano in Swanton's lounge-bar, beneath a framed advertisement for Power's whiskey. Chas Flynn, the best man, had opened two packets of confetti: it lay thickly on the remains of the wedding-cake, on the surface of the bar and the piano, on the table and the two small chairs that the lounge-bar contained, and on the tattered green and red linoleum.

The wedding guests, themselves covered in confetti, stood in groups. Father Hogan, who had conducted the service in the Church of the Immaculate Conception, stood with Mrs Atty, the mother of the bride, and Mrs Cornish, the mother of the bridegroom, and Mrs Tracy, a sister of Mrs Atty's.

Mrs Tracy was the stoutest of the three women, a farmer's widow who lived eight miles from the town. In spite of the jubilant nature of the occasion, she was dressed in black, a colour she had affected since the death of her husband three years ago. Mrs Atty, bespectacled, with her grey hair in a bun, wore a flowered dress – small yellow and blue blooms that blended easily with the confetti. Mrs Cornish was in pink, with a pink hat. Father Hogan, a big red-complexioned man, held a tumbler containing whiskey and water in equal measures; his companions sipped Winter's Tale sherry.

Artie Cornish, the bridegroom, drank stout with his friends Eddie Boland and Chas Flynn, who worked in the town's bacon factory, and Screw Doyle, so called because he served behind the counter in Phelan's hardware shop. Artie, who worked in a shop himself – Driscoll's Provisions and Bar – was a freckled man of twenty-eight, six years older than his bride. He was heavily built, his bulk encased now in a suit of navy-blue serge, similar to the suits that all the other men were wearing that morning in Swanton's lounge-bar. In the opinion of Mr Driscoll, his employer, he was a conscientious shopman, with a good memory for where commodities were kept on the shelves. Customers occasionally found him slow.

The fathers of the bride and bridegroom, Mr Atty and Mr Cornish, were talking about greyhounds, keeping close to the bar. They shared a feeling of unease, caused by being in the lounge-bar of Swanton's, with women present, on a Saturday morning. 'Bring us two more big ones,' Mr Cornish requested of Kevin, a youth behind the bar, hoping that this addition to his consumption of whiskey would relax matters. They wore white carnations in the button-holes of their suits, and stiff white collars which were reddening their necks. Unknown to one another, they shared the same thought: a wish that the bride and groom would soon decide to bring the occasion to an end by going to prepare themselves for their journey to Cork on the half-one bus. Mr Atty and Mr Cornish, bald-headed men of fifty-three and fifty-five, had it in mind to spend the remainder of the day in Swanton's lounge-bar, celebrating in their particular way the union of their children.

The bride, who had been Teresa Atty and was now Teresa Cornish, had a round, pretty face and black, pretty hair, and was a month and a half pregnant. She stood in the corner of the lounge with her friends, Philomena Morrissey and Kitty Rouche, both of whom had been bridesmaids. All three of them were attired in their wedding finery, dresses they had feverishly worked on to get finished in time for the wedding. They planned to alter the dresses and have them dyed so that later on they could go to parties in them, even though parties were rare in the town.

'I hope you'll be happy, Teresa,' Kitty Roche whispered. 'I hope you'll be all right.' She couldn't help giggling, even though she didn't want to. She giggled because she'd drunk a glass of gin and Kia-Ora orange, which Screw Doyle had said would steady her. She'd been nervous in the church. She'd tripped twice on the walk down the aisle.

'You'll be marrying yourself one of these days,' Teresa whispered, her cheeks still glowing after the excitement of the ceremony. 'I hope you'll be happy too, Kit.'

But Kitty Roche, who was asthmatic, did not believe she'd ever marry. She'd be like Miss Levis, the Protestant woman on the Cork road, who'd never got married because of tuberculosis. Or old Hannah Flood, who had a bad hip. And it wasn't just that no one would want to be saddled with a diseased wife: there was also the fact that the asthma caused a recurrent skin complaint on her face and neck and hands.

Teresa and Philomena drank glasses of Babycham, and Kitty drank Kia-Ora with water instead of gin in it. They'd known each other all their lives. They'd been to the Presentation Nuns together, they'd taken First Communion together. Even when they'd left the Nuns, when Teresa had gone to work in the Medical Hall and Kitty Roche and Philomena in Keane's drapery, they'd continued to see each other almost every day.

'We'll think of you, Teresa,' Philomena said. 'We'll pray for you.' Philomena, plump and pale-haired, had every hope of marrying and had even planned her dress, in light lemony lace, with a Limerick veil. Twice in the last month she'd gone out with Des Foley the vet, and even if he was a few years older than he might be and had a car that smelt of cattle disinfectant, there was more to be said for Des Foley than for many another.

Teresa's two sisters, much older than Teresa, stood by the piano and the framed Power's advertisement, between the two windows of the lounge-bar. Agnes, in smart powder-blue, was tall and thin, the older of the two; Loretta, in brown, was small. Their own two marriages, eleven and nine years ago, had been consecrated by Father Hogan in the Church of the Immaculate Conception and celebrated afterwards in this same lounge-bar. Loretta had married a man who was no longer mentioned because he'd gone to England and had never come back. Agnes had married George Tobin, who was at present sitting outside the lounge-bar in a Ford Prefect, in charge of his and Agnes's three small children. The Tobins lived in Cork now, George being the manager of a shoe-shop there. Loretta lived with her parents, like an unmarried daughter again.

'Sickens you,' Agnes said 'She's only a kid, marrying a goop like that. She'll be stuck in this dump of a town for ever.'

Loretta didn't say anything. It was well known that Agnes's own marriage had turned out well: George Tobin was a tee-totaller and had no interest in either horses or greyhounds. From where she stood Loretta could see him through the window, sitting patiently in the Ford Prefect, reading a comic to his children. Loretta's marriage had not been consummated.

'Well, though I've said it before I'll say it again,' said Father Hogan. 'It's a great day for a mother.'

Mrs Atty and Mrs Cornish politely agreed, without speaking. Mrs Tracy smiled.

'And for an aunt too, Mrs Tracy. Naturally enough.'

Mrs Tracy smiled again. 'A great day,' she said.

'Ah, I'm happy for Teresa,' Father Hogan said. 'And for Artie, too, Mrs Cornish; naturally enough. Aren't they as fine a couple as ever stepped out of this town?'

'Are they leaving the town?' Mrs Tracy asked, confusion breaking in her face. 'I thought Artie was fixed in Driscoll's.'

'It's a manner of speaking, Mrs Tracy,' Father Hogan

explained. 'It's a way of putting the thing. When I was marrying them this morning I looked down at their two faces and I said to myself, "Isn't it great God gave them life?"'

The three women looked across the lounge, at Teresa standing with her friends Philomena and Kitty Roche, and then at Artie, with Screw Doyle, Eddie Boland and Chas Flynn.

'He has a great career in front of him in Driscoll's,' Father Hogan pronounced. 'Will Teresa remain on in the Medical Hall, Mrs Atty?'

Mrs Atty replied that her daughter would remain for a while in the Medical Hall. It was Father Hogan who had persuaded Artie of his duty when Artie had hesitated. Mrs Atty and Teresa had gone to him for advice, he'd spoken to Artie and to Mr and Mrs Cornish, and the matter had naturally not been mentioned on either side since.

'Will I get you another glassful, Father?' enquired Mrs Tracy, holding out her hand for the priest's tumbler.

'Well, it isn't every day I'm honoured,' said Father Hogan with his smile, putting the tumbler into Mrs Tracy's hand.

At the bar Mr Atty and Mr Cornish drank steadily on. In their corner Teresa and her bridesmaids talked about weddings that had taken place in the Church of the Immaculate Conception in the past, how they had stood by the railings of the church when they were children, excited by the finery and the men in serge suits. Teresa's sisters whispered, Agnes continuing about the inadequacy of the man Teresa had just married. Loretta whispered without actually forming words. She wished her sister wouldn't go on so because she didn't want to think about any of it, about what had happened to Teresa, and what would happen to her again tonight, in a hotel in Cork. She'd fainted when it had happened to herself, when he'd come at her like a farm animal. She'd fought like a mad thing.

It was noisier in the lounge-bar than it had been. The voices of the bridegroom's friends were raised; behind the bar young Kevin had switched on the wireless. *Take my hand*, cooed a soft male voice, *take my whole life too*.

'Bedad, there'll be no holding you tonight, Artie,' Eddie Boland whispered thickly into the bridegroom's ear. He nudged Artie in the stomach with his elbow, spilling some Guinness. He laughed uproariously.

'We're following you in two cars,' Screw Doyle said. 'We'll be waiting in the double bed for you.' Screw Doyle laughed also, striking the floor repeatedly with his left foot, which was a habit of his when excited. At a late hour the night before he'd told Artie that once, after a dance, he'd spent an hour in a field with the girl whom Artie had agreed to marry. 'I had a great bloody ride of her,' he'd confided.

'I'll have a word with Teresa,' said Father Hogan, moving away from Teresa's mother, her aunt and Mrs Cornish. He did not, however, cross the lounge immediately, but paused by the bar, where Mr Cornish and Mr Atty were. He put his empty tumbler on the bar itself, and Mr Atty pushed it towards young Kevin, who at once refilled it.

'Well, it's a great day for a father,' said Father Hogan. 'Aren't they a tip-top credit to each other?'

'Who's that, Father?' enquired Mr Cornish, his eyes a little bleary, sweat hanging from his cheeks.

Father Hogan laughed. He put his tumbler on the bar again, and Mr Cornish pushed it towards young Kevin for another refill.

In their corner Philomena confided to Teresa and Kitty Roche that she wouldn't mind marrying Des Foley the vet. She'd had four glasses of Babycham. If he asked her this minute, she said, she'd probably say yes. 'Is Chas Flynn nice?' Kitty Roche asked, squinting across at him.

On the wireless Petula Clark was singing 'Downtown'. Eddie Boland was whistling 'Mother Macree'. 'Listen, Screw,' Artie said, keeping his voice low although it wasn't necessary. 'Is that true? Did you go into a field with Teresa?'

Loretta watched while George Tobin in his Ford Prefect turned a page of the comic he was reading to his children. Her sister's voice continued in its abuse of the town and its people, in particular the shopman who had got Teresa pregnant. Agnes hated the town and always had. She'd met George Tobin at a dance in Cork and had said to Loretta that in six months' time she'd be gone from the town for ever. Which was precisely what had happened, except that marriage had made her less nice than she'd been. She'd hated the town in a jolly way once, laughing over it. Now she hardly laughed at all.

'Look at him,' she was saying. 'I doubt he knows how to hold a knife and fork.'

Loretta ceased her observation of her sister's husband through the window and regarded Artie Cornish instead. She looked away from him immediately because his face, so quickly replacing the face of George Tobin, had caused in her mind a double image which now brutally persisted. She felt a sickness in her stomach, and closed her eyes and prayed. But the double image remained: George Tobin and Artie Cornish coming at her sisters like two farmyard animals and her sisters fighting to get away. 'Dear Jesus,' she whispered to herself. 'Dear Jesus, help me.'

'Sure it was only a bit of gas,' Screw Doyle assured Artie. 'Sure there was no harm done, Artie.'

In no way did Teresa love him. She had been aware of that when Father Hogan had arranged the marriage, and even before that, when she'd told her mother that she thought she was pregnant and had then mentioned Artie Cornish's name. Artie Cornish was much the same as his friends: you could be walking along a road with Screw Doyle or Artie Cornish and you could hardly tell the difference. There was nothing special about Artie Cornish, except that he always added up the figures twice when he was serving you in Driscoll's. There was nothing bad about him either, any more than there was anything bad about Eddie Boland or Chas Flynn or even Screw Doyle. She'd said privately to Father Hogan that she didn't love him or feel anything for him one way or the other: Father Hogan had replied that in the circumstances all that line of talk was irrelevant.

When she was at the Presentation Convent Teresa had imagined her wedding, and even the celebration in this very lounge-bar. She had imagined everything that had happened that morning, and the things that were happening still. She had imagined herself standing with her bridesmaids as she was standing now, her mother and her aunt drinking sherry, Agnes and Loretta being there too, and other people, and music. Only the bridegroom had been mysterious, some faceless, bodiless presence, beyond imagination. From conversations she had had with Philomena and Kitty Roche, and with her sisters, she knew that they had imagined in a similar way. Yet Agnes had settled for George Tobin because George Tobin was employed in Cork and could take her away from the town. Loretta, who had been married for a matter of weeks, was going to become a nun.

Artie ordered more bottles of stout from young Kevin. He didn't want to catch the half-one bus and have to sit beside her all the way to Cork. He didn't want to go to the Lee Hotel when they could just as easily have remained in the town, when he could just as easily have gone in to Driscoll's tomorrow and continued as before. It would have been different if Screw Doyle hadn't said he'd been in a field with her: you could pretend a bit on the bus, and in the hotel, just to make the whole thing go. You could pretend like you'd been pretending ever since Father Hogan had laid down the law, you could make the best of it like Father Hogan had said.

He handed a bottle of stout to Chas Flynn and one to Screw Doyle and another to Eddie Boland. He'd ask her about it on the bus. He'd repeat what Screw Doyle had said and ask her if it was true. For all he knew the child she was carrying was Screw Doyle's child and would be born with Screw Doyle's thin nose, and everyone in the town would know when they looked at it. His mother had told him when he was sixteen never to trust a girl, never to get involved, because he'd be caught in the end. He'd get caught because he was easy-going, because he didn't possess the smartness of Screw Doyle and some of the others. 'Sure, you might as well marry Teresa as anyone else,' his father had said after Father Hogan had called to see them about the matter. His mother had said things would never be the same between them again.

Eddie Boland sat down at the piano and played 'Mother Macree', causing Agnes and Loretta to move to the other side of the lounge-bar. In the motor-car outside the Tobin children asked their father what the music was for.

'God go with you, girl,' Father Hogan said to Teresa, motioning Kitty Roche and Philomena away. 'Isn't it a grand thing that's happened, Teresa?' His red-skinned face, with the shiny false teeth so evenly arrayed in it, was close to hers. For a moment she thought he might kiss her, which of course was ridiculous, Father Hogan kissing anyone, even at a wedding celebration.

'It's a great day for all of us, girl.'

When she'd told her mother, her mother said it made her feel sick in her stomach. Her father hit her on the side of the face. Agnes came down specially from Cork to try and sort the matter out. It was then that Loretta had first mentioned becoming a nun.

'I want to say two words,' said Father Hogan, still standing beside her, but now addressing everyone in the lounge-bar. 'Come over here alongside us, Artie. Is there a drop in everyone's glass?'

Artie moved across the lounge-bar, with his glass of stout. Mr Cornish told young Kevin to pour out a few more measures. Eddie Boland stopped playing the piano.

'It's only this,' said Father Hogan. 'I want us all to lift our glasses to Artie and Teresa. May God go with you, the pair of you,' he said, lifting his own glass.

'Health, wealth and happiness,' proclaimed Mr Cornish from the bar.

'And an early night,' shouted Screw Doyle. 'Don't forget to draw the curtains, Artie.'

They stood awkwardly, not holding hands, not even touching. Teresa watched while her mother drank the remains of her sherry, and while her aunt drank and Mrs Cornish drank. Agnes's face was disdainful, a calculated reply to the coarseness of Screw Doyle's remarks. Loretta was staring ahead of her, concentrating her mind on her novitiate. A quick flush passed over the roughened countenance of Kitty Roche. Philomena laughed, and all the men in the lounge-bar, except Father Hogan, laughed.

'That's sufficient of that talk,' Father Hogan said with contrived severity. 'May you meet happiness halfway,' he added, suitably altering his intonation. 'The pair of you, Artie and Teresa.'

Noise broke out again after that. Father Hogan shook hands

with Teresa and then with Artie. He had a funeral at half-past three, he said: he'd better go and get his dinner inside him.

'Goodbye, Father,' Artie said. 'Thanks for doing the job.'

'God bless the pair of you,' said Father Hogan, and went away.

'We should be going for the bus,' Artie said to her. 'It wouldn't do to miss the old bus.'

'No, it wouldn't.'

'I'll see you down there. You'll have to change your clothes.'

'Yes.'

'I'll come the way I am.'

'You're fine the way you are, Artie.'

He looked at the stout in his glass and didn't raise his eyes from it when he spoke again. 'Did Screw Doyle take you into a field, Teresa?'

He hadn't meant to say it then. It was wrong to come out with it like that, in the lounge-bar, with the wedding-cake still there on the piano, and Teresa still in her wedding-dress, and confetti everywhere. He knew it was wrong even before the words came out; he knew that the stout had angered and befuddled him.

'Sorry,' he said. 'Sorry, Teresa.'

She shook her head. It didn't matter: it was only to be expected that a man you didn't love and who didn't love you would ask a question like that at your wedding celebration.

'Yes,' she said. 'Yes, he did.'

'He told me. I thought he was codding. I wanted to know.'

'It's your baby, Artie. The other thing was years ago.'

He looked at her. Her face was flushed, her eyes had tears in them.

'I had too much stout,' he said.

They stood where Father Hogan had left them, drawn away from their wedding guests. Not knowing where else to look, they looked together at Father Hogan's black back as he left the lounge-bar, and then at the perspiring, naked heads of Mr Cornish and Mr Atty by the bar.

At least they had no illusions, she thought. Nothing worse could happen than what had happened already, after Father Hogan had laid down the law. She wasn't going to get a shock like Loretta had got. She wasn't going to go sour like Agnes had gone when she'd discovered that it wasn't enough just to marry a man for a purpose, in order to escape from a town. Philomena was convincing herself that she'd fallen in love with an elderly vet, and if she got any encouragement Kitty Roche would convince herself that she was mad about anyone at all.

For a moment as Teresa stood there, the last moment before she left the lounge-bar, she felt that she and Artie might make some kind of marriage together because there was nothing that could be destroyed, no magic or anything else. He could ask her the question he had asked, while she stood there in her wedding dress: he could ask her and she could truthfully reply, because there was nothing special about the occasion, or the lounge-bar all covered in confetti.

Office Romances

'Oh no, I couldn't,' Angela said in the outer office. 'Really, Mr Spelle. Thank you, though.'

'Don't you drink then, Miss Hosford? Nary a drop at all?' He laughed at his own way of putting it. He thought of winking at her as he laughed, but decided against it: girls like this were sometimes scared out of their wits by a wink.

'No, it's not that, Mr Spelle – '

'It's just that it's a way of getting to know people. Everyone else'll be down in the Arms, you know.'

Hearing that, she changed her mind and quite eagerly put the grey plastic cover on her Remington International. She'd refused his invitation to have a drink because she'd been flustered when he'd come into the outer office with his right hand poked out for her to shake, introducing himself as Gordon Spelle. He hadn't said anything about the other people from the office being there: in a matter of seconds he'd made the whole thing sound romantic, a tête-à-tête with a total stranger. Any girl's reaction would be to say she couldn't.

'Won't be a moment, Mr Spelle,' she said. She picked up her handbag from the floor beside her chair and walked with it from the office. Behind her, she heard the office silence broken by a soft whistling: Gordon Spelle essaying 'Smoke Gets in Your Eyes'.

Angela had started at C.S. & E. at half-past nine that morning, having been interviewed a month ago by Miss

Ivygale, her immediate employer. Miss Ivygale was a slender woman of fifty or thereabouts, her face meticulously made up. Her blue-grey hair was worked on daily by a hairdresser, a Mr Patric, whom twice that day she'd mentioned to Angela, deploring the fact that next March he was planning to leave the Elizabeth Salon. At C.S. & E. Miss Ivygale occupied an inner office that was more luxuriously appointed than the outer one where Angela sat with her filing cabinets and her Remington International. On the windowsill of the outer office Miss Ivygale's last secretary, whom she referred to as Sue, had left a Busy Lizzie in a blue-glazed pot. There was a calendar that showed Saturdays and Sundays in red, presented by the Michelin Tyre Company.

In a small lavatory Angela examined her face in the mirror over the wash-basin. She sighed at her complexion. Her eyes had a bulgy look because of her contact lenses. The optician had said the bulgy look would go when the lids became used to the contact lenses, but as far as she was concerned it never had. 'No, no, you're imagining it, Miss Hosford,' the optician had said when she'd gone back after a month to complain that the look was still there.

In the lavatory she touched one or two places on her cheeks with Pure Magic and powdered over it. She rubbed lipstick into her lips and then pressed a tissue between them. She ran a comb through her hair, which was fair, and fluffy because she'd washed it the night before: it was her best feature, she considered, a pretty shade, soft and naturally curly.

'I like your dress, Miss Hosford,' he said when she returned to the outer office. 'Fresh as a flower it looks.' He laughed at his own description of the blue-and-white dress she was wearing. The blue parts were flowers of a kind, he supposed, a type of blue geranium they appeared to be, with blue leaves sprouting out of blue stems. Extraordinary, the tasteless stuff a girl like this would sometimes wear.

'Thank you,' she said.

'We don't bother much with surnames at C.S. and E.' he told her as they walked along a green-carpeted corridor to a lift. 'All right to call you Angela, Miss Hosford?'

'Oh, yes, of course.'

He closed the lift doors. He smiled at her. He was a tall, sleek man who had something the matter with his left eye, a kind of droop in the upper lid and a glazed look in the eye itself, a suggestion of blindness. Another oddness about him, she thought in the lift, was his rather old-fashioned suit. It was a pepper-coloured suit with a waistcoat, cut in an Edwardian style. His manners were old-fashioned too, and the way he spoke had a pedantic air to it that recalled the past: Edwardian again perhaps, she didn't know. It seemed right that he had whistled 'Smoke Gets in Your Eyes' rather than a current pop song.

'I suppose it's your first job, Angela?'

'Oh, heavens, no!'

'I'd say you were twenty.'

'Twenty-six, actually.'

He laughed. 'I'm thirty-eight myself.'

They left the lift and walked together through the elegant reception area of C.S. and E. When she'd walked through it for her interview Angela had been reminded of the lounge of a large, new hotel: there were sofas and armchairs covered in white ersatz leather, and steel-framed reproductions of paintings by Paul Klee on rust-coloured walls, and magazines on steel-topped tables. When Angela had come for her interview, and again when she'd arrived at C.S. and E. that morning, there'd been a beautiful black-haired girl sitting at the large reception desk, which was upholstered here and there in the same ersatz leather as the sofas and the armchairs. But at this time of the evening, five to six, the beautiful black-haired girl was not there.

'I'd really have said it was your first job,' he said when they reached the street. He smiled at her. 'Something about you.'

She knew what he meant. She was often taken to be younger than she was, it had something to do with being small: five foot one she was, with thin, small arms that she particularly disliked. And of course there was her complexion, which was a schoolgirl complexion in the real sense, since schoolgirls rather than adults tended to be bothered with pimples. 'Attack them from inside, Miss Hosford,' her doctor had advised. 'Avoid all sweets and chocolate, avoid cakes and biscuits with your coffee. Lots of lemon juice, fresh fruit, salads.' She ate lots of fruit and salads anyway, just in case she'd get fat, which would have been the last straw. She naturally never ate sweet things.

'Horrid being new,' he said. 'Like your first day at school.'

The street, fashionably situated just off Grosvenor Square, was busy with people impatient to be home: it was a cold night in November, not a night for loitering. Girls in suede boots or platform shoes had turned up the collars of their coats. Some carried bundles of letters which had been signed too late to catch the afternoon dispatch boys. In the harsh artificial light their faces were pale, sometimes garish with make-up: the light drew the worst out of girls who were pretty, and killed the subtleties of carefully-chosen lipstick and make-up shades. God alone knew, Angela said to herself, what it did to her. She sighed, experiencing the familiar feeling of her inferiority complex getting the upper hand.

'Hullo, Gordon,' a man in a black overcoat said to Gordon Spelle. The man had been walking behind them for some time, while Angela had been listening to Gordon Spelle going on about the first day he'd spent at school. Miserable beyond measure he'd been.

'God, it's chilly,' the man said, dropping into step with them and smiling at Angela.

'Angela Hosford,' Gordon Spelle said. 'She's come to work for Pam Ivygale.'

'Oh, Pam, dear Pam!' the man said. He laughed in much the same way as Gordon Spelle was given to laughing, or so it seemed to Angela. His black overcoat had a little rim of black fur on its collar. His hair was black also. His face in the distorting street-light had a purple tinge, and Angela guessed that in normal circumstances it was a reddish face.

'Tommy Blyth,' Gordon Spelle said.

They entered a public house at the corner of a street. It was warm there, and crowded, and quite attractively noisy. Fairy lights were draped on a Christmas tree just inside the door because Christmas was less than six weeks away. Men like Tommy Blyth, in overcoats with furred collars and with reddish faces, were standing by a coal fire with glasses in their hands. One of them had his right arm round the waist of C.S. and E.'s black-haired receptionist.

'What's your poison, Angela?' Gordon Spelle asked, and she said she'd like some sherry.

'Dry?'

'Oh, it doesn't matter – well, medium, actually.'

He didn't approach the bar but led her into a far corner and sat her down at a table. It was less crowded there and rather dimly lit. He said he wouldn't be a minute.

People were standing at the bar, animatedly talking. Some of the men had taken off their overcoats. All of them were wearing suits, most of them grey or blue but a few of a more extravagant shade, like Gordon Spelle's. Occasionally a particular man, older and stouter than his companions, laughed raucously, swaying backwards on his heels. On a bar-stool to this man's right, in a red wool dress with a chiffon scarf at her throat, sat Miss Ivygale. The red wool coat that had been hanging just inside the outer office door all day hung on the arm of the raucous man: Miss Ivygale, Angela deduced, was intent on staying a while, or at least as long as the man was agreeable to looking after her coat for her. 'You'll find it friendly at C.S. and E.,' Miss Ivygale had said. 'A generous firm.' Miss Ivygale looked as though she'd sat on her bar-stool every night for the past twenty-three years, which was the length of time she'd been at C.S. and E.

'Alec Hemp,' Gordon Spelle said, indicating the man who had Miss Ivygale's coat on his arm.

The name occurred on C.S. and E.'s stationery: *A. R. Hemp*. It was there with other names, all of them in discreet italics, strung out along the bottom of the writing paper that had *C.S. and E.* and the address at the top: *S. P. Bakewell, T. P. Cooke, N. N. E. Govier, I. D. Jackson, A. F. Norris, P. Onniman, A. R. Hemp*, the directors of the C.S. and E. board.

'That's been going on for years,' Gordon Spelle said. He handed her her sherry and placed on the table in front of him a glass of gin and Britvic orange juice. His droopy eye had closed, as if tired. His other, all on its own, looked a little beady.

'Sorry?'

'Pam Ivygale and Alec Hemp.'

'Oh.'

'It's why she never married anyone else.'

'I see.'

Miss Ivygale's brisk manner in the office and her efficient probing when she'd interviewed Angela had given Angela the impression that she lived entirely for her work. There was no hint of a private life about Miss Ivygale, and certainly no hint of any love affair beyond a love affair with C.S. and E.

'Alec,' Gordon Spelle said, 'has a wife and four children in Brighton.'

'I see.'

'Office romance.' His droopy eye opened and gazed bleakly

at her, contrasting oddly with the busyness of the other eye. He said it was disgraceful that all this should be so, that a woman should be messed up the way Mr Hemp for twenty-three years had messed up Miss Ivygale. Everyone knew, he said, that Alec Hemp had no intention of divorcing his wife: he was stringing Miss Ivygale along. 'Mind you, though,' he added, 'she's tricky.'

'She seems very nice – '

'Oh, Pam's all right. Now, tell me all about yourself.'

Angela lived in a flat with two other girls, a ground-floor flat in what had once been a private house in Putney. She'd lived there for three years, and before that she'd lived in a similar flat in another part of Putney, and before that in a hostel. Every six or seven weeks she went home for the week-end, to her parents in Exeter, Number 4 Carhampton Road. When she'd qualified as a shorthand typist at the City Commercial College in Exeter the College had found her a position in the offices of a firm that manufactured laminates. Three years later, after some months' discussion and argument with her parents, she'd moved to London, to the offices of a firm that imported and marketed German wine. From there, she'd moved to the firm called C.S. and E.

'You can hear it in your voice,' Gordon Spelle said. 'Exeter and all that.'

She laughed. 'I thought I'd lost it.'

'It's nice, a touch of the West Countries.'

The laminates firm had been a dull one, or at least a dull one for a girl to work in. But her parents hadn't understood that. Her parents, whom she liked and respected very much, had been frightened by the idea of her going to London, where there was loose living, so other parents had told them, and drinking and drugs, and girls spending every penny they had on clothes and rarely eating a decent meal. The German wine firm had turned out to be a dull place for a girl to work in too, or so at least it seemed after a few years. Often, though, while finding it dull, Angela had felt that it suited her. With her poor complexion and her bulging contact lenses and her small, thin arms, it was a place to crouch away in. Besides herself, two elderly women were employed in the office, and there was Mr Franklin and Mr Snyder, elderly also. Economy was practised in the office, the windows seemed always to be dusty, electric-light bulbs were of a low wattage. On the mornings when a new pimple cruelly erupted on her neck or one of her cheeks, Angela had hurried from bus to tube and was glad when she reached the dingy office of the wine firm and lost herself in its shadows. Then a girl in the flat introduced her to Pure Magic, so good at disguising imperfections of the skin. But although it did not, as in an advertisement, change Angela's life and could do nothing at all for her thin arms, it did enough to draw her from the dinginess of the wine firm. A girl in the flat heard of the vacancy with Miss Ivygale at C.S. and E. and, not feeling like a change herself, persuaded Angela to apply for it. The shared opinion of the girls in the flat was that Angela needed drawing out. They liked her and were sorry for her: no joke at all, they often said to one another, to have an inferiority complex like Angela's. The inferiority complex caused nerviness in her, one of them diagnosed, and the nerviness caused her bad complexion. In actual fact, her figure and her arms were perfectly all right, and her hair was really pretty the way it curled. Now that she'd at last stopped wearing spectacles she really looked quite presentable, even if her eyes did tend to bulge a little.

'Oh, you'll like it at C.S. and E.' Gordon Spelle said. 'It's really friendly, you know. Sincerely so.'

He insisted on buying her another drink and while he was at the bar she wondered when, or if, she was going to meet the people he'd mentioned, the other employees of C.S. and

E. Miss Ivygale had narrowed her eyes in her direction and then had looked away, as if she couldn't quite place her. The black-haired receptionist had naturally not remembered her face when she'd come into the bar with the two men. The only person Gordon Spelle had so far introduced her to was the man called Tommy Blyth, who had joined the group around the fire and was holding the hand of a girl.

'It's the C.S. and E. pub,' Gordon Spelle said when he returned with the drinks. 'There isn't a soul here who isn't on the strength.' He smiled at her, his bad eye twitching. 'I like you, you know.' She smiled back at him, not knowing how to reply. He picked up her left hand and briefly squeezed it.

'Don't trust that man, Angela,' Miss Ivygale said, passing their table on her way to the Ladies. She stroked the back of Gordon Spelle's neck. 'Terrible man,' she said.

Angela was pleased that Miss Ivygale had recognised her and had spoken to her. It occurred to her that her immediate employer was probably shortsighted and had seen no more than the outline of a familiar face when she'd peered across the bar at her.

'Come on, have a drink with us,' Miss Ivygale insisted on her way back from the Ladies.

'Oh, it's all right, Pam,' Gordon Spelle said quickly, but Miss Ivygale stood there, waiting for them to get up and accompany her. 'You watch your step, my boy,' she said to Gordon Spelle as they all three made their way together. Gordon Spelle told her she was drunk.

'This is my secretary, Alec,' Miss Ivygale said at the bar. 'Replacing Sue. Angela Hosford.'

Mr Hemp shook Angela's hand. He had folded Miss Ivygale's red coat and placed it on a bar-stool. He asked Angela what she was drinking and while she was murmuring that she wouldn't have another one Gordon Spelle said a medium sherry and a gin and Britvic orange for himself. Gordon Spelle was looking cross, Angela noticed. His bad eye closed again. He was glaring at Miss Ivygale with the other one.

'Cheers, Angela,' Mr Hemp said. 'Welcome to C.S. and E.'

'Thank you, Mr Hemp.'

People were leaving the bar, waving or calling out good-night to the group she was with. A man paused to say something to Mr Hemp and then stayed to have another drink. By the fire the receptionist and another girl listened while Tommy Blyth told them about car radios, advising which kind to buy if they ever had to.

'I brought her in here to have a simple drink,' Gordon Spelle was protesting to Miss Ivygale, unsuccessfully attempting to keep his voice low. 'So's the poor girl could meet a few people.'

Miss Ivygale looked at Angela and Angela smiled at her uneasily, embarrassed because they were talking about her. Miss Ivygale didn't smile back, and it couldn't have been that Miss Ivygale didn't see her properly this time because the distance between them was less than a yard.

'You watch your little step, my boy,' Miss Ivygale warned again, and this time Gordon Spelle leaned forward and kissed her on the cheek. 'All right, my love?' he said.

Miss Ivygale ordered Mr Hemp another Bell's whisky and one for herself, reminding the barman that the measures they were drinking were double measures. 'What're you on, Dil?' she asked the man who was talking to Mr Hemp. 'No, no, must go,' he said.

'Bell's I think he's on,' the barman said, pouring a third large whisky.

'And a gin and Britvic for Gordon,' Miss Ivygale said. 'And a medium sherry.'

'Oh, really,' murmured Angela.

'Nonsense,' Miss Ivygale said.

In the lavatory Gordon Spelle swore as he urinated. Typical of bloody Pam Ivygale to go nosing in like that. He wouldn't have brought the girl to the Arms at all if he'd thought Ivygale would be soaked to the gills, hurling abuse about like bloody snowballs. God alone knew what kind of a type the girl thought he was now. Girls like that had a way of thinking you a sexual maniac if you so much as took their arm to cross a street. There'd been one he'd known before who'd come from the same kind of area, Plymouth or Bristol or somewhere. Bigger girl actually, five foot ten she must have been, fattish. 'Touch of the West Countries', he'd said when she'd opened her mouth, the first time he'd used the expression. Tamar Dymond she'd been called, messy bloody creature.

Gordon Spelle combed his hair and then decided that his tie needed to be reknotted. He removed his pepper-coloured jacket and his waistcoat and took the tie off, cocking up the collar of his striped blue shirt in order to make the operation easier. His wife, Peggy, would probably be reading a story to the younger of their two children, since she generally did so at about seven o'clock. As he reknotted his tie, he imagined his wife sitting by the child's bed reading a Topsy and Tim book.

'Oh, say you're going to Luton,' Miss Ivygale said. 'Tell her it's all just cropped up in the last fifteen minutes.'

Mr Hemp shook his head. He pointed out that rather often recently he'd telephoned his wife at seven o'clock to say that what had cropped up in the last fifteen minutes was the fact that unexpectedly he had to go to Luton. Mr Hemp had moved away from the man called Dil, closer to Miss Ivygale. They were speaking privately, Mr Hemp in a lower voice than Miss Ivygale. The man called Dil was talking to another man.

Standing by herself and not being spoken to by anyone, Angela was feeling happy. It didn't matter that no one was speaking to her, or paying her any other kind of attention. She felt warm and friendly, quite happy to be on her own while Gordon Spelle was in the Gents and Mr Hemp and Miss Ivygale talked to each other privately. She liked him, she thought as she stood there: she liked his old-fashioned manners and the way he'd whistled 'Smoke Gets in Your Eyes', and his sympathy over her being new. She smiled at him when he returned from the Gents. It was all much nicer than the German wine firm, or the laminates firm.

'Hullo,' he said in a whisper, staring at her.

'It was nice of you to bring me here,' she said, whispering also.

'Nice for me, too,' said Gordon Spelle.

Mr Hemp went away to telephone his wife. The telephone was behind Angela, in a little booth against the wall. The booth was shaped like a sedan chair, except that it didn't have any shafts to carry it by. Angela had noticed it when she'd been sitting down with Gordon Spelle. She hadn't known then that it contained a telephone and had wondered at the presence of a sedan chair in a bar. But several times since then people had entered it and each time a light had come on, revealing a telephone and a pile of directories.

'Because they only told me ten minutes ago,' Mr Hemp was saying. 'Because the bloody fools couldn't make their minds up, if you can call them minds.'

Gordon Spelle squeezed her hand and Angela squeezed back because it seemed a friendly thing to do. She felt sorry for him because he had only one good eye. It was the single defect in his handsome face. It gave him a tired look, and suggested suffering.

'I wish you'd see it my way,' Mr Hemp was saying crossly in the sedan chair. 'God damn it, I don't *want* to go to the bloody place.'

'I really must go,' Angela murmured, but Gordon Spelle continued to hold her hand. She didn't want to go. 'I really must,' she said again.

In the Terrazza, where the waiters wore striped blue-and-white jerseys and looked like sailors at a regatta, Mr Hemp and Miss Ivygale were well known. So was Gordon Spelle. The striped waiters greeted them affectionately, and a man in a dark suit addressed all three of them by name. He bowed at Angela. 'How d'you do?' he said, handing her a menu.

'*Petto di pollo sorpresa*,' Gordon Spelle recommended. 'Chicken with garlic in it.'

'Garlic? Oh – '

'He always has it,' Miss Ivygale said, pointing with the menu at Gordon Spelle. 'You'll be all right, dear.'

'What're you having, darling?' Mr Hemp asked Miss Ivygale. In the taxi on the way to the Terrazza he had sat with his arm around her and once, as though they were in private, he'd kissed her on the mouth, making quite a lot of noise about it. Angela had been embarrassed and so, she imagined, had Gordon Spelle.

'*Gamberone al spiedo*,' Miss Ivygale ordered.

'Cheers,' Mr Hemp said, lifting a glass of white wine into the air.

'I think I'm a bit drunk,' Angela said to Gordon Spelle and he wagged his head approvingly. Mr Hemp said he was a bit drunk himself, and Miss Ivygale said she was drunk, and Gordon Spelle pointed out that you only live once.

'Welcome to C.S. and E.,' Mr Hemp said, lifting his glass again.

The next morning, in the flat in Putney, Angela told her flat-mates about the delicious food at the Terrazza and how she couldn't really remember much else. There'd certainly been a conversation at the restaurant table, and in a taxi afterwards she remembered Gordon Spelle humming and then Gordon Spelle had kissed her. She seemed to remember him saying that he'd always wanted to be a dance-band leader, although she wasn't sure if she'd got that right. There were other memories of Gordon Spelle in the taxi, which she didn't relate to her flat-mates. There'd been, abruptly, his cold hand on the flesh of one of her thighs, and her surprise that the hand could have got there without her noticing. At another point there'd been his cold hand on the flesh of her stomach. 'Look, you're not married or anything?' she remembered herself saying in sudden alarm. She remembered the noise of Gordon Spelle's breathing and his tongue penetrating her ear. 'Married?' he'd said at some other point, and had laughed.

Feeling unwell but not unhappy, Angela vividly recalled the face and clothes of Gordon Spelle. She recalled his hands, which tapered and were thin, and his sleek hair and droopy eye. She wondered how on earth she was going to face him after what had happened in the taxi, or how she was going to face Miss Ivygale because Miss Ivygale, she faintly remembered, had fallen against a table on their way out of the restaurant, upsetting plates of soup and a bottle of wine. When Angela had tried to help her to stand up again she'd used unpleasant language. Yet the dim memories didn't worry Angela in any real way, not like her poor complexion sometimes worried her, or her contact lenses. Even though she was feeling unwell, she only wanted to smile that morning. She wanted to write a letter to her parents in Carhampton Road, Exeter, and tell them she'd made a marvellous decision when she'd decided to leave the German wine business and go to C.S. and E. She should have done it years ago, she wanted to tell them, because everyone at C.S. and E. was so friendly and because you only lived once. She wanted to tell them about Gordon Spelle, who had said in the taxi that he thought he was falling in love with her, which was of course an exaggeration.

She drank half a cup of Nescafé and caught a thirty-seven bus. Sitting beside an Indian on the lower deck, she thought about Gordon Spelle. On the tube to Earl's Court she thought of him again, and on the Piccadilly line between Earl's Court and Green Park she went on thinking about him. When she closed her eyes, as she once or twice did, she seemed to be with him in some anonymous place, stroking his face and comforting him because of his bad eye. She walked from the tube station, past the Rootes' Group car showrooms and Thos Cook's in Berkeley Street, along Lansdowne Row with its pet shops and card shop and coffee shops, past the Gresham Arms, the C.S. and E. pub. It was a cold morning, but the cold air was pleasant. Pigeons waddled on the pavements, cars drew up at parking-meters. Fresh-faced and shaven, the men of the night before hurried to their offices. She wouldn't have recognised Tommy Blyth, she thought, or the man called Dil, or even Mr Hemp. Girls in suede boots hurried, also looking different in the morning light. She was being silly, she said to herself in Carlos Place: he probably said that to dozens of girls.

In Angela's life there had been a few other men. At the age of twelve she had been attracted by a youth who worked in a newsagent's. She'd liked him because he'd always been ready to chat to her and smile at her, two or three years older he'd been. At fourteen she'd developed a passion for an American actor called Don Ameche whom she'd seen in an old film on television. For several weeks she'd carried with her the memory of his face and had lain in bed at night imagining a life with him in a cliff-top house she'd invented, in California. She'd seen herself and Don Ameche running into the sea together, as he had run with an actress in the film. She'd seen them eating breakfast together, out in the open, on a sunny morning. But Don Ameche, she'd suddenly realised, was sixty or seventy now.

When Angela had first come to London a man who'd briefly been employed in the German wine business used occasionally to invite her to have a cup of coffee with him at the end of the day, just as Gordon Spelle had invited her to have a drink. But being with this man wasn't like being with Gordon Spelle: the man was a shabby person who was employed in some lowly capacity, who seemed to Angela, after the third time they'd had coffee together, to be mentally deficient. One Monday morning he didn't turn up for work, and was never heard of again.

There'd been another man, more briefly, in Angela's life, a young man called Ted Apwell whom she'd met at a Saturday-night party given by a friend of one of her flatmates. She and Ted Apwell had paired off when the party, more or less at an end, had become uninhibited. At half-past three in the morning she'd allowed herself to be driven home by Ted Apwell, knowing that it was to his home rather than hers they were going. He'd taken her clothes off and in a half-hearted, inebriated way had put an end to her virginity, on a hearth-rug in front of a gas fire. He'd driven her on to her flat, promising – too often, she realised afterwards – that he'd telephone her on Monday. She'd found him hard to forget at first, not because she'd developed any great fondness for him but because of his nakedness and her own on the hearth-rug, the first time all that had happened. There hadn't, so far, been a second time.

Miss Ivygale did not come in that morning. Angela sat alone in the outer office, with nothing to do because there were no letters to type. A tea-lady arrived at a quarter-past ten and poured milky coffee on to two lumps of sugar in a cup she'd earlier placed on Angela's desk. 'Pam not in this morning?' she said, and Angela said no, Miss Ivygale wasn't.

At ten-past twelve Gordon Spelle entered the outer office. 'Red roses,' he lilted, 'for a blue lady. Oh, Mr Florist, please . . .' He laughed, standing by the door. He closed the door and crossed to her desk and kissed her. If anyone had asked her in that moment she'd have said that her inferiority complex was a thing of the past. She felt pretty when Gordon Spelle kissed her, not knowing what everyone else knew, that Gordon Spelle was notorious.

They had lunch in a place called the Coffee Bean, more modest than the Terrazza. Gordon Spelle told her about his childhood, which had not been happy. He told her about coming to C.S. and E. nine years ago, and about his earlier ambition to be a dance-band leader. 'Look,' he said when they'd drunk a carafe of Sicilian wine. 'I want to tell you, Angela: I'm actually married.'

She felt a coldness in her stomach, as though ice had somehow become lodged there. The coldness began to hurt her, like indigestion. All the warmth of her body had moved into her face and neck. She hated the flush that had come to her face and neck because she knew it made her look awful.

'Married?' she said.

He'd only laughed last night in the taxi, she remembered: he hadn't actually said he wasn't married, not that she could swear to it. He'd laughed and given the impression that married was the last thing he was, so that she'd woken up that morning with the firmly-established thought that Gordon Spelle, a bachelor, had said he loved her and had embraced her with more passion than she'd ever permitted in another man or youth. In the moments of waking she'd even been aware of thinking that one day she and Gordon Spelle might be married, and had imagined her parents in their best clothes, her father awkward, giving her away. It was all amazing; incredible that Gordon Spelle should have picked her out when all around him, in C.S. and E. and in the other offices, there were beautiful girls.

'I didn't dare tell you,' he said. 'I tried to, Angela. All last night I tried to, but I couldn't. In case you'd go away.'

They left the Coffee Bean and walked about Grosvenor Square in bitter November sunshine. Men were tidying the flowerbeds. The people who had hurried from their offices last night and had hurried into them this morning, and out of them for lunch, were hurrying back to them again.

'I'm in love with you, Angela,' he said, and again she felt it was incredible. She might be dreaming, she thought, but knew she was not.

They walked hand in hand, and she suddenly remembered Mr Hemp telephoning in the sedan chair, cross and untruthful with his wife. She imagined Gordon Spelle's wife and saw her as a hard-faced woman who was particular about her house, who didn't let him smoke in certain rooms, who'd somehow prevented him from becoming a dance-band leader. She seemed to be older than Gordon Spelle, with hair that was quite grey and a face that Angela remembered from a book her father used to read her as a child, the face of a farmyard rat.

'She's a bit of an invalid, actually,' Gordon Spelle said. 'She isn't well most of the time and she's a ball of nerves anyway. She couldn't stand a separation, Angela, or anything like that: I wouldn't want to mislead you, Angela, like Alec Hemp – '

'Oh, Gordon.'

He looked away from her and with his face still averted he said he wasn't much of a person. It was all wrong, being in love with her like this, with a wife and children at home. He would never want her to go on waiting for him, as Pam Ivygale had waited for twenty-three years.

'Oh, love,' she said.

The ice had gone from her stomach, and her face had cooled again. He put his arms around her, one hand on her hair, the other pressing her body into his. He whispered, but she couldn't hear what he said and the words didn't seem important. The hurrying people glanced at them, surprised to witness a leisurely embrace, in daylight on a path in Grosvenor Square.

'Oh, love,' she said again.

The cold had brought out the defects on her face: beneath heavily-applied make-up he noticed that the skin was pimply and pitted. Affected by the cold also, her eyes were red-rimmed. She reminded him of Dolores Birkett, a girl who'd been at C.S. and E. three years ago.

They returned to the office. He released her hand and took her arm instead. He'd see her at half-past five, he said in the lift. He kissed her in the lift because there was no one else in it. His mouth was moist and open. No one ever before had kissed her like he did, as though far more than kisses were involved, as though his whole being was passionate for hers. 'I love you terribly,' he said.

All afternoon, with no real work to do, she thought about it, continuing to be amazed. It was a mystery, a gorgeous mystery that became more gorgeous the more she surveyed the facts. The facts were gorgeous themselves: nicer, she considered, than any of the other facts of her life. In prettily coloured clothes the girls of C.S. and E. walked the green-carpeted corridors from office to office, their fingernails gleaming, their skins like porcelain, apparently without pores. In their suede boots or their platform shoes they queued for lunchtime tables in the Coffee Bean, or stood at five-past six in the warm bar of the Gresham Arms. Their faces were nicer than her face, their bodies more lissom, their legs and arms more suavely elegant. Yet she had been chosen.

She leafed through files, acquainting herself further with the affairs of Miss Ivygale's office. She examined without interest the carbon copies of letters in buff-coloured folders. The faint, blurred type made no sense to her and the letters themselves seemed as unimportant as the flimsy paper they were duplicated on. In a daydream that was delicious his tapering hands again caressed her. 'I love you terribly, too,' she said.

At four o'clock Miss Ivydale arrived. She'd been working all day in her flat, she said, making notes for the letters she now wished to dictate. Her manner was businesslike, she didn't mention the evening before. 'Dear Sir,' she said. 'Further to yours of the twenty-ninth . . .'

Angela made shorthand notes and then typed Miss Ivygale's letters. He did not love his wife; he had hinted that he did not love his wife; no one surely could kiss you like that, no one could put his arms around you in the broad daylight in Grosvenor Square, and still love a wife somewhere. She imagined being in a room with him, a room with an electric fire built into the wall, and two chintz-covered armchairs and a sofa covered in the same material, with pictures they had chosen together, and ornaments on the mantelpiece. 'No, I don't love her,' his voice said. 'Marry me, Angela,' his voice said.

'No, no, that's really badly done,' Miss Ivygale said. 'Type it again, please.'

You couldn't blame Miss Ivygale. Naturally Miss Ivygale was cross, having just had her share of Mr Hemp, one night out of so many empty ones. She smiled at Miss Ivygale when she handed her the retyped letter. Feeling generous and euphoric, she wanted to tell Miss Ivygale that she was still attractive at fifty, but naturally she could not do that.

'See they catch the post,' Miss Ivygale sourly ordered, handing her back the letters she'd signed.

'Yes, yes, of course, Miss Ivygale – '

'You'll need to hurry up.'

She took the letters to the dispatch-room in the basement and when she returned to the outer office she found that Miss Ivygale had already left the inner one. She put the grey plastic cover on her Remington International and went to the lavatory to put Pure Magic on her face. 'I wonder who's kissing her now,' Gordon Spelle was murmuring when she entered the outer office again. 'I wonder who's showing her how.'

He put his arms around her. His tongue crept between her teeth, his hands caressed the outline of her buttocks. He led her into Miss Ivydale's office, an arm around her waist, his lips damply on her right ear. He was whispering something about Miss Ivygale having left for the Gresham Arms and about having to lock the door because the cleaners would be coming round. She heard the door being locked. The light went out and the office was dark except for the glow of the street lamps coming through two uncurtained windows. His mouth was working on hers again, his fingers undid the zip at the side of her skirt. She closed her eyes, saturated by the gorgeousness of the mystery.

Take it easy, he said to himself when he had her on the floor, remembering the way Dolores Birkett had suddenly shouted out, in discomfort apparently although at the time he'd assumed it to be pleasure. A Nigerian cleaner had come knocking at the door when she'd shouted out the third or fourth time. 'Oh, God, I love you,' he whispered to Angela Hosford.

*   *   *

She had vodka and lime in the Gresham Arms because she felt she needed pulling together and one of the girls in the flat had said that vodka was great for that. It had been very painful on the floor of Miss Ivygale's office, and not even momentarily pleasurable, not once. It had been less painful the other time, with Ted Apwell on the hearth-rug. She wished it didn't always have to be on a floor, but even so it didn't matter – nor did the pain, nor the apprehension about doing it in Miss Ivygale's office. All the time he'd kept saying he loved her, and as often as she could manage it she'd said she loved him too.

'Must go,' he said now with sudden, awful abruptness. He buttoned the jacket of his pepper-coloured suit. He kissed her on the lips, in full view of everyone in the Gresham Arms. She wanted to go with him but felt she shouldn't because the drink he'd just bought her was scarcely touched. He'd drunk his own gin and Britvic in a couple of gulps.

'Sorry for being so grumpy,' Miss Ivygale said.

The Gresham Arms was warm and noisy, but somehow not the same at all. The men who'd been there last night were there again: Tommy Blyth and the man called Dil and all the other men – and the black-haired receptionist and all the other girls. Mr Hemp was not. Mr Hemp was hurrying back to his wife, and so was Gordon Spelle.

'What're you drinking?' Miss Ivygale asked her.

'Oh no, no. I haven't even started this one, thanks.'

But Miss Ivygale, whose own glass required refilling, insisted. 'Sit down, why don't you?' Miss Ivygale suggested, indicating the bar-stool next to hers. 'Take off your coat. It's like a furnace in here.'

Slowly Angela took off her coat. She sat beside her immediate employer, still feeling painful and in other ways aware of what had occurred on Miss Ivygale's office floor. They drank together and in time they both became a little drunk. Angela felt sorry for Miss Ivygale then, and Miss Ivygale felt sorry for Angela, but neither of them said so. And in the end, when Angela asked Miss Ivygale why it was that Gordon Spelle had picked her out, Miss Ivygale replied that it was because Gordon Spelle loved her. What else could she say? Miss Ivygale asked herself. How could she say that everyone knew that Gordon Spelle chose girls who were unattractive because he believed such girls, deprived of sex for long periods at a time, were an easier bet? Gordon Spelle was notorious, but Miss Ivygale naturally couldn't say it, any more than she'd been able to say it to Dolores Birkett or Tamar Dymond or Sue, or any of the others.

'Oh, it's beautiful!' Angela cried suddenly, having drunk a little more. She was referring, not to her own situation, but to the fact that Miss Ivygale had wasted half a lifetime on a hopeless love. Feeling happy herself, she wanted Miss Ivygale to feel happy also.

Miss Ivygale did not say anything in reply. She was fifty and Angela was twenty-six: that made a difference where knowing what was beautiful was concerned. The thing about Gordon Spelle was that with the worst possible motives he performed an act of charity for the girls who were his victims. He gave them self-esteem, and memories to fall back on – for the truth was too devious for those closest to it to guess, and too cruel for other people ever to reveal to them. The victims of Gordon Spelle left C.S. and E. in the end because they believed the passion of his love for them put him under a strain, he being married to a wife who was ill. As soon as each had gone he looked around for someone else.

'And beautiful for you too, my dear,' Miss Ivydale murmured, thinking that in a way it was, compared with what she had herself. She'd been aware for twenty-three years of being used by the man she loved: self-esteem and memories were better than knowing that, no matter how falsely they came.

'Let's have two for the road,' mumured Miss Ivygale, and ordered further drinks.

Mr McNamara

'How was he?' my mother asked on the morning of my thirteenth birthday.

She spoke while pouring tea into my father's extra-large breakfast cup, the last remaining piece of a flowered set, *Ville de Lyon* clematis on a leafy ground. My father had a special knife and fork as well, the knife another relic of the past, the fork more ordinary, extra-strong because my father was always breaking forks.

'Oh, he's well enough,' he said on the morning of my thirteenth birthday, while I sat patiently. 'The old aunt's kicking up again.'

My mother, passing him his tea, nodded. She remarked that in her opinion Mr McNamara's aunt should be placed in an asylum, which was what she always said when the subject of Mr McNamara's aunt, reputedly alcoholic, cropped up.

My mother was tallish and slender, but softly so. There was nothing sharp or angular about my mother, nothing wiry or hard. She had misty blue eyes and she seemed always to be on the point of smiling. My father, in contrast, was bulky, a man with a brown face and a brown forehead stretching back where hair once had been, with heavy brown-backed hands and eyes the same shade of blue mist as my mother's. They were gentle with one another in a way that was similar also, and when they disagreed or argued their voices weren't ever raised. They could be angry with us, but not with one another. They meted out punishments for us jointly, sharing disapproval or disappointment. We felt doubly ashamed when our misdemeanours were uncovered.

'The train was like a Frigidaire,' my father said. 'Two hours late at the halt. Poor Flannagan nearly had pneumonia waiting.' The whole country had ivy growing over it, he said, like ivy on a gravestone. Eating bacon and sausages with his special knife and fork, he nodded in agreement with himself. 'Ivy-clad Ireland,' he said when his mouth was momentarily empty of food. 'Anthracite motor-cars, refrigerators on the Great Southern Railway. Another thing, Molly: it's the opinion in Dublin that six months' time will see foreign soldiers parading themselves on O'Connell Street. German or English, take your pick, and there's damn all Dev can do about it.'

My mother smiled at him and sighed. Then, as though to cheer us all up, my father told a story that Mr McNamara had told him, about a coal merchant whom Mr McNamara had apparently known in his youth. The story had to do with the ill-fitting nature of the coal merchant's artificial teeth, and the loss of the teeth when he'd once been swimming at Ringsend. Whenever my father returned from a meeting with Mr McNamara he brought us back such stories, as well as the current opinion of Mr McNamara on the state of the nation and the likelihood of the nation becoming involved in the war. 'The opinion in Dublin' was the opinion of Mr McNamara, as we all knew. Mr McNamara drove a motor-car powered by gas because there wasn't much petrol to be had. The gas, so my father said, was manufactured by anthracite in a burner stuck on to the back of Mr McNamara's Ford V-8.

Returning each time from Dublin, my father bore messages and gifts from Mr McNamara, a tin of Jacob's biscuits or bars of chocolate. He was a man who'd never married and who lived on inherited means, in a house in Palmerston Road, with members of his family – the elderly alcoholic aunt who should have been in an asylum, a sister and a brother-in-law. The sister, now Mrs Matchette, had earlier had theatrical ambitions, but her husband, employed in the National Bank, had persuaded her away from them. My father had never actually met Mr McNamara's insane aunt or Mrs Matchette or her husband: they lived through Mr McNamara for him, at second hand, and for us they lived through my father, at a further remove. We had a vivid image of all of them, Mrs Matchette thin as a blade of grass, endlessly smoking and playing patience, her husband small and solemn, neatly moustached, with dark neat hair combed straight back from what Mr McNamara had called a 'squashed forehead'. Mr McNamara himself we imagined as something of a presence: prematurely white-haired, portly, ponderous in speech and motion. Mr McNamara used to frequent the bar of a hotel called Fleming's, an old-fashioned place where you could get snuff as well as tobacco, and tea, coffee and Bovril as well as alcoholic drinks. It was here that my father met him on his visits to Dublin. It was a comfort to go there, my father said, when his business for the day was done, to sit in a leather chair and listen to the chit-chat of his old companion. The bar would fill with smoke from their Sweet Afton cigarettes, while my father listened to the latest about the people in the house in Palmerston Road, and the dog they had, a spaniel called Wolfe Tone, and a maid called Trixie O'Shea, from Skibbereen. There was ritual about it, my father smoking and listening, just as a day or so later he'd smoke and we'd listen ourselves, at breakfast-time in our house in the country.

There were my three sisters and myself: I was the oldest, the only boy. We lived in a house that had been in the family for several generations, three miles from Curransbridge, where the Dublin train halted if anyone wanted it to, and where my father's granary and mill were. Because of the shortage of petrol, my father used to walk the three miles there and back every day. Sometimes he'd persuade Flannagan, who worked in the garden for us, to collect him in the dog-cart in the evening, and always when he went to Dublin he arranged for Flannagan to meet the train he returned on. In the early hours of the morning I'd sometimes hear the rattle of the dog-cart on the avenue and then the wheels on the gravel outside the front of the house. At breakfast-time the next morning my father would say he was glad to be back again, and kiss my mother with the rest of us. The whole thing occurred once every month or so, the going away in the first place, the small packed suitcase in the hall, my father in his best tweed suit, Flannagan and the dog-cart. And the returning a few days later: breakfast with Mr McNamara, my sister Charlotte used to say.

As a family we belonged to the past. We were Protestants in what had become Catholic Ireland. We'd once been part of an ascendancy, but now it was not so. Now there was the income from the granary and the mill, and the house we lived in: we sold grain and flour, we wielded no power. 'Proddy-woddy green-guts,' the Catholic children cried at us in Curransbridge. 'Catty, Catty, going to mass,' we whispered back, 'riding on the devil's ass.' They were as good as we were. It had not always been assumed so, and it sometimes seemed part of all the changing and the shifting of this and that, that Mr McNamara, so honoured in our house, was a Catholic himself. 'A liberal, tolerant man,' my father used to say. 'No trace of the bigot in him.' In time, my father used to say, religious differences in Ireland wouldn't exist. The war would sort the whole matter out, even though as yet Ireland wasn't involved in it. When the war was over, and whether there was involvement or not, there wouldn't be any patience with religious differences. So, at least, Mr McNamara appeared to argue.

Childhood was all that: my sisters, Charlotte, Amelia and Frances, and my parents gentle with each other, and Flannagan in the garden and Bridget our maid, and the avuncular spirit of Mr McNamara. There was Miss Ryan as well, who arrived every morning on an old Raleigh bicycle, to teach the four of us, since the school at Curransbridge was not highly thought of by my parents.

The house itself was a Georgian rectangle when you looked straight at it, spaciously set against lawns which ran back to the curved brick of the kitchen-garden wall, with a gravel sweep in front, and an avenue running straight as a die for a mile and a half through fields where sheep grazed. My sisters had some world of their own which I knew I could not properly share. Charlotte, the oldest of them, was five years younger than I was, Amelia was six and Frances five.

'Ah, he was in great form,' my father said on the morning of my thirteenth birthday. 'After a day listening to rubbish it's a pleasure to take a ball of malt with him.'

Frances giggled. When my father called a glass of whiskey a ball of malt Frances always giggled, and besides it was a giggly occasion. All my presents were sitting there on the sideboard, waiting for my father to finish his breakfast and to finish telling us about Mr McNamara. But my father naturally took precedence: after all, he'd been away from the house for three days, he'd been cold and delayed on the train home, and attending to business in Dublin was something he disliked in any case. This time, though, as well as his business and the visit to Fleming's Hotel to see Mr McNamara, I knew he'd bought the birthday present that he and my mother would jointly give me. Twenty minutes ago he'd walked into the dining-room with the wrapped parcel under his arm. 'Happy birthday, boy,' he'd said, placing the parcel on the sideboard beside the other three, from my sisters. It was the tradition in our house – a rule of my father's – that breakfast must be over and done with, every scrap eaten, before anyone opened a birthday present or a Christmas present.

'It was McNamara said that,' my father continued. 'Ivy-clad Ireland. It's the neutral condition of us.'

It was my father's opinion, though not my mother's, that Ireland should have acceded to Winston Churchill's desire to man the Irish ports with English soldiers in case the Germans got in there first. Hitler had sent a telegram to de Valera apologising for the accidental bombing of a creamery, which was a suspicious gesture in itself. Mr McNamara, who also believed that de Valera should hand over the ports to Churchill, said that any gentlemanly gesture on the part of the German Führer was invariably followed by an act of savagery. Mr McNamara, in spite of being a Catholic, was a keen admirer of the House of Windsor and of the English people. There was no aristocracy in the world to touch the English, he used to say, and no people, intent on elegance, succeeded as the English upper classes did. Class-consciousness in England was no bad thing, Mr McNamara used to argue.

My father took from the side pocket of his jacket a small wrapped object. As he did so, my sisters rose from the breakfast table and marched to the sideboard. One by one my presents were placed before me, my parents' brought from the sideboard by my mother. It was a package about two and a half feet long, a few inches in width. It felt like a bundle of twigs and was in fact the various parts of a box-kite. Charlotte had bought me a book called *Dickon the Impossible*, Amelia a kaleidoscope. 'Open mine exceedingly carefully,' Frances said. I did, and at first I thought it was a pot of jam. It was a goldfish in a jar.

'From Mr McNamara,' my father said, pointing at the smallest package. I'd forgotten it, because already the people who normally gave me presents were accounted for. 'I happened to mention,' my father said, 'that today was a certain day.'

It was so heavy that I thought it might be a lead soldier, or a horseman. In fact it was a dragon. It was tiny and complicated, and it appeared to be made of gold, but my father assured me it was brass. It had two green eyes that Frances said were emeralds, and small pieces let into its back which she said looked like rubies. 'Priceless,' she whispered jealously. My father laughed and shook his head. The eyes and the pieces in the brass back were glass, he said.

I had never owned so beautiful an object. I watched it being passed from hand to hand around the breakfast table, impatient to feel it again myself. 'You must write at once to Mr McNamara,' my mother said. 'It's far too generous of him,' she added, regarding my father with some slight disapproval, as though implying that my father shouldn't have accepted the gift. He vaguely shook his head, lighting a Sweet Afton. 'Give me the letter when you've done it,' he said. 'I have to go up again in a fortnight.'

I showed the dragon to Flannagan, who was thinning beetroot in the garden. I showed it to Bridget, our maid. 'Aren't you the lucky young hero?' Flannagan said, taking the dragon in a soil-caked hand. 'You'd get a five-pound note for that fellow, anywhere you cared to try.' Bridget polished it with Brasso for me.

That day I had a chocolate birthday cake, and sardine sandwiches, which were my favourite, and brown bread and greengage jam, a favourite also. After tea all the family watched while my father and I tried to fly the kite, running with it from one end of a lawn to the other. It was Flannagan who got it up for us in the end, and I remember the excitement of the string tugging at my fingers, and Bridget crying out that she'd never seen a thing like that before, wanting to know what it was for. 'Don't forget, dear, to write to Mr McNamara first thing in the morning,' my mother reminded me when she kissed me goodnight. I wouldn't forget, I promised, and didn't add that of all my presents, including the beautiful green and yellow kite, I liked the dragon best.

But I never did write to Mr McNamara. The next day was a different kind of day, a grim nightmare of a day during all of which someone in the house was weeping, and often several of us together. My father, so affectionate towards all of us, was no longer alive.

The war continued and Ireland continued to play no part in it. Further accidental German bombs were dropped and further apologies were sent to de Valera by the German Führer. Winston Churchill continued to fulminate about the ports, but the prophecy of Mr McNamara that foreign soldiers would parade in O'Connell Street did not come true.

Knitting or sewing, my mother listened to the BBC news with a sadness in her eyes, unhappy that elsewhere death was occurring also. It was no help to any of us to be reminded that people in Britain and Europe were dying all the time now, with the same sudden awfulness as my father had.

Everything was different after my father died. My mother and I began to go for walks together. I'd take her arm, and sometimes her hand, knowing she was lonely. She talked about him to me, telling me about their honeymoon in Venice, the huge square where they'd sat drinking chocolate, listening to the bands that played there. She told me about my own birth, and how my father had given her a ring set with amber which he'd bought in Louis Wine's in Dublin. She would smile at me on our walks and tell me that even though I was only thirteen I was already taking his place. One day the house would be mine, she pointed out, and the granary and the mill. I'd marry, she said, and have children of my own, but I didn't want even to think about that. I didn't want to marry; I wanted my mother always to be there with me, going on walks and telling me about the person we all missed so much. We were still a family, my sisters and my mother and myself, Flannagan in the garden, and Bridget. I didn't want anything to change.

After the death of my father Mr McNamara lived on, though in a different kind of way. The house in Palmerston Road, with Mr McNamara's aunt drinking in an upstairs room, and the paper-thin Mrs Matchette playing patience instead of being successful in the theatre, and Mr Matchette with his squashed forehead, and Trixie O'Shea from Skibbereen, and the spaniel called Wolfe Tone: all of them remained quite vividly alive after my father's death, as part of our memory of him. Fleming's Hotel remained also, and all the talk there'd been there of the eccentric household in Palmerston Road. For almost as long as I could remember, and certainly as long as my sisters could remember, our own household had regularly been invaded by the other one, and after my father's death my sisters and I often recalled specific incidents retailed in Fleming's Hotel and later at our breakfast table. There'd been the time when Mr McNamara's aunt had sold the house to a man she'd met outside a public house. And the time when Mrs Matchette appeared to have fallen in love with Garda Molloy, who used to call in at the kitchen for Trixie O'Shea every night. And the time the spaniel was run over by a van and didn't die. All of it was preserved, with Mr McNamara himself, white-haired and portly in the smoke-brown bar of Fleming's Hotel, where snuff could be bought, and Bovril as well as whiskey.

A few months after the death my mother remarked one breakfast-time that no doubt Mr McNamara had seen the obituary notice in the *Irish Times*. 'Oh, but you should write,' my sister Frances cried out in her excitable manner. My mother shook her head. My father and Mr McNamara had been bar-room friends, she pointed out: letters in either direction would not be in order. Charlotte and Amelia agreed with this opinion, but Frances still protested. I couldn't see that it mattered. 'He gave us all that chocolate,' Frances cried, 'and the biscuits.' My mother said again that Mr McNamara was not the kind of man to write to about a death, nor the kind who would write himself. The letter that I was to have written thanking him for the dragon was not mentioned. Disliking the writing of letters, I didn't raise the subject myself.

At the end of that year I was sent to a boarding-school in the Dublin mountains. Miss Ryan continued to come to the house on her Raleigh to teach my sisters, and I'd have far preferred to have remained at home with her. It could not be: the boarding-school in the Dublin mountains, a renowned Protestant monument, had been my father's chosen destiny for me and that was that. If he hadn't died, leaving home might perhaps have been more painful, but the death had brought with it practical complications and troubles, mainly concerned with the running of the granary and the mill: going away to school was slight compared with all that, or so my mother convinced me.

The headmaster of the renowned school was a small, red-skinned English cleric. With other new boys, I had tea with him and his wife in the drawing-room some days after term began. We ate small ham-paste sandwiches and Battenburg cake. The headmaster's wife, a cold woman in grey, asked me what I intended to do – 'in life', as she put it. I said I'd run a granary and a mill at Curransbridge; she didn't seem interested. The headmaster told us he was in *Who's Who*. Otherwise the talk was of the war.

Miss Ryan had not prepared me well. 'Dear boy, whoever taught you French?' a man with a pipe asked me, and did not stay to hear my answer. 'Your Latin, really!' another man exclaimed, and the man who taught me mathematics warned me never to set my sights on a profession that involved an understanding of figures. I sat in the back row of the class with other boys who had been ill-prepared for the renowned school.

I don't know when it was – a year, perhaps, or eighteen months after my first term – that I developed an inquisitiveness about my father. Had he, I wondered, been as bad at everything as I was? Had some other man with a pipe scorned his inadequacy when it came to French? Had he felt, as I did, a kind of desperation when faced with algebra? You'd *have* to know a bit about figures, I used, almost miserably, to say to myself: you'd have to if you hoped to run a granary and a mill. Had he been good at mathematics?

I asked my mother these questions, and other questions like them. But my mother was vague in her replies and said she believed, although perhaps she was wrong, that my father had not been good at mathematics. She laughed when I asked the questions. She told me to do my best.

But the more I thought about the future, and about myself in terms of the man whose place I was to take, the more curious I became about him. In the holidays my mother and I still went on our walks together, through the garden and then into the fields that stretched behind it, along the banks of the river that flowed through Curransbridge. But my mother spoke less and less about my father because increasingly there was less to say, except with repetition. I imagined the huge square in Venice and the cathedral and the bands playing outside the cafés. I imagined hundreds of other scenes, her own varied memories of their relationship and their marriage. We often walked in silence now, or I talked more myself, drawing her into a world of cross-country runs, and odorous changing-rooms, and the small headmaster's repeated claim that the food we ate had a high calorific value. School was ordinarily dreary: I told her how we smoked wartime American cigarettes in mud huts specially constructed for the purpose and how we relished the bizarre when, now and again, it broke the monotony. There was a master called Mr Dingle, whose practice it was to enquire of new boys the colour and nature of their mother's night-dresses. In the oak-panelled dining-hall that smelt of mince and the butter that generations had flicked on to the ceiling, Mr Dingle's eye would glaze as he sat at the end of a Junior House table while one boy after another fuelled him with the stuff of fantasies. On occasions when parents visited the school he would observe through cigarette smoke the mothers of these new boys, stripping them of their skirts and blouses in favour of the night clothes that their sons had described for him. There was another master, known as Buller Achen, who was reputed to take a sensual interest in the sheep that roamed the mountainsides, and a boy called Testane-Hackett who was possessed of the conviction that he was the second son of God. In the dining-hall a gaunt black-clad figure, a butler called Tripp, hovered about the high table where the headmaster and the prefects sat, assisted by a maid, said to be his daughter, who was known to us as the Bicycle. There was Fisher Major, who never washed, and Strapping, who disastrously attempted to treat some kind of foot ailment with mild acid. My mother listened appreciatively, and I often saw in her eyes the same look that had been there at breakfast-time when my father spoke of Fleming's Hotel and Mr McNamara. 'How like him you are!' she now and again murmured, smiling at me.

At Curransbridge I stood in his office above the mill, a tiny room now occupied by the man my mother had chosen to look after things, a Mr Devereux. In the house I rooted through the belongings he'd left behind; I stared at photographs of him. With Flannagan and my sisters I flew the kite he'd bought me that last time he'd been to Dublin. I polished the small brass dragon that his bar-room companion had given him to give to me. 'It's the boy's birthday,' I imagined him saying in the brown bar of Fleming's Hotel, and I imagined the slow movement of Mr McNamara's hand as he drew the dragon from his pocket. It was inevitable, I suppose, that sooner or later I should seek out Fleming's Hotel.

'An uncle,' I said to the small headmaster. 'Passing through Dublin, sir.'

'Passing? Passing?' He had a Home Counties accent and a hard nasal intonation. 'Passing?' he said again, giving the word an extra vowel sound.

'On his way to Galway, sir. He's in the R.A.F., sir. I think he'd like to see me, sir, because my father – '

'Ah, yes, yes. Back in time for Chapel, please.'

Fleming's Hotel, it said in the telephone directory, 21 *Wheeler Street*. As I cycled down from the mountains, I didn't know what I was going to do when I got there.

It was a narrow, four-storey building in a terrace with others, a bleak-looking stone façade. The white woodwork of the windows needed a coat of paint, the glass portico over the entrance doors had a dusty look. It was on this dusty glass that the name *Fleming's Hotel* was picked out in white enamel letters stuck to the glass itself. I cycled past the hotel twice, glancing at the windows – a dozen of them, the four at the top much smaller than the others – and at the entrance doors. No one left or entered. I propped the bicycle against the edge of the pavement some distance away from the hotel, outside what seemed to be the street's only shop, a greengrocer's. There were pears in the window. I went in and bought one.

I wheeled the bicycle away from the shop and came, at the end of the street, to a canal. Slowly I ate the pear, and then I took my red and green school cap from my head and wheeled my bicycle slowly back to Fleming's Hotel. I pushed open one of the entrance doors and for a split second I heard my father's voice again, describing what I now saw: the smokiness of the low-ceilinged hall, a coal fire burning, and a high reception counter with the hotel's register open on it, and a brass bell beside the register. There were brown leather armchairs in the hall and a brown leather bench running along one wall. Gas lamps were lit but even so, and in spite of the fact that it was four o'clock in the afternoon, the hall was dim. It was empty of other people and quiet. A tall grandfather clock ticked, the fire occasionally hissed. There was a smell of some kind of soup. It was the nicest, most comfortable hall I'd ever been in.

Beyond it, I could see another coal fire, through an archway. That was the bar where they used to sit, where for all I knew Mr McNamara was sitting now. I imagined my father crossing the hall as I crossed it myself. The bar was the same as the hall, with the same kind of leather chairs, and a leather bench and gas lamps and a low ceiling. There were net curtains pulled across the two windows, and one wall was taken up with a counter, with bottles on shelves behind it, and leather-topped stools in front of it. There was a woman sitting by the fire drinking orange-coloured liquid from a small glass. Behind the bar a man in a white jacket was reading the *Irish Independent*.

I paused in the archway that divided the bar from the hall. I was under age. I had no right to take a further step and I didn't know what to do or to say if I did. I didn't know what drink to order. I didn't know if in the dim gaslight I looked a child.

I went to the bar and stood there. The man didn't look up from his newspaper. *Smithwick's Ale* were words on the labels of bottles: I would ask for a Smithwick's Ale. All I wanted was to be allowed to remain, to sit down with the beer and to think about my father. If Mr McNamara did not come today he'd come another day. Frances had been right: he should have been written to. I should have written to him myself, to thank my father's friend for his present.

'Good evening,' the barman said.

'Smithwick's, please,' I said as casually as I could. Not knowing how much the drink might be, I placed a ten-shilling note on the bar.

'Drop of lime in it, sir?'

'Lime? Oh, yes. Yes, please. Thanks very much.'

'Choppy kind of day,' the barman said.

I took the glass and my change, and sat down as far as possible from where the woman was sitting. I sat so that I was facing both the bar and the archway, so that if Mr McNamara came in I'd see him at once. I'd have to leave at six o'clock in order to be safely back for Chapel at seven.

I finished the beer. I took an envelope out of my pocket and drew pieces of holly on the back of it, a simple art-form that Miss Ryan had taught all of us. I took my glass to the bar and asked for another Smithwick's. The barman had a pale, unhealthy-seeming face, and wire-rimmed glasses, and a very thin neck. 'You do want the best, don't you?' he said in a joky kind of voice, imitating someone. 'Bird's Custard,' he said in the same joky way, 'and Bird's Jelly de Luxe.' My father had mentioned this barman: he was repeating the advertisements of Radio Eireann. 'You do want the best, don't you?' he said again, pushing the glass of beer towards me. By the fire, the woman made a noise, a slight, tired titter of amusement. I laughed myself, politely too.

When I returned to my armchair I found the woman was looking at me. I wondered if she could be a prostitute, alone in a hotel bar like that. A boy at school called Yeats claimed that prostitutes hung about railway stations mostly, and on quays. But there was of course no reason why you shouldn't come across one in a bar.

Yet she seemed too quietly dressed to be a prostitute. She was wearing a green suit and a green hat, and there was a coat made of some kind of fur draped over a chair near the chair she sat on. She was a dark-haired woman with an oval face. I'd no idea what age she was: somewhere between thirty and forty, I imagined: I wasn't good at guessing people's ages.

The Smithwick's Ale was having an effect on me. I wanted to giggle. How extraordinary it would be, I thought, if a prostitute tried to sell herself to me in my father's and Mr McNamara's hotel. After all, there was no reason at all why some prostitutes shouldn't be quietly-dressed, probably the more expensive ones were. I could feel myself smiling, holding back the giggle. Naturally enough, I thought, my father hadn't mentioned the presence of prostitutes in Fleming's Hotel. And then I thought that perhaps, if he'd lived, he would have told me one day, when my sisters and my mother weren't in the room. It was the kind of thing, surely, that fathers did tell sons.

I took the envelope I'd drawn the holly on out of my pocket and read the letter it contained. They were managing, my mother said. Miss Ryan had had a dose of 'flu, Charlotte and Amelia wanted to breed horses, Frances didn't know what she wanted to do. His rheumatics were slowing Flannagan down a bit in the garden. Bridget was insisting on sweeping the drawing-room chimney. *It'll be lovely at Christmas*, she wrote. *So nice being all together again.*

The oval-faced woman put on her fur coat, and on her way from the bar she passed close to where I was sitting. She looked down and smiled at me.

'Hills of the North, rejoice!' we sang in chapel that night. 'Valley and lowland, sing!'

I smelt of Smithwick's Ale. I knew I did because as we'd stood in line in Cloisters several other boys had remarked on it. As I sang, I knew I was puffing the smell all over everyone else. 'Like a bloody brewery,' Gahan Minor said afterwards.

'. . . this night,' intoned the small headmaster nasally, 'and for ever more.'

'Amen,' we all replied.

Saturday night was a pleasant time. After Chapel there were two and a half hours during which you could do more or less what you liked, provided the master on duty knew where you were. You could work in the Printing Shop or read in the Library, or take part in a debate, such as that this school is an outpost of the British Empire, or play billiards or do carpentry, or go to the model railway club or the music-rooms. At half-past nine there was some even freer time, during which the master on duty didn't have to know where you were. Most boys went for a smoke then.

After Chapel on the Saturday night after I'd visited Fleming's Hotel I read in the Library. I read *Jane Eyre*, but all the time the oval face of the woman in the hotel kept appearing in my mind. It would stay there for a few seconds and then fade, and then return. Again and again, as I read *Jane Eyre*, she passed close to my chair in the bar of Fleming's Hotel, and looked down and smiled at me.

The end of that term came. The Sixth Form and Remove did

Macbeth on the last two nights, A. McC. P. Jackson giving what was generally regarded as a fine performance as Banquo. Someone stole the secondhand Penguin I'd bought from Grace Major to read on the train, *Why Didn't They Ask Evans?* Aitcheson and Montgomery were found conversing in the shower-room in the middle of the night.

On the journey home I was unable to stop thinking about Fleming's Hotel. A man in the carriage lent me a copy of *Barrack Variety*, but the jokes didn't seem funny. It was at moments like these that the truth most harshly mocked me. Ever since I'd found the hotel, ever since the woman had stared at me, it had been a part of every day, and for whole nights in my long, cheerless dormitory I had been unable to sleep. My father's voice had returned to me there, telling again the stories of his friend, and reminding me of his friend's opinions. My father had disagreed with my mother in her view that de Valera should not hand over the ports to Churchill, preferring to share the view of his friend. At school and on the train, and most of all when I returned home, the truth made me feel ill, as though I had 'flu.

That Christmas morning we handed each other our presents, after we'd eaten, still observing my father's rule. We thought of him then, they in one way, I in another. 'Oh, my dear, how lovely!' my mother whispered over some ornament I'd bought her in a Dublin shop. I had thrown the dragon with the green glass eyes far into a lake near the school, unable to understand how my father had ever brought it to the house, or brought bars of chocolate or tins of Jacob's biscuits. To pass to his children beneath my mother's eyes the gifts of another woman seemed as awful a sin as any father could commit, yet somehow it was not as great as the sin of sharing with all of us this other woman's eccentric household, her sister and her sister's husband, her alcoholic aunt, a maid and a dog. 'That's Norah McNamara,' the barman's voice seemed to say again at our breakfast table, and I imagined them sitting there, my father and she, in that comfortable bar, and my father listening to her talk of the house in Palmerston Road and of how she admired the English aristocracy. I watched my mother smile that Christmas morning, and I wanted to tell the truth because the truth was neat and without hypocrisy: I wanted carefully to say that I was glad my father was dead.

Instead I left the breakfast table and went to my bedroom. I wept there, and then washed my face in cold water from the jug on my wash-stand. I hated the memory of him and how he would have been that Christmas morning; I hated him for destroying everything. It was no consolation to me then that he had tried to share with us a person he loved in a way that was different from the way he loved us. I could neither forgive nor understand. I felt only bitterness that I, who had taken his place, must now continue his deception, and keep the secret of his lies and his hypocrisy.

Afternoon Dancing

Every summer since the war the two couples had gone to
Southend in September, staying in Mr Roope's Prospect
Hotel. They'd known each other since childhood: Poppy and
Albert, Alice and Lenny. They'd been to the same schools,
they'd all been married in the summer of 1938. They rented
houses in the same street, Paper Street, S.E.4., Poppy and
Albert Number 10, and Alice and Lenny Number 41. They
were all in their mid-fifties now, and except for Poppy they'd
all run to fat a bit. Len was a printer, Albert was employed by
the London Electricity Board, as a cable-layer. Every night
the two men had a few drinks together in the Cardinal Wolsey
in Northbert Road, round the corner from Paper Street.
Twice a week, on Wednesdays and Fridays, the wives went to
Bingo. Alice's children – Beryl and Ron – were now married
and had children of their own. Poppy's son, George, married
also, had gone to Canada in 1969.

Poppy was very different from Alice. Alice was timid, she'd
never had Poppy's confidence. In middle age Poppy was a
small, wiry woman with glasses, the worrying kind you might
think to look at her, only Poppy didn't worry at all. Poppy was
always laughing, nudging Alice when they were together on a
bus, drawing attention to some person who amused her.
'Poppy Edwards, you're a holy terror!' Miss Curry of Tat-
terall Elementary School had pronounced forty years ago, and
in lots of ways Poppy was a holy terror still. She'd been a
slap-happy mother and was a slap-happy wife, not caring

much what people thought if her child wasn't as meticulously turned out as other children, or if Albert's sandwiches were carelessly made. Once, back in 1941 when Albert was in the army, she'd begun to keep company with a man who was an air-raid warden, whose bad health had prevented him from joining one of the armed forces. When the war came to an end she was still involved with this man and it had seemed likely then that she and Albert would not continue to live together. Alice had been worried about it all, but then, a month before Albert was due to be demobbed, the man had been knocked down by an army truck in Holborn and had instantly died. Albert remained in ignorance of everything, even though most people in Paper Street knew just what had been going on and how close Albert had come to finding himself wifeless. In those days Poppy had been a slim, small girl in her twenties, with yellow hair that looked as though it had been peroxided but which in fact hadn't, and light-blue mischievous eyes. Alice had been plumper, dark-haired and reliable-looking, pretty in her nice-girl way. Beryl and Ron had not been born yet.

During the war, with their two husbands serving in Italy and Africa together, Poppy had repeatedly urged Alice to let her hair down a bit, as she herself was doing with the air-raid warden. They were all going to be blown up, she argued, and if Alice thought that Lenny and Albert weren't chancing their arms with the local talent in Italy and Africa then Alice definitely had another think coming. But Alice, even after Lenny confessed that he'd once chanced his arm through physical desperation, couldn't bring herself to emulate the easy attitudes of her friend. The air-raid warden was always producing friends for her, men whose health wasn't good either, but Alice chatted politely to each of them and made it clear that she didn't wish for a closer relationship. With peace and the death of the air-raid warden, Poppy calmed down a bit, and the birth of her child eighteen months later calmed her down further.

But even so she was still the same Poppy, and in late middle age when she suggested that she and Alice should take up dancing again the idea seemed to Alice to be just like all the other ideas Poppy had had in the past: when they were seven, to take Mrs Grounds' washing off her line and peg it up on Mrs Bond's; when they were ten, to go to Woolworth's with Davie Rickard and slip packets of carrots from the counter into the pockets of his jacket; at fifteen, to write anonymous letters to every teacher who'd ever had anything to do with them; at sixteen, to cut the hair of people in the row in front of them in the Regal Cinema. 'Dancing?' Alice said. 'Oh, Poppy, whatever would they say?'

Whatever would the two husbands say, she meant, and the other wives of Paper Street and Beryl and Ron? Going to Bingo was one thing and quite accepted. Going dancing at fifty-four was a different kettle of fish altogether. Before their marriages they had often gone dancing: they had been taken to dance-halls on Saturday nights by the men they later married, and by other men. Every June, all four of them went dancing once or twice in Southend, even though the husbands increasingly complained that it made them feel ridiculous. But what Poppy had in mind now wasn't the Grand Palais in Southend or the humbler floors of thirty years ago, or embarrassed husbands, or youths treading over your feet: what Poppy had in mind was afternoon dancing in a place in the West End, without the husbands or anyone else knowing a thing about it. 'Tea-time foxtrots,' Poppy said. 'The Tottenham Court Dance-Rooms. All the rage, they are.' And in the end Alice agreed.

They went quite regularly to the Tottenham Court Dance-Rooms, almost every Tuesday. They dressed up as they used to dress up years ago; with discretion they applied rouge and eye-shadow. Alice put on a peach-coloured corset in an effort to trim down her figure a bit, and curled the hair that had once been fair and now was grey. It looked a bit frizzy when she curled it now, the way it had never done when she was a girl, but although the sight of it sometimes depressed her she accepted the middle-aged frizziness because there was nothing she could do about it. Poppy's hair had become rather thin on the top of her head, but she didn't seem to notice and Alice naturally didn't mention the fact. In middle age Poppy always kept her grey hair dyed a brightish shade of chestnut, and when Alice once read in a magazine that excessive dying eventually caused a degree of baldness she didn't mention it either, fearing that in Poppy's case the damage was already done. On their dancing afternoons they put on headscarves and pulled their coats carefully about them, to hide the finery beneath. Poppy wore spectacles with gold-coloured trim on the orange frames, her special-occasion spectacles she called them. They always walked quickly away from Paper Street.

In the dance-rooms they had tea on the balcony as soon as they arrived, at about a quarter-to-three. There was a lot of scarlet plush on the balcony, and scarlet lights. There were little round tables with paper covers on them, for convenience. When they'd had tea and Danish pastries and a few slices of Swiss roll they descended one of the staircases that led to the dance-floor and stood chatting by a pillar. Sometimes men came up to them and asked if one or other would like to dance. They didn't mind if men came up or not, or at least they didn't mind particularly. What they enjoyed was the band, usually Leo Ritz and his Band, and looking at the other dancers and the scarlet plush and having tea. Years ago they'd have danced together, just for the fun of it, but somehow they felt too old for that, at fifty-four. An elderly man with rather long grey hair once danced too intimately with Alice and she'd had to ask him to release her. Another time a middle-aged man, not quite sober, kept following them about, trying to buy them Coca-Cola. He was from Birmingham, he told them; he was in London on business and had had lunch with people who were making a cartoon film for his firm. He described the film so that they could look out for it on their television screens: it was an advertisement for wallpaper paste, which was what his firm manufactured. They were glad when this man didn't appear the following Tuesday.

Other men were nicer. There was one who said his name was Sidney, who was lonely because his wife had left him for a younger man; and another who was delicate, a Mr Hawke. There was a silent, bald-headed man whom they both liked dancing with because he was so good at it, and there was Grantly Palmer, who was said to have won awards for dancing in the West Indies.

Grantly Palmer was a Jamaican, a man whom neither of them had agreed to dance with when he'd first asked them because of his colour. He worked as a barman in a club, he told them later, and because of that he rarely had the opportunity to dance at night. He'd often thought of changing his job since dancing meant so much to him, but bar work was all he knew. In the end they became quite friendly with Grantly Palmer, so much so that whenever they entered the dance-rooms he'd hurry up to them smiling, neat as a new pin. He'd dance with one and then the other. Tea had to wait, and when eventually they sat down to it he sat with them and insisted on paying. He was always attentive, pressing Swiss roll on both of them and getting them cigarettes from the coin machine. He talked about the club where he worked, the Rumba Rendezvous in Notting Hill Gate, and often tried to persuade them to give it a try. They giggled quite girlishly at that, wondering what their husbands would say about their attending the Rumba Rendezvous, a West Indian Club. Their husbands would have been astonished enough if they knew they went afternoon tea-dancing in the Tottenham Court Dance-Rooms.

Grantly Palamer was a man of forty-two who had never married, who lived alone in a room in Maida Vale. He was a born bachelor, he told the two wives, and would not have appreciated home life, with children and all that it otherwise implied. In his youth he had played the pins, he informed them with an elaborate, white smile, meaning by this that he'd had romantic associations. He would laugh loudly when he said it. He'd been naughty in his time, he said.

Whenever he talked like that, with his eyes blazing excitedly and his teeth flashing, Alice couldn't help thinking that Grantly Palmer was a holy terror just like Poppy had been and still in a way was, the male equivalent. She once said this to Poppy and immediately regretted it, fearing that Poppy would take offence at being likened to a black man, but Poppy hadn't minded at all. Poppy had puffed at a tipped Embassy and had made Alice blush all over her neck by saying that in her opinion Grantly Palmer fancied her. 'Skin and bone he'd think me,' Poppy said. 'Blacks like a girl they can get their teeth into.' They were on the upper deck of a bus at the time and Poppy had laughed shrilly into her cigarette smoke, causing people to glance amusedly at her. She peered through her gold-trimmed spectacles at the people who looked at her, smiling at them. 'My friend has a fella in love with her,' she said to the conductor, shouting after him as he clattered down the stairs. 'A holy terror she says he is.'

He was cheeky, Alice said, the way he always insisted on walking off the dance-floor hand in hand with you, the way he'd pinch your arm sometimes. But her complaints were half-hearted because the liberties Grantly Palmer took were never offensive: it wasn't at all the same as having a drunk pulling you too close to him and slobbering into your hair. 'You'll lose him, Alice,' Poppy cried now and again in shrill mock-alarm as they watched him paying attentions to some woman who was new to the dance-rooms. Once he'd referred to such a person, asking them if they'd noticed her, a stout woman in pink, an unmarried short-hand typist he said she was. 'My, my,' he said in his Jamaican drawl, shaking his head. 'My, my.' They never saw the unmarried shorthand typist again, but Poppy said he'd definitely been implying something, that he'd probably enticed her to his room in Maida Vale. 'Making you jealous,' Poppy said.

The men whom Alice and Poppy had married weren't at all like Grantly Palmer. They were quiet men, rather similar in appearance and certainly similar in outlook. Both were of medium build, getting rather bald in their fifties, Alice's Lenny with a moustache, Poppy's Albert without. They were keen supporters of Crystal Palace Football Club, and neither of them, according to Poppy, knew anything about women. The air-raid warden had known about women, Poppy said, and so did Grantly Palmer. 'He wants you to go out with him,' she said to Alice. 'You can see it in his eyes.' One after-noon when he was dancing with Alice he asked her if she'd consider having a drink on her own with him, some evening when she wasn't doing anything better. She shook her head when he said that, and he didn't ever bring the subject up again. 'He's mad for you,' Poppy said when she told her of this invitation. 'He's head over heels, love.' But Alice laughed, unable to believe that Grantly Palmer could possibly be mad for a corseted grandmother of fifty-four with unmanageable grey hair.

Without much warning, Poppy died. During a summer holi-day at Mrs Roope's Prospect Hotel she'd complained of pains, though not much, because that was not her way. 'First day back you'll see Dr Pace,' Albert commanded. Two months later she died one night, without waking up.

After the death Alice was at a loss. For almost fifty years Poppy had been her friend. The affection between them had increased as they'd watched one another age and as their companionship yielded more memories they could share. Their children – Alice's Beryl and Ron, and Poppy's George – had played together. There'd been the business of George's emigration to Canada, and Alice's comforting of Poppy because of it. There'd been the marriage of Ron and then of Beryl, and Poppy's expression of Alice's unspoken thought, that Ron's Hilda wasn't good enough for him, too bossy for any man really, and Poppy's approval of Beryl's Tony, an approval that Alice shared.

Alice had missed her children when they'd gone, just as Poppy had missed George. 'Oh Lord, I know, dear!' Poppy cried when Alice wept the day after Beryl's wedding. Beryl had lived at home until then, as Ron had until his marriage. It was a help, being able to talk to Poppy about it, and Poppy so accurately understanding what Alice felt.

After Poppy's death the silence she'd prevented when Alice's children had grown up fell with a vengeance. It icily surrounded Alice and she found it hard to adapt herself to a life that was greyer and quieter, to days going by without Poppy dropping in or she herself dropping in on Poppy, without the cups of Maxwell House coffee they'd had together, and the cups of tea, and the biscuits and raspberry-jam sandwich cake, which Poppy had been fond of. Once, awake in the middle of the night, she found herself thinking that if Lenny had died she mightn't have missed him so much. She hated that thought and tried, unsuccessfully, to dispel it from her mind. It was because she and Poppy had told one another everything, she kept saying to herself, the way you couldn't really tell Lenny. But all this sounded rather lame, and when she said to herself instead that it was because she and Poppy had known one another all their lives it didn't sound much better: she and Lenny had known one another all their lives, too. For six months after the death she didn't go to Bingo, unable to face going on her own. It didn't even occur to her to go afternoon dancing.

The first summer after the death, Alice and Lenny and Albert went as usual to the Prospect Hotel in Southend. There seemed to the two men to be no good reason why they shouldn't, although when they arrived there Albert was suddenly silent and Alice could see that he was more upset than he'd imagined he would be. But after a day he was quite himself again, and when it wasn't necessary to cheer him up any more she began to feel miserable herself. It wasn't so much because of the death, but because she felt superfluous without Poppy. She realised gradually, and the two men realised even more gradually, that on previous holidays there had been no conversation that was general to all four of them: the men had talked to each other and so had their wives. The men did their best now to include Alice, but it was difficult and awkward.

She took to going for walks by herself, along the front and down the piers, out to the sea and back again. It was then, that summer at Southend, that Alice began to think about Grantly Palmer. It had never occurred to her before that he didn't even know that Poppy had died, even though they'd all three been such good friends on Tuesday afternoons at the Tottenham Court Dance-Rooms. She wondered what he thought, if he'd been puzzled by their sudden absence, or if he still attended the dance-rooms himself. One night in the Prospect Hotel, listening to the throaty breathing of her husband, she suddenly and quite urgently wanted to tell Grantly Palmer about Poppy's death. She suddenly felt that it was his due, that she'd been unkind not ever to have informed him. Poppy would wish him to know, she said to herself; it was bad that she'd let down her friend in this small way. In the middle of that night, while still listening to Lenny's breathing, she resolved to return to the Tottenham Court Dance-Rooms and found herself wondering if Leo Ritz and his Band would still be playing there.

'Breakfasts've gone down a bit,' Albert said on the way back to London, and Lenny reminded him that Mrs Roope had had a bit of family trouble. 'Dropped Charlie Cooke, I see,' Lenny said, referring to a Crystal Palace player. He handed Albert the *Daily Mirror*, open at the sports page. 'Dare say they'll be back to normal next year,' Albert said, still referring to the breakfasts.

In Paper Street, a week after their return, she put on her peach-coloured corset and the dress she'd worn the first time they'd gone afternoon dancing – blue-green satin, with a small array of sequins at the shoulders and the breast. It felt more silent than ever in the house in Paper Street, because in the past Poppy used to chat and giggle in just the same way as she had as a girl, lavishly spraying scent on herself, a habit she'd always had also. Alice closed the door of Number 41 behind her and walked quickly in Paper Street, feeling guiltier than she had when the guilt could be shared. She'd tell some lie if someone she knew said she was looking smart. She'd probably say she was going to Bingo, which was what they'd both said once when Mrs Tedman had looked them up and down, as though suspecting the finery beneath. You could see that Mrs Tedman hadn't believed that they were going to Bingo, but Poppy said it didn't matter what Mrs Tedman thought. It was all a bit frightening without Poppy, but then everything was something else without Poppy, dull or silent or frightening. Alice caught a bus, and at a quarter-to-three she entered the dance-rooms.

'Well, well!' Grantly Palmer said, smiling his bright smile. 'Well, well, stranger lady!'

'Hullo, Mr Palmer.'

'Oh, child, child!'

'Hullo, Grantly.'

It had always been a joke, the business of Christian names between the three of them. 'Alice and Poppy!' he'd said the first time they'd had tea together. 'My, my, what charmin' names!' They'd just begun to use his own Christian name when Poppy had died. 'Funny name, Grantly,' Poppy had remarked on the bus after he'd first told them, but soon it had become impossible to think of him as anything else.

'Where's Poppy, dear?'

'Poppy died, Grantly.'

She told him all about it, about last year's holiday at Southend and the development of the illness and then the funeral. 'My God!' he said, staring into her eyes. 'My God, Alice.'

The band was playing 'Lullaby of Broadway': middle-aged women, in twos or on their own, stood about, sizing up the men who approached them, in the same expert way as she and Poppy had sized men up in their time. 'Let's have a cup of tea,' Grantly Palmer said.

They had tea and Swiss roll slices and Danish pastries. They talked about Poppy. 'Was she happy?' he asked. And Alice said her friend had been happy enough.

In silence on the balcony they watched the dancers rotating below them. He wasn't going to dance with her, she thought, because Poppy had died, because the occasion was a solemn one. She was aware of disappointment. Poppy had been dead for more than a year, after all.

'It's a horrible thing,' he said. 'A friend dying. In the prime of her life.'

'I miss her.'

'Of course, Alice.'

He reached across the tea-table and seized one of her hands. He held it for a moment and then let it go. It was a gesture that reminded her of being a girl. On television men touched girls' hands in that way. How nice, she suddenly thought, the chap called Ashley was in *Gone with the Wind*. She'd seen the film with Poppy, revived a few years back, Leslie Howard playing Ashley.

He went away and returned with another pot of tea and a plate of Swiss roll slices. Leo Ritz and his Band were playing 'September Love'.

'I thought I'd never lay eyes on you again, Alice.'

He regarded her solemnly. He didn't smile when he said that the very first time he'd met her he'd considered her a very nice person. He was wearing a suit made of fine, black corduroy. His two grey hands were gripping his tea-cup, nursing it.

'I came back to tell you about Poppy, Grantly.'

'I kept on hoping you'd come back. I kept on thinking about you.' He nodded, lending emphasis to this statement. Without drinking from it, he placed his tea-cup on the table and pulled his chair in a bit, nearer to hers. She could feel some part of his legs, an ankle-bone it felt like. Then she felt one of his hands, beneath the table, touching her right knee and then touching the left one.

She didn't move. She gazed ahead of her, feeling through the material of her dress the warmth of his flesh. The first time they'd had tea with him he'd told a joke about three Jamaican clergymen on a desert island and she and Poppy had laughed their heads off. Even when it had become clear to Poppy and herself that what he was after was sex and not love, Poppy had still insisted that she could chance her arm with him. It was as though Poppy wanted her to go out with Grantly Palmer because she herself had gone out with the air-raid warden.

His hand remained on her left knee. She imagined it there, the thin grey hand on the blue satin material of her dress. It moved, pushing back the satin, the palm caressing, the tip of the thumb pressing into her thigh.

She withdrew her leg, smiling to cover the unfriendliness of this decision. She could feel warmth all over her neck and her cheeks and around her eyes. She could feel her eyes beginning to water. On her back and high up on her forehead, beneath the grey frizz of her hair, she felt the moisture of sweat.

He looked away from her. 'I always liked you, Alice,' he said. 'You know? I liked you better than Poppy, even though I liked Poppy too.'

It was different, a man putting his hand on your knee: it was different altogether from the natural intimacy of dancing, when anything might have been accidental. She wanted to go away now; she didn't want him to ask her to dance with him. She imagined him with the pink woman, fondling her knees under a table before taking her to Maida Vale. She saw herself in the room in Maida Vale, a room in which there were lilies growing in pots, although she couldn't remember that he'd ever said he had lilies. There was a thing like a bedspread hanging on one of the walls, brightly coloured, red and blue and yellow. There was a gas fire glowing and a standard lamp such as she'd seen in the British Home Stores, and a bed with a similar brightly-coloured cloth covering it, and a table and two upright chairs, and a tattered green screen behind which there'd be a sink and a cooking stove. In the room he came to her and took her coat off and then undid the buttons of her dress. He lifted her petticoat over her head and unhooked her peach-coloured corset and her brassière.

'Will you dance with me, Alice?'

She shook her head. Her clothes were sticking to her now. Her armpits were clammy.

'Won't you dance, dear?'

She said she'd rather not, not today. Her voice shivered

and drily crackled. She'd just come to tell him about Poppy, she said again.

'I'd like to be friends with you, Alice. Now that Poppy has – '

'I have to go home, Grantly. I have to.'

'Don't go, darling.'

His hands had crossed the table again. They held her wrists; his teeth and his eyes flashed at her, though not in a smiling way. She shouldn't have come, her own voice kept protesting in the depths of her mind, like an echo. It had all been different when there were three of them, all harmless flirtation, with Poppy giggling and pretending, just fun.

There was excitement in his face. He released her wrists, and again, beneath the table, she felt one of his legs against hers. He pushed his chair closer to the table, a hand moved on her thigh again.

'No, no,' she said.

'I looked for you. I don't know your other name, you know. I didn't know Poppy's either. I didn't know where you lived. But I looked for you, Alice.'

He didn't say how he'd looked for her, but repeated that he had, nodding emphatically.

'I thought if I found you we'd maybe have a drink one night. I have records in my room I'd like you to hear, Alice. I'd like to have your opinion.'

'I couldn't go to your room – '

'It would be just like sitting here, Alice. It would be quite all right.'

'I couldn't ever, Grantly.'

What would Beryl and Ron say if they could see her now, if they could hear the conversation she was having, and see his hand on her leg? She remembered them suddenly as children, Beryl on the greedy side yet refusing to eat fish in any shape or form, Ron having his nails painted with Nail-Gro because he bit them. She remembered the birth of Ron and how it had been touch and go because he'd weighed so little. She remembered the time Beryl scalded herself on the electric kettle and how Lenny had rung 999 because he said it would be the quickest way to get attention. She remembered the first night she'd been married to Lenny, taking her clothes off under a wrap her mother had given her because she'd always been shy about everything. All she had to do, she said to herself, was to stand up and go.

His hands weren't touching her any more. He moved his body away from hers, and she looked at him and saw that the excitement had gone from his face. His eyes had a dead look. His mouth had a melancholy twist to it.

'I'm sorry,' she said.

'I fancied you that first day, Alice. I always fancied you, Alice.'

He was speaking the truth to her and it was strange to think of it as the truth, even though she had known that in some purely physical way he desired her. It was different from being mad for a person, and yet she felt that his desiring her was just as strange as being mad for her. If he didn't desire her she'd have been able to return to the dance-rooms, they'd have been able to sit here on the balcony, again and again, she telling him more about Poppy and he telling her more about himself, making one another laugh. Yet if he didn't desire her he wouldn't want to be bothered with any of that.

'Can't fancy black girls,' he said, with his head turned well away from her. 'White women, over sixty if it's possible. Thirteen stone or so. That's why I go to the dance-rooms.' He turned to face her and gazed morosely at her eyes. 'I'm queer that way,' he said. 'I'm a nasty kind of black man.'

She could feel sickness in her stomach, and the skin of her back, which had been so damp with sweat, was now cold. She picked up her handbag and held it awkwardly for a moment, not knowing what to say. 'I must go,' she said eventually, and her legs felt shaky when she stood on them.

He remained at the table, all his politeness gone. He looked bitter and angry and truculent. She thought he might insult her. She thought he might shout loudly at her in the dance-rooms, calling her names and abusing her. But he didn't. He didn't say anything at all to her. He sat there in the dim, tinted light, seeming to slump from one degree of disappointment to a deeper one. He looked crude and pathetic. He looked another person.

Again, as she stood there awkwardly, she thought about the room in Maida Vale, which she'd furnished with lilies and brightly-coloured cloths. Again his grey hands undid her corset and her brassière, and just for a moment it seemed that there wouldn't have been much wrong in letting him admire her in whatever way he wanted to. It was something that would disgust people if they knew; Beryl and Ron would be disgusted, and Lenny and Albert naturally enough. Grantly Palmer would disgust them, and she herself, a grandmother, would disgust them for permitting his attentions. There was something wrong with Grantly Palmer, they'd all say: he was sick and dirty, as he even admitted himself. Yet there were always things wrong with people, things you didn't much care for and even were disgusted by, like Beryl being greedy and Ron biting his nails, like the way Lenny would sometimes blow his nose without using a handkerchief or a tissue. Even Poppy hadn't been perfect: on a bus it had sometimes been too much, her shrillness and her rushy ways, so clearly distasteful to other people sitting there.

Alice wanted to tell Grantly Palmer all that. Desperately she tried to form an argument in her mind, a conversation with herself that had as its elements the greediness of her daughter and her son's bitten nails and her husband clearing the mucus from his nose at the sink, and she herself agreeing to be the object of perversion. But the elements would not connect, and she felt instinctively that she could not transform them into coherent argument. The elements spun dizzily in her mind, the sense she sought from them did not materialise.

'Goodbye,' she said, knowing he would not answer. He was ashamed of himself; he wanted her to go. 'Goodbye,' she said again. 'Goodbye, Grantly.'

She moved away from him, forcing herself to think about the house in Paper Street, about entering it and changing her clothes before Lenny returned. She'd bought two chops that morning and there was part of a packet of frozen beans in the fridge. She saw herself peeling potatoes at the sink, but at the same time she could feel Grantly Palmer behind her, still sitting at the table, ashamed when he need not be. She felt ashamed herself for having tea with him, for going to see him when she shouldn't, just because Poppy was dead and there was no one else who was fun to be with.

Leo Ritz and his Band were playing 'Scatterbrain' as she left the dance-rooms. The middle-aged dancers smiled as they danced, some of them humming the tune.

Last Wishes

In the neighbourhood Mrs Abercrombie was a talking point.
Strangers who asked at Miss Dobbs' Post Office and Village
Stores or at the Royal Oak were told that the wide entrance
gates on the Castle Cary road were the gates to Rews Manor,
where Mrs Abercrombie lived in the past, with servants. No
one from the village except old Dr Ripley and a window-
cleaner had seen her since 1947, the year of her husband's
death. According to Dr Ripley, she'd become a hypochondriac.

But even if she had, and in spite of her desire to live as a
recluse, Mrs Abercrombie continued to foster the grandeur
that made Rews Manor, nowadays, seem old-fashioned.
Strangers were told that the interior of the house had to be
seen to be believed. The staircase alone, in white rose-veined
marble, was reckoned to be worth thousands; the faded carpets had come from Persia; all the furniture had been in the
Abercrombie family for four or five generations. On every
second Sunday in the summer the garden was open to
visitors and the admission charges went to the Nurses.

Once a week Plunkett, the most important of Mrs Abercrombie's servants, being her butler, drove into the village
and bought stamps and cigarettes in the post office and stores.
It was a gesture more than anything else, Miss Dobbs considered, because the bulk of the Rews Manor shopping was
done in one or other of the nearby towns. Plunkett was about
fifty, a man with a sandy appearance who drove a pre-war

Wolseley and had a pleasant, easy-going smile. The window-cleaner reported that there was a Mrs Plunkett, a uniformed housemaid, but old Dr Ripley said the uniformed maid was a person called Tindall. There were five servants at Rews Manor, Dr Ripley said, if you counted the two gardeners, Mr Apse and Miss Bell, and all of them were happy. He often repeated that Mrs Abercrombie's servants were happy, as though making a point: they were pleasant people to know, he said, because of their contentment. Those who had met Plunkett in the village agreed, and strangers who had come across Mr Apse and Miss Bell in the gardens of Rews Manor found them pleasant also, and often envied them their dispositions.

In the village it was told how there'd always been Abercrombies at Rews Manor, how the present Mrs Abercrombie's husband had lived there alone when he'd inherited it – until he married at forty-one, having previously not intended to marry at all because he suffered from a blood disease that had killed his father and his grandfather early in their lives. It was told how the marriage had been a brief and a happy one, and how there'd been no children. Mrs Abercrombie's husband had died within five years and had been buried in the grounds of Rews Manor, near the azaleas.

'So beautifully kept, the garden,' visitors to the neighbourhood would marvel. 'That gravel in front, not a stone out of place! Those lawns and rose-bushes!' And then, intrigued by the old-fashioned quality of the place, they'd hear the story of this woman whose husband had inopportunely died, who existed now only in the world of her house and gardens, who lived in the past because she did not care for the present. People wove fantasies around this house and its people; to those who were outside it, it touched on fantasy itself. It was real because it was there and you could see it, because you could see the man called Plunkett buying stamps in the post office, but its reality was strange, as exotic as a coloured orchid. In the nineteen-sixties and -seventies, when life often had a grey look, the story of Rews Manor cheered people up, both those who told it and those who listened. It created images in minds and it affected imaginations. The holidaymakers who walked through the beautifully-kept garden, through beds of begonias and roses, among blue hydrangeas and potentilla and witch-hazel and fuchsia, were grateful. They were grateful for the garden and for the story that went with them, and later they told the story themselves, with conjectured variations.

At closer quarters, Rews Manor was very much a world of its own. In 1948, at the time of Mr Abercrombie's death, Mr Apse, the gardener, worked under the eighty-year-old Mr Marriott, and when Mr Marriott died Mrs Abercrombie promoted Mr Apse and advertised for an assistant. There seemed no reason why a woman should not be as suitable as a man and so Miss Bell, being the only applicant, was given the post. Plunkett had also been advertised for when his predecessor, Stubbins, had become too old to carry on. The housemaid, Tindall, had been employed a few years after the arrival of Plunkett, as had Mrs Pope, who cooked.

The servants all lived in, Mr Apse where he had always lived, in a room over the garage, Miss Bell next door to him. The other three had rooms in a wing of the house which servants, in the days when servants were more the thing, had entirely occupied. They met for meals in the kitchen and sometimes they would sit there in the evenings. The room which once had been the servants' sitting-room had a dreariness about it: in 1956 Plunkett moved the television set into the kitchen.

Mr Apse was sixty-three now and Miss Bell was forty-five.

Mrs Pope was fifty-nine, Tindall forty-three. Plunkett, reckoned in the village to be about fifty, was in fact precisely that. Plunkett, who had authority over the indoor servants and over Mr Apse and Miss Bell when they were in the kitchen, had at the time of Mrs Abercrombie's advertisement held a position in a *nouveau riche* household in Warwickshire. He might slowly have climbed the ladder and found himself, when death or age had made a gap for him, in charge of its servants. He might have married and had children. He might have found himself for the rest of his life in the butler's bungalow, tucked out of sight on the grounds, growing vegetables in his spare time. But for Plunkett these prospects hadn't seemed quite right. He didn't want to marry, nor did he wish to father children. He wanted to continue being a servant because being a servant made him happy, yet the stuffiness of some households was more than he could bear and he didn't like having to wait for years before being in charge. He looked around, and as soon as he set foot in Rews Manor he knew it was exactly what he wanted, a small world in which he had only himself to blame if the food and wine weren't more than up to scratch. He assisted Mrs Abercrombie in her choosing of Mrs Pope as cook, recognising in Mrs Pope the long-latent talents of a woman who sought the opportunity to make food her religion. He also assisted in the employing of Tindall, a fact he had often recalled since, on the nights he spent in her bed.

Mrs Pope had cooked in a YWCA until she answered the advertisement. The raw materials she was provided with had offered her little opportunity for the culinary experiments she would have liked to attempt. For twenty years she had remained in the kitchens of the YWCA because her husband, now dead, had been the janitor. In the flat attached to the place she had brought up two children, a boy and a girl, both of them now married. She'd wanted to move to somewhere nicer when Winnie, the girl, had married a traveller in stationery, but her husband had refused point-blank, claiming that the YWCA had become his home. When he died, she hadn't hesitated.

Miss Bell had been a teacher of geography, but had been advised for health considerations to take on outdoor work. Having always enjoyed gardening and knowing quite a bit about it, she'd answered Mrs Abercrombie's advertisement in *The Times*. She'd become used to living in, in a succession of boarding-schools, so that living in somewhere else suited her quite well. Mr Apse was a silent individual, which suited her also. For long hours they would work side by side in the vegetable garden or among the blue hydrangeas and azaleas that formed a shrubbery around the house, neither of them saying anything at all.

Tindall had worked as a packer in a frozen-foods factory. There'd been trouble in her life in that the man she'd been engaged to when she was twenty-two, another employee in the factory, had made her pregnant and had then, without warning, disappeared. He was a man called Bert Fask, considerate in every possible way, quiet and seemingly reliable. Everyone said she was lucky to be engaged to Bert Fask and she had imagined quite a happy future. 'Don't matter a thing,' he said when she told him she was pregnant, and he fixed it that they could get married six months sooner than they'd intended. Then he disappeared. She'd later heard that he'd done the same thing with other girls, and when it became clear that he didn't intend to return she began to feel bitter. Her only consolation was the baby, which she still intended to have even though she didn't know how on earth she was going to manage. She loved her unborn child and she longed for its birth so that she herself could feel loved again. But the child, two months premature, lived for only sixteen hours. That blow was a terrible one, and it was when endeavouring to get over it that she'd come across Mrs Abercrombie's advertisement, on a page of a newspaper that a greengrocer had wrapped a beetroot in. That chance led her to a contentment she hadn't known before, to a happiness that was different only in detail from the happinesses of the other servants.

On the morning of July 12th, 1974, a Friday, Tindall knocked on Mrs Abercrombie's bedroom door at her usual time of eight forty-five. She carried into the room Mrs Abercrombie's breakfast tray and the morning mail, and placed the tray on the Queen Anne table just inside the door. She pulled back the bedroom's six curtains. 'A cloudy day,' she said.

Mrs Abercrombie, who had been reading Butler's *Lives of the Saints*, extinguished her bedside light. She remarked that the wireless the night before had predicted that the weather would be unsettled: rain would do the garden good.

Tindall carried the tray to the bed, placed it on the mahogany bed-table and settled the bed-table into position. Mrs Abercrombie picked up her letters. Tindall left the room.

Letters were usually bills, which were later passed to Plunkett to deal with. Plunkett had a housekeeping account, into which a sum of money was automatically transferred once a month. Mrs Abercrombie's personal requirements were purchased from this same account, negligible since she had ceased to buy clothes. It was Tindall who noticed when she needed a lipstick refill or lavender water or more hairpins. Tindall made a list and handed it to Plunkett. For years Mrs Abercrombie herself hadn't had the bother of having to remember, or having to sign a cheque.

This morning there was the monthly account from the International Stores and one from the South-Western Electricity Board. The pale brown envelopes were identification enough: she put them aside unopened. The third envelope contained a letter from her solicitors about her will.

*   *   *

In the kitchen, over breakfast, the talk turned to white raspberries. Mr Apse said that in the old days white raspberries had been specially cultivated in the garden. Tindall, who had never heard of white raspberries before, remarked that the very idea of them gave her the creeps. 'More flavour really,' Miss Bell said quietly.

Plunkett, engrossed in the *Daily Telegraph*, did not say anything. Mrs Pope said she'd never had white raspberries and would like to try them. She'd be more than grateful, she added, if Mr Apse could see his way to putting in a few canes. But Mr Apse had relapsed into his more familiar mood of silence. He was a big man, slow of movement, with a brown bald head and tufts of grey hair about his ears. He ate bacon and mushrooms and an egg in a slow and careful manner, occasionally between mouthfuls drinking tea. Miss Bell nodded at Mrs Pope, an indication that Mr Apse had heard the request about the raspberries and would act upon it.

'Like slugs they sound,' Tindall said.

Miss Bell, who had small tortoiseshell glasses and was small herself, with a weather-beaten face, said that they did not taste like slugs. Her father had grown white raspberries, her mother had made a delicious dish with them, mixing them with loganberries and baking them with a meringue top. Mrs Pope nodded. She'd read a recipe like that once, in Mrs Beeton it might have been; she'd like to try it out.

In the *Daily Telegraph* Plunkett read that there was a strike of television technicians and a strike of petrol hauliers. The sugar shortage was to continue and there was likely to be a shortage of bread. He sighed without making a sound. Staring at print he didn't feel like reading, he recalled the warmth of Tindall's body the night before. He glanced round the edge of the newspaper at her: there was a brightness in her eyes, which was always there the morning after he'd visited her in bed. She'd wept twice during the four hours he'd spent: tears of fulfilment he'd learnt they were, but all the same he could never prevent himself from comforting her. Few words passed between them when they came together in the night; his comforting consisted of stroking her hair and kissing her damp cheeks. She had narrow cheeks, and jet-black hair which she wore done up in a knot during the day but which tumbled all over the pillows when she was in bed. Her body was bony, which he appreciated. He didn't know about the tragedy in her life because she'd never told him; in his eyes she was a good and efficient servant and a generous woman, very different from the sorrowful creature who'd come looking for employment eighteen years ago. She had never once hinted at marriage, leaving him to deduce that for her their arrangement was as satisfactory as it was for him.

'Moussaka for dinner,' Mrs Pope said, rising from the breakfast table. 'She asked for it special.'

'No wonder, after your last one,' Miss Bell murmured. The food at the schools where she'd taught geography had always been appalling: grey-coloured mince and soup that smelt, huge sausage-rolls for Sunday tea, cold scrambled egg.

'Secret is, cook it gently,' Mrs Pope said, piling dishes into the sink. 'That's all there's to it if you ask me.'

'Oh no, no,' Miss Bell murmured, implying that there was a great deal more to moussaka than that. She carried her own dishes to the sink. Mrs Pope had a way with moussaka, she added in her same quiet way, which was why Mrs Abercrombie had asked for it again.

Tindall chewed her last corner of toast and marmalade. She felt just slightly sore, pleasantly so, as she always did after a visit from Plunkett. Quite remarkable he sometimes was in the middle of the night, yet who'd have thought he'd know a thing about any of it?

Mr Apse left the kitchen and Miss Bell followed him. Tindall carried her dishes to the sink and assisted Mrs Pope with the washing up. At the table Plunkett lit his first cigarette of the day, lingering over a last cup of tea.

As she did every morning after breakfast, Mrs Abercrombie recalled her husband's death. It had taken place on a fine day in March, a day with a frost in the early morning and afterwards becoming sunny, though still cold. He'd had a touch of 'flu but was almost better; Dr Ripley had suggested his getting up in time for lunch. But by lunch-time he was dead, with the awful suddenness that had marked the deaths of his father and his grandfather, nothing to do with 'flu at all. She'd come into their bedroom, with the clothes she'd aired for him to get up into.

Mrs Abercrombie was sixty-one now; she'd been thirty-four at the time of the death. Her life for twenty-seven years had been a memorial to her brief marriage, but death had not cast unduly gloomy shadows, for after the passion of her sorrow there was some joy at least in her sentimental memories. Her own death preoccupied her now: she was going to die because with every day that passed she felt more weary. She felt herself slipping away and even experienced slight pains in her body, as if some ailment had developed in order to hurry her along. She'd told Dr Ripley, wondering if her gallstones were playing up, but Dr Ripley said there was nothing the matter with her. It didn't comfort her that he said it because she didn't in the least mind dying. She had a belief that after death she would meet again the man who had himself died so abruptly, that the interrupted marriage would somehow continue. For twenty-seven years this hope had been the consolation that kept her going. That and the fact that she had provided a home for Mr Apse and Miss Bell, and Mrs Pope and Tindall and Plunkett, all of whom had grown older with her and had shared with her the beauty of her husband's house.

'I shall not get up today,' she murmured on the morning of July 12th. She did not, and in fact did not ever again get up.

They were thrown into confusion. They stood in the kitchen looking at one another, only Plunkett looking elsewhere, at the Aga that for so long now had been Mrs Pope's delight. No one had expected Mrs Abercrombie to die, having been repeatedly assured by Dr Ripley that there was nothing the matter with her. The way she lived, so carefully and so well looked after, there had seemed no reason why she shouldn't last for another twenty years at the very least, into her eighties. In bed at night, on the occasions when he didn't visit Tindall's bed, Plunkett had worked out that if Mrs Abercrombie lived until she was eighty, Miss Bell would be seventy-four and Mrs Pope seventy-eight. Tindall, at sixty-two, would presumably be beyond the age of desire, as he himself no doubt would be at sixty-nine. Mr Apse, so grizzled and healthy did he sometimes seem, might still be able to be useful in the garden, at eighty-two. It seemed absurd to Plunkett on the morning of July 12th that Mrs Abercrombie had died twenty years too soon. It also seemed unfair.

It seemed particularly unfair because, according to the letter which Mrs Abercrombie had that morning received from her solicitors, she had been in the process of altering her will. Mrs Abercrombie had once revealed to Plunkett that it had been her husband's wish, in view of the fact that there were no children, that Rews Manor should eventually pass into the possession of a body which was engaged in the study of rare grasses. It was a subject that had interested him and which he had studied in considerable detail himself. 'There'll be legacies of course,' Mrs Abercrombie had reassured Plunkett, 'for all of you.' She'd smiled when she'd said that and Plunkett had bowed and murmured in a way that, years ago, he'd picked up from Hollywood films that featured English butlers.

But in the last few weeks Mrs Abercrombie had apparently had second thoughts. Reading between the lines of the letter from her solicitors, it was clear to Plunkett that she'd come to consider that legacies for her servants weren't enough. *We assume your wish to be,* the letter read, *that after your death your servants should remain in Rews Manor, retaining the house as it is and keeping the gardens open to the public. That this should be so until such time as Mr Plunkett should have reached retirement age, i.e. sixty-five years or, in the event of Mr Plunkett's previous death, that this arrangement should continue until the year 1990. At either time, the house and gardens should be disposed of as in your current will and the servants remaining should receive the legacies as previously laid down. We would be grateful if you would confirm at your convenience that we are correct in this interpretation of your wishes: in which case we will draw up at once the necessary papers.* But her convenience had never come because she had left it all too late. With the typewritten sheet in his hand, Plunkett had felt a shiver of bitterness. He'd felt it again, with anger, when he'd looked at her dead face.

'Grass,' he said in the kitchen. 'They'll be studying grass here.'

The others knew what he was talking about. They, like he, believing that Mrs Abercrombie would live for a long time yet, had never paused to visualise Rews Manor in that far-off future. They did so now, since the future was bewilderingly at hand. Contemporary life closed in upon the house and garden that had belonged to the past. They saw the house without its furniture since such furniture would be unsuitable in a centre for the studying of grasses. They saw, in a vague way, men in shirtsleeves, smoking pipes and carrying papers. Tindall saw grasses laid out for examination on a long trestle table in the hall. Mr Apse saw roses uprooted from the garden, the blue hydrangeas disposed of, and small seed-beds neatly laid out, for the cultivation of special grass. Miss Bell had a vision of men with a bulldozer, but she could not establish their activity with more precision. Mrs Pope saw caterers' packs on the kitchen table and in the cold room and the store cupboards: transparent plastic bags containing powdered potatoes in enormous quantities, fourteen-pound tins of instant coffee, dried mushrooms and dried all-purpose soup. Plunkett saw a laboratory in the drawing-room.

'I must telephone Dr Ripley,' Plunkett said, and the others thought, but did not say it, that it was too late for Dr Ripley to be of use.

'You have to,' Plunkett said, 'when a person dies.'

He left the kitchen, and Mrs Pope began to make coffee. The others sat down at the table, even though it was half-past eleven in the morning. There were other houses, Tindall said to herself, other country houses where life would be quiet and more agreeable than life in a frozen-foods firm. And yet other houses would not have him coming to her bedroom, for she could never imagine his suggesting that they should go somewhere together. That wasn't his way; it would be too binding, too formal, like a proposal of marriage. And she wouldn't have cared to be Mrs Plunkett, for she didn't in the least love him.

'Poor thing,' Mrs Pope said, pouring her boiling water on to the coffee she had ground, and for a moment Tindall thought the reference was to her.

'Yes,' Miss Bell whispered, 'poor old thing.' She spoke in a kind way, but her words, sincerely meant, did not sound so in the kitchen. Somewhere in the atmosphere that the death had engendered there was resentment, a reflection of the bitterness it had engendered in Plunkett. There was a feeling that Mrs Abercrombie, so considerate in her lifetime, had let them down by dying. Even while she called her a poor old thing, Miss Bell wondered what she should do now. Many employers might consider the idea of a woman gardener eccentric, and certainly other men, more set in their ways than Mr Apse, mightn't welcome a female assistant.

Mrs Pope thought along similar lines. You became used to a place, she was reflecting as she poured the coffee into cups, and there'd be few other places where you could cook so grandly for a single palate, where you were appreciated every day of your life. 'Bloody inedible,' she'd heard a girl exclaim in a corridor of the YWCA, referring to carefully poached haddock in a cream sauce.

'The doctor'll be here at twelve,' Plunkett sombrely announced, re-entering the kitchen from the back hall. 'I left a message; I didn't say she'd died.'

He sat down at the table and waited while Mrs Pope filled his coffee-cup. Tindall placed the jug of hot milk beside him and for a moment the image of her fingers on the flowered surface of the china caused him to remember the caressing of those fingers the night before. He added two lumps of sugar and poured the milk. He felt quite urgent about Tindall, which he never usually did at half-past eleven on a morning after. He put it down to the upset of the death, and the fact that he was idle when normally on a Friday morning he'd be going through the stores with Mrs Pope.

'Doctor'll sign a death warrant,' Mrs Pope said. 'There'll be the funeral.'

Plunkett nodded. Mrs Abercrombie had a cousin in Lincolnshire and another in London, two old men who once, twelve years ago, had spent a weekend in Rews Manor. Mrs Abercrombie hadn't corresponded with them after that, not caring for them, Plunkett imagined. The chances were they were dead by now.

'No one much to tell,' Mrs Pope said, and Miss Bell mentioned the two cousins. He'd see if they were alive, Plunkett said.

It was while saying that, and realising as he said it the pointlessness of summoning these two ancient men to a funeral, that he had his idea: why should not Mrs Abercrombie's last wishes be honoured, even if she hadn't managed to make them legal? The idea occurred quickly and vividly to him, and immediately he regretted his telephoning of Dr Ripley. But as soon as he regretted it he realised that the telephoning had been essential. Dr Ripley was a line of communication with the outside world and had been one for so long that it would seem strange to other people if a woman, designated a hypochondriac, failed to demand as regularly as before the attentions of her doctor. It would seem stranger still to Dr Ripley.

Yet there was no reason why Mrs Abercrombie should not be quietly buried beside the husband she had loved, where she was scheduled to be buried anyway. There was no reason that Plunkett could see why the household should not then proceed as it had in the past. The curtains of the drawing-room would be drawn when next the window-cleaner came, Dr Ripley would play his part because he'd have no option.

'I see no harm in it,' Plunkett said.

'In what?' Mrs Pope enquired, and then, speaking slowly to break the shock of his idea, he told them. He told them about the letter Mrs Abercrombie had received that morning from her solicitors. He took it from an inside pocket and showed it to them. They at first thought it strange that he should be carrying Mrs Abercrombie's correspondence on his person, but as the letter passed among them, they understood.

'Oh no,' Miss Bell murmured, her small brown face screwed up in distaste. Mrs Pope shook her head and said she couldn't be a party to deception. Mr Apse did not say anything. Tindall half shook her head.

'It was what she clearly wished,' Plunkett explained. 'She had no intention of dying until she'd made this stipulation.'

'Death waits for no one's wishes,' Mr Apse pointed out in a ponderous voice.

'All we are doing,' Plunkett said, 'is to make it wait.'

'But there's Dr Ripley,' Tindall said, and Mrs Pope added that a doctor couldn't ever lend himself to anything shady. It surprised Mrs Pope that Plunkett had made such an extraordinary suggestion, just as it surprised Miss Bell. Tindall and Mr Apse were surprised also, but more at themselves for thinking that what Plunkett was suggesting was only a postponement of the facts, not a suppression.

'But, Plunkett, what exactly are you wanting to do?' Mrs Pope cried out, suddenly shrill.

'She must be buried as she said. She spoke to us all of it, that she wished to be laid down by Mr Abercrombie in the garden.'

'But you have to inform the authorities,' Miss Bell whispered, and Mrs Pope, still shrill, said there had to be a coffin and a funeral.

'I'd make a coffin,' Plunkett replied swiftly. 'There's the timber left over from the drawing-room floorboards. Beautiful oak, plenty of it.'

They knew he could. They'd seen him making other things, a step-ladder and bird-boxes, and shelves for the store-room.

'I was with her one day,' Plunkett said, not telling the truth now. 'We were standing in the garage looking at the timber. "You could make a coffin out of that," she said. "I don't suppose you've ever made a coffin, Plunkett." Those were her exact words. Then she turned and went away: I knew what she meant.'

They believed this lie because to their knowledge he had never lied before. They believed that Mrs Abercrombie had spoken of a coffin, but Miss Bell and Mrs Pope considered that she had only spoken in passing, without significance. Mr Apse and Tindall, wishing to believe that the old woman had been giving a hint to Plunkett, saw no reason to doubt that she had.

'I really couldn't,' Miss Bell said, 'be a party to anything like that.'

For the first time in their association Plunkett disliked Miss Bell. He'd always thought her a little field-mouse of a thing, all brown creases he imagined her body would be, like her face. Mrs Abercrombie had asked him what he'd thought when Miss Bell had answered the advertisement for an assistant gardener. 'She's been a teacher,' Mrs Abercrombie had said, handing him Miss Bell's letter, in which it was stated that Miss Bell was qualified to teach geography but had been medically advised to seek outdoor work. 'No harm in seeing her,' he'd said, and had promised to give Mrs Abercrombie his own opinion after he'd opened the hall-door to the applicant and received her into the hall.

'You would not be here, Miss Bell,' he said now, 'if I hadn't urged Mrs Abercrombie that it wasn't peculiar to employ a woman in the garden. She was dead against it.'

'But that's no reason to go against the law,' Mrs Pope cried, shrill again. 'Just because she took a woman into the garden doesn't mean anything.'

'You would not be here yourself, Mrs Pope. She was extremely reluctant to have a woman whose only experience in the cooking line was in a hostel. It was I who had an instinct about your letter, Mrs Pope.'

'There's still Dr Ripley,' Miss Bell said, feeling that all the protestation and argument were anyway in vain because Dr Ripley was shortly due in the house and would put an end to all this absurdity. Dr Ripley would issue a death certificate and would probably himself inform a firm of undertakers. The death of Mrs Abercrombie had temporarily affected Plunkett, Miss Bell considered. She'd once read in the *Daily Telegraph* of a woman who'd wished to keep the dead body of her husband under glass.

'Of course there's Dr Ripley,' Mrs Pope said. She spoke sharply and with a trace of disdain in her voice. If Mrs Abercrombie had let them down by dying before her time, then Plunkett was letting them down even more. Plunkett had always been in charge, taking decisions about everything, never at a loss. It was ironic that he should be the one to lose his head now.

'It is Dr Ripley I'm thinking about,' Plunkett said. 'People will say he neglected her.'

There was a silence then in the kitchen. Mrs Pope had begun to lick her lips, a habit with her when she was about to speak. She changed her mind and somehow, because of what had been said about Dr Ripley, found herself less angry. Everyone liked the old doctor, even though they'd often agreed in the kitchen that he was beyond it.

When Plunkett said that Dr Ripley might have neglected Mrs Abercrombie, guilt nibbled at Miss Bell. There was a time two years ago when she'd cut her hand on a piece of metal embedded in soil. She'd gone to Dr Ripley with it and although he'd chatted to her and been extremely kind his treatment hadn't been successful. A week later her whole arm had swelled up and Plunkett had insisted on driving her to the out-patients' department of a hospital. She was lucky to keep the arm, an Indian doctor had pronounced, adding that someone had been careless.

Mrs Pope recalled the affair of Miss Bell's hand, and Mr Apse recalled the occasion, and so did Tindall. In the snow once Dr Ripley's old Vauxhall had skidded on the drive and

Mr Apse had had to put gravel under the back wheels to get it out of the ditch. It had puzzled Mr Apse that the skid had occurred because, as far as he could see, there'd been no cause for Dr Ripley to apply his brakes. It had occurred to him afterwards that the doctor hadn't quite known what he was doing.

'It's a terrible thing for a doctor to be disgraced,' Plunkett said. 'She thought the world of him, you know.'

The confusion in the kitchen was now considerable. The shock of the death still lingered and with it, though less than before, the feeling of resentment. There was the varying reaction to Plunkett's proposal that Mrs Abercrombie's remains should be quietly disposed of. There was concern for Dr Ripley, and a mounting uneasiness that caused the concern to give way to a more complicated emotion: it wasn't simply that the negligence of Dr Ripley had brought about a patient's death, it seemed that his negligence must be shared, since they had known he wasn't up to it and had not spoken out.

'Her death will cause unhappiness all round,' Plunkett said. 'Which she didn't wish at all. He'd be struck off.'

Dr Ripley had attended Miss Bell on a previous occasion, a few months after her arrival in Rews Manor. She'd come out in spots which Dr Ripley had diagnosed as German measles. He had been called in when Tindall had influenza in 1960. He'd been considerate and efficient about a tiresome complaint of Mrs Pope's.

The two images of Dr Ripley hovered in the kitchen: a man firm of purpose and skilful in his heyday, moustached and smart but always sympathetic, a saviour who had become a medical menace.

'She died of gallstones,' Plunkett said, 'which for eight or nine years she suffered from, a fact he always denied. She'd be still alive if he'd treated her.'

'We don't know it was gallstones,' Miss Bell protested quietly.

'We would have to say. We would have to say that she complained of gallstones.' Plunkett looked severe. 'If he puts down pneumonia on the death certificate we would have to disagree. After all,' he continued, his severity increasing with each word, 'he could kill other people too.'

He looked from one face to another and saw that the mind behind each was lost in the confusion he had created. He, though, could see his way through the murk of it. Out of the necessary chaos he could already see the order he desired, and it seemed to him now that everything else he had ever experienced paled beside the excitement of the idea he'd been visited by.

'We must bargain with Dr Ripley,' he said, 'for his own sake. She would not have wished him to be punished for his negligence, any more than she would wish us to suffer through her unnecessary death. We must put it all to Dr Ripley. He must sign a death certificate in her room this morning and forget to hand it in. I would be satisfied with that.'

'Forget?' Miss Bell repeated, aghast and totally astonished.

'Or leave it behind here and forget that he has left it behind. Any elderly behaviour like that, it's all of a piece. I'm sure there's no law that says she can't be quietly put away in the garden, and the poor old chap'll be long since dead before anyone thinks to ask a question. We would have saved his bacon for him and be looked after ourselves, just as she wished. No one would bother about any of it in a few years' time, and we'd have done no wrong by burying her where she wished to be. Only the old chap would be a bit amiss by keeping quiet about a death, but he'd be safely out of business by then.'

Mr Apse remembered a lifetime's association with the garden of Rews Manor, and Mrs Pope recalled the cheerless kitchens of the YWCA, and Miss Bell saw herself kneeling in a flower-bed on an autumn evening, taking begonia tubers from the earth. There could be no other garden for Mr Apse, and for Miss Bell no other garden either, and no other kitchen for Mrs Pope. Plunkett might propose to her, Tindall said to herself, just in order to go on sharing beds with her, but the marriage would not be happy because it was not what they wanted.

'There's the will,' Miss Bell said, whispering so low that her words were almost incomprehensible. 'There's the will she has signed.'

'In time,' Plunkett said, 'the will shall naturally come into its own. That is what she intended. We should all be properly looked after, and then the grass merchants will take over, as laid down. When the place is no longer of use to us.' He added that he felt he had been visited, that the idea had quite definitely come from outside himself rather than from within. Regretful in death, he said, Mrs Abercrombie had expressed herself to him because she was cross with herself, because she was worried for her servants and for the old doctor.

'He let her die of neglected gallstones,' Plunkett repeated with firm conviction. 'A most obvious complaint.'

In the hall the doorbell rang, a clanging sound, for the bell was of an old-fashioned kind.

'Well?' Plunkett said, looking from one face to another.

'We don't know that it was gallstones,' Miss Bell protested again. 'She only mentioned gallstones. Dr Ripley said – '

'Oh, for heaven's sake, Miss Bell!'

He glared at Miss Bell with dislike in his face. They'd been through all that, he said: gallstones or something else, what did it matter? The woman was dead.

'It's perfectly clear to all of us, Miss Bell, that Mrs Abercrombie would not have wished her death to cause all this fuss. That's the only point I'm making. In my opinion, apparently not shared by you, Mrs Abercrombie was a woman of remarkable sensitivity. And kindness, Miss Bell. Do you really believe that she would have wished to inflict this misery on a harmless old doctor?' He paused, staring at Miss Bell, aware that the dislike in his face was upsetting her. 'Do you really believe she wished to deprive us of our home? Do you believe that Mrs Abercrombie was unkind?'

Miss Bell did not say anything, and in the silence the door-bell pealed again. Mrs Pope was aware that her head had begun to ache. Mr Apse took his pipe from his pocket and put it on the table. He cut slivers from a plug of tobacco and rubbed them together in the palm of his left hand. Tindall watched him, thinking that she had never seen him preparing his pipe in the kitchen before.

'You're mad!' Miss Bell suddenly cried. 'The whole thing has affected you, Plunkett. It's ridiculous what you're saying.' The blood had gone to her face and neck, and showed in dark blotches beneath her weathered skin. Her eyes, usually so tranquil, shone fierily in her anger. She didn't move, but continued to stand at the corner of the kitchen table, just behind Mr Apse, who was looking up at her, astonished.

'How can we possibly do such a thing?' Miss Bell shrieked. 'It's a disgusting, filthy kind of thing to suggest. Her body's still warm and you can stand there saying that everything should be falsified. You don't care tuppence for Dr Ripley, it's not Dr Ripley who matters to you. They could hang him for murder – '

'I did not say Dr Ripley would be hanged.'

'You implied it. You implied the most terrible things.'

The power left her voice as she uttered the last three words. Her eyes closed for a moment and when she opened them again she was weeping.

'Now, now, my dear,' Mrs Pope said, going to her and putting a hand on her arm.

'I am only thinking of Mrs Abercrombie's wishes,' Plunkett said, unmoved and still severe. 'Her wishes didn't say the old doctor should be hounded.'

Mrs Pope continued to murmur consolation. She sat Miss Bell down at the table. Tindall went to a drawer in the dresser and took from it a number of household tissues which she placed in front of Miss Bell. Mr Apse pressed the shredded tobacco into his pipe.

'I see no reason at all not to have a private household funeral,' Plunkett said. He spoke slowly, emphasising the repetition in his statement, summing everything up. What right had the stupid little creature to create a ridiculous fuss when the other three would easily now have left everything in his hands? It wasn't she who mattered, or she who had the casting vote: it was old Ripley, still standing on the doorstep.

'No,' Miss Bell whispered. 'No, no.'

It was a nightmare. It was a nightmare to be crouched over the kitchen table, with Mrs Pope's hand on her shoulder and tissues laid out in front of her. It was a nightmare to think that Mr Apse wouldn't have cared what they did with Mrs Abercrombie, that Tindall wouldn't have cared, that Mrs Pope was coming round to Plunkett's horrible suggestions. It was a nightmare to think of the doctor being blackmailed by Plunkett's oily tongue. Plunkett was like an animal, some creature out of which a devil of hell had come.

'Best maybe to have a chat with the doctor,' Miss Bell heard Mrs Pope's voice say, and heard the agreement of Tindall, soothing, like a murmur. She was aware of Mr Apse nodding his head. Plunkett said:

'I think that's fair.'

'No. No, no,' Miss Bell cried.

'Then what is fair, Miss Bell?' Mrs Pope, quite sharply, asked.

'Mrs Abercrombie is dead. It must be reported.'

'That's the doctor's job,' Plunkett pointed out. 'It don't concern us.'

'The doctor'll know,' Tindall said, considering it odd that Plunkett had all of a sudden used bad grammar, a lapse she had never before heard from him.

Without saying anything else, Plunkett left the kitchen.

Dr Ripley, who had pulled the bell four times, was pulling it again when Plunkett opened the hall-door. The butler, Dr Ripley thought, was looking dishevelled and somewhat flushed. Blood pressure, he automatically said to himself, while commenting on the weather.

'She died,' Plunkett said. 'I wanted to tell you in person, Doctor.'

They stood for a moment while Plunkett explained the circumstances, giving the time of death as nine-thirty or thereabouts.

'I'm really sorry,' Dr Ripley said. 'Poor dear.'

He mounted the stairs, with Plunkett behind him. Never again would he do so, he said to himself, since he, too, knew that the house was to pass into the possession of an organisation which studied grasses. In the bedroom he examined the body and noted that death was due to simple heart failure, a brief little attack, he reckoned, judging by her countenance and the unflustered arrangement of her body. He sighed over the corpse, although he was used to corpses. It seemed a lifetime, and indeed it was, since he had attended her for a throat infection when she was a bride.

'Heart,' Dr Ripley said on the landing outside the bedroom. 'She was very beautiful, you know. In her day, Plunkett.'

Plunkett nodded. He stood aside to allow the doctor to precede him downstairs.

'She'll be happy,' Dr Ripley said. 'Being still in love with her husband.'

Again Plunkett nodded, even though the doctor couldn't see him. 'We wondered what best to do,' he said.

'Do?'

'You'll be issuing a certificate?'

'Well yes, of course.'

'It was that we were wondering about. The others and myself.'

'Wondering?'

'I'd like a chat with you, Doctor.'

Dr Ripley, who hadn't turned his head while having this conversation, reached the hall. Plunkett stepped round him and led the way to the drawing-room.

'A glass of sherry?' Plunkett suggested.

'Well, that's most kind of you, Plunkett. In the circumstances – '

'I think she'd have wished you to have one, sir.'

'Yes, maybe she would.'

Plunkett poured from a decanter and handed Dr Ripley the glass. He waited for the doctor to sip before he spoke.

'She sent a message to you, Doctor. Late last night she rang her bell and asked for me. She said she had a feeling she might die in the night. "If I do," she said, "I don't want him blamed." '

'Blamed? Who blamed? I don't understand you, Plunkett.'

'I asked her that myself. "Who blamed?" I said, and she said: "Dr Ripley." '

Plunkett watched while a mouthful of sherry was consumed. He moved to the decanter and carried it to Dr Ripley's glass. Mrs Abercrombie had had a heart attack, Dr Ripley said. He couldn't have saved her even if he'd been called in time.

'Naturally, we didn't send for you last night, sir, even though she said that. On account of your attitude, Doctor.'

'Attitude?'

'You considered her a hypochondriac, sir.'

'Mrs Abercrombie was.'

'No, sir. She was a sick woman.'

Dr Ripley finished his second glass of sherry and crossed the drawing-room to the decanter. He poured some more, filling the glass to the brim.

'I'm afraid,' he said, 'I've no idea what you're talking about, Plunkett.'

In the kitchen they did not speak. Mrs Pope made more coffee and put pieces of shortbread on a plate. No one ate the shortbread, and Miss Bell shook her head when Mrs Pope began to refill her coffee-cup.

'Bovril, dear?' Mrs Pope suggested, but Miss Bell rejected Bovril also.

The garden had an atmosphere, different scents came out at different times of year, varying also from season to season. It was in the garden that she'd realised how unhappy she'd been, for eleven years, teaching geography. Yet even if the garden were Paradise itself you couldn't just bury a dead woman in it and pretend she hadn't died. Every day of your life you'd pass the mound, your whole existence would be a lie.

'I'll go away,' Miss Bell said shakily, in a whisper. 'I'll pack and go. I promise you, I'll never tell a thing.'

To Dr Ripley's astonishment, Mrs Abercrombie's butler accused him of negligence and added that it would have been Mrs Abercrombie's desire to hush the matter up. He said that Mrs Abercrombie would never have wished to disgrace an old man.

'What I'm suggesting,' Plunkett said, 'is that you give the cause of death to suit yourself and then become forgetful.'

'Forgetful?'

'Leave the certificate behind you, sir, as if in error.'

'But it has to be handed in, Plunkett. Look here, there's no disgrace involved, or negligence or anything else. You haven't been drinking, have you?'

'It's a decision we came to in the kitchen, Doctor. We're all agreed.'

'But for heaven's sake, man – '

'Mrs Abercrombie's wish was that her body should be buried in the shrubbery, beside her husband's. That can be quietly done. Your good name would continue, Doctor, without a stain. Whether or not you take on further patients is your own affair.'

Dr Ripley sat down. He stared through wire-rimmed spectacles at a man he had always considered pleasant. Yet this same man was now clearly implying that he was more of an undertaker than a doctor.

'What I am saying, sir, is that Rews Manor shall continue as Mrs Abercrombie wished it to. What I am saying is that you and we shall enter into the small conspiracy that Mrs Abercrombie is guiding us towards.'

'Guiding?'

'Since her death she has been making herself felt all over the house. Read that, sir.'

He handed Dr Ripley the letter from Mrs Abercrombie's solicitors, which Dr Ripley slowly read and handed back. Plunkett said:

'It would be disgraceful to go against the wishes of the recently dead, especially those of a person like Mrs Abercrombie, who was kindness itself – to all of us, and to you, sir.'

'You're suggesting that her death should be suppressed, Plunkett? So that you and the others may remain here?'

'So that you may not face charges, sir.'

'But, for the Lord's sake, man, I'd face no charges. I've done nothing at all.'

'A doctor can be in trouble for doing nothing, when he should be doing everything, when he should be prolonging life instead of saying his patients are imagining things.'

'But Mrs Abercrombie did – '

'In the kitchen we're all agreed, sir. We remember, Doctor. We remember Miss Bell's hand a few years ago, that she nearly died of. Criminal neglect, they said in the out-patients'. Another thing, we remember the time we had to get your car out of the ditch.'

'I skidded. There was ice – '

'I have seen you drunk, Doctor,' Plunkett said, 'at half-past ten in the morning.'

Dr Ripley stared harder at Plunkett, believing him now to be insane. He didn't say anything for a moment and then, recovering from his bewilderment, he spoke quietly and slowly. There was a perfectly good explanation for the skid on the icy snow of the drive: he'd braked to avoid a blackbird that was limping about in front of him. He'd never in his life been drunk at half-past ten in the morning.

'You know as well as I do,' Plunkett continued, as though he were deaf or as though the doctor hadn't spoken, 'you know as well as I do that Mrs Abercrombie wouldn't rest if she was responsible for getting you into the Sunday papers.'

In the kitchen they did not reply when Miss Bell said she'd pack and go. They didn't look at her, and she knew they were thinking that she wouldn't be able to keep her word. They were thinking she was hysterical and frightened, and that the weight of so eccentric a secret would prove too much for her.

'It's just that Mrs Abercrombie wanted to change her will, dear,' Mrs Pope said.

'Yes,' said Mr Apse.

They spoke gently, in soft tones like Miss Bell's own. They looked at her in a gentle way, and Tindall smiled at her, gently also. They'd be going against Mrs Abercrombie as soon as she was dead, Tindall said, speaking as softly as the others had spoken. They must abide by what had been in Mrs Abercrombie's heart, Mr Apse said.

Again Miss Bell wondered what she would do when she left the garden, and wondered then if she had the right to plunge these people into unhappiness. With their faces so gently disposed before her, and with Plunkett out of the room, she saw for the first time their point of view. She said to herself that Plunkett would return to normal, since all her other knowledge of him seemed to prove that he was not a wicked man. Certainly there was no wickedness in Mrs Pope or Mr Apse, or in Tindall; and was it really so terrible, she found herself wondering then, to take from Mrs Abercombie what she had wished to give? Did it make sense to quibble now when you had never quibbled over Dr Ripley's diagnosis of hypochondria?

Miss Bell imagined the mound in the shrubbery beside the other mound, and meals in the kitchen, the same as ever, and visitors in the garden on a Sunday, and the admission charges still passed on to the Nurses. She imagined, as often she had, growing quite old in the setting she had come to love.

'A quiet little funeral,' Mrs Pope said. 'She'd have wanted that.'

'Yes,' Mr Apse said.

In her quiet voice, not looking at anyone, Miss Bell apologised for making a fuss.

*　　*　　*

To Dr Ripley's surprise, Plunkett took a packet of cigarettes from his pocket and lit one. He blew out smoke. He said:

'Neglected gallstones: don't wriggle out of it, Doctor.' His voice was cool and ungracious. He regarded Dr Ripley contemptuously. 'What about Bell's hand? That woman near died as well.'

For a moment Dr Ripley felt incapable of a reply. He remembered the scratch on Miss Bell's hand, a perfectly clean little wound. He'd put some iodine on it and a sticking-plaster dressing. He'd told her on no account to go poking it into her flower-beds, but of course she'd taken no notice.

'Miss Bell was extremely foolish,' he said at length, speaking quietly. 'She should have returned to me the moment the complication began.'

'You weren't to be found, Doctor. You were in the bar of the Clarence Hotel or down in the Royal Oak, or the Rogues' Arms – '

'I am not a drunkard, Plunkett. I was not negligent in the matter of Miss Bell's hand. Nor was I negligent over Mrs Abercrombie. Mrs Abercrombie suffered in no way whatsoever from gallstone trouble. Her heart was a little tired; she had a will to die and she died.'

'That isn't true, Doctor. She had a will to live, as this letter proves. She had a will to get matters sorted out – '

'If I were you, Plunkett, I'd go and lie down for a while.'

Dr Ripley spoke firmly. The astonishment that the butler had caused in him had vanished, leaving him unflustered and professional. His eyes behind their spectacles stared steadily into Plunkett's. He didn't seem at all beyond the work he did.

'Your car skidded,' Plunkett said, though without his

previous confidence. 'You were whistled to the gills on Christmas booze that day – '

'That's offensive and untrue, Plunkett.'

'All I'm saying, sir, is that it'd be better for all concerned – '

'I'd be obliged if you didn't speak to me in that manner, Plunkett.'

To Plunkett's horror, Dr Ripley began to go. He placed his empty sherry glass on the table beside the decanter. He buttoned his jacket.

'Please, sir,' Plunkett said, changing his tone a little and hastening towards the sherry decanter. 'Have another glassful, sir.'

Dr Ripley ignored the invitation. 'I would just like to speak to the others,' he said, 'before I go.'

'Of course. Of course, sir.'

It was, Dr Ripley recognised afterwards, curiosity that caused him to make that request. Were the others in the same state as Plunkett? Had they, too, changed in a matter of hours from being agreeable people to being creatures you could neither like nor respect nor even take seriously? Would they, too, accuse him to his face of negligence and drunkenness?

In the kitchen the others rose to their feet when he entered.

'Doctor's here to have a word,' Plunkett said. He added that Dr Ripley had come to see their point of view, a statement that Dr Ripley didn't contradict immediately. He said instead that he was sorry that Mrs Abercrombie had died.

'Oh, so are we, sir,' Mrs Pope cried. 'We're sorry and shaken, sir.'

But in the kitchen Dr Ripley didn't feel their sorrow, any more than he had felt sorrow emanating from Plunkett in the drawing-room. In the kitchen there appeared to be fear in the eyes of quiet Mr Apse and in the eyes of Mrs Pope and the softly-spoken Miss Bell, and in the eyes of Tindall. It was fear, Dr Ripley suddenly realised, that had distorted Plunkett and continued to distort him, though differently now. Fear had bred greed in them, fear had made them desperate, and had turned them into fools.

'Dr Ripley'll see us through,' Plunkett said.

When he told the truth, they didn't say anything at all. Not even Plunkett spoke, and for a moment the only sound in the kitchen was the soft weeping of Miss Bell.

'Her wishes were clear,' Dr Ripley said. 'She died when she knew she'd made them so, when she received the letter this morning. Her wishes would have been honoured in law, even though they weren't in a will.'

They stood like statues in the kitchen. The weeping of Miss Bell ceased; there was no sound at all. They would none of them remain in the house now, Dr Ripley thought, because of their exposure one to another. In guilt and deception they had imagined they would remain, held together by their aberration. But now, with the memory of their greed and the irony of their error, there would be hatred and shame among them.

He wanted to comfort them, but could not. He wanted to say that they should forget what had taken place since Mrs Abercrombie's death, that they should attempt to carry out her wishes. But he knew it was too late for any of that. He turned and went away, leaving them still standing like statues. It was strange, he thought as he made his way through the house, that a happiness which had been so rich should have trailed such a snare behind it. And yet it seemed cruelly fitting that the loss of so much should wreak such damage in pleasant, harmless people.

Mrs Acland's Ghosts

Mr Mockler was a tailor. He carried on his business in a house that after twenty-five years of mortgage arrangements had finally become his: 22 Juniper Street, S.W.17. He had never married and since he was now sixty-three it seeemd likely that he never would. In an old public house, the Charles the First, he had a drink every evening with his friends Mr Uprichard and Mr Tile, who were tailors also. He lived in his house in Juniper Street with his cat Sam, and did his own cooking and washing and cleaning: he was not unhappy.

On the morning of October 19th, 1972, Mr Mockler received a letter that astonished him. It was neatly written in a pleasantly rounded script that wasn't difficult to decipher. It did not address him as 'Dear Mr Mockler', nor was it signed, nor conventionally concluded. But his name was used repeatedly, and from its contents it seemed to Mr Mockler that the author of the letter was a Mrs Acland. He read the letter in amazement and then read it again and then, more slowly, a third time.

Dr Scott-Rowe is dead, Mr Mockler. I know he is dead because a new man is here, a smaller, younger man, called Dr Friendman. He looks at us, smiling, with his unblinking eyes. Miss Acheson says you can tell at a glance that he has practised hypnosis.

They're so sure of themselves, Mr Mockler: beyond the limits of their white-coated world they can accept nothing. I am a woman imprisoned because I once saw ghosts. I am paid for by the man who was my husband, who writes out monthly cheques for the peaches they bring to my room, and the beef olives and the *marrons glacés*. 'She must above all things be happy,' I can imagine the stout man who was my husband saying, walking with Dr Scott-Rowe over the sunny lawns and among the rosebeds. In this house there are twenty disturbed people in private rooms, cosseted by luxury because other people feel guilty. And when we walk ourselves on the lawns and among the rosebeds we murmur at the folly of those who have so expensively committed us, and at the greater folly of the medical profession: you can be disturbed without being mad. Is this the letter of a lunatic, Mr Mockler?

I said this afternoon to Miss Acheson that Dr Scott-Rowe was dead. She said she knew. All of us would have Dr Friendman now, she said, with his smile and his tape recorders. 'May Dr Scott-Rowe rest in peace,' said Miss Acheson: it was better to be dead than to be like Dr Friendman. Miss Acheson is a very old lady, twice my age exactly: I am thirty-nine and she is seventy-eight. She was committed when she was eighteen, in 1913, a year before the First World War. Miss Acheson was disturbed by visions of St Olaf of Norway and she still is. Such visions were an embarrassment to Miss Acheson's family in 1913 and so they quietly slipped her away. No one comes to see her now, no one has since 1927.

'You must write it all down,' Miss Acheson said to me when I told her, years ago, that I'd been committed because I'd seen ghosts and that I could prove the ghosts were real because the Rachels had seen them too. The Rachels are living some normal existence somewhere, yet they were terrified half out of their wits at the time and I wasn't frightened at all. The trouble nowadays, Miss Acheson says and I quite agree, is that if you like having ghosts near you people think you're round the bend.

I was talking to Miss Acheson about all this yesterday and she said why didn't I do what Sarah Crookham used to do? There's nothing the matter with Sarah Crookham, any more than there is with Miss Acheson or myself: all that Sarah Crookham suffers from is a broken heart. 'You must write it all down,' Miss Acheson said to her when she first came here, weeping, poor thing, every minute of the day. So she wrote it down and posted it to A. J. Rawson, a person she found in the telephone directory. But Mr Rawson never came, nor another person Sarah Crookham wrote to. I have looked you up in the telephone directory, Mr Mockler. It is nice to have a visitor.

'You must begin at the beginning,' Miss Acheson says, and so I am doing that. The beginning is back a bit, in January 1949, when I was fifteen. We lived in Richmond then, my parents and one brother, George, and my sisters Alice and Isabel. On Sundays, after lunch, we used to walk all together in Richmond Park with our dog, a Dalmatian called Salmon. I was the oldest and Alice was next, two years younger, and George was eleven and Isabel eight. It was lovely walking together in Richmond Park and then going home to Sunday tea. I remember the autumns and winters best, the cosiness of the coal fire, hot sponge cake and special Sunday sandwiches, and little buns that Alice and I always helped to make on Sunday mornings. We played Monopoly by the fire, and George would always have the ship and Anna the hat and Isabel the racing-car and Mummy the dog. Daddy and I would share the old boot. I really loved it.

I loved the house: 17 Lorelei Avenue, an ordinary suburban house built some time in the early nineteen-twenties, when Miss Acheson was still quite young. There were bits of stained glass on either side of the hall-door and a single

stained glass pane, Moses in the bulrushes, in one of the landing windows. At Christmas especially it was lovely: we'd have
the Christmas tree in the hall and always on Christmas Eve,
as long as I can remember, there'd be a party. I can remember
the parties quite vividly. There'd be people standing round
drinking punch and all the children would play hide-and-seek
upstairs, and nobody could ever find George. It's George, Mr
Mockler, that all this is about. And Alice, of course, and Isabel.

When I first described them to Dr Scott-Rowe he said
they sounded marvellous, and I said I thought they probably were, but I suppose a person can be prejudiced in
family matters of that kind. Because they were, after all, my
brother and my two sisters and because, of course, they're
dead now. I mean, they were probably ordinary children, just
like any children. Well, you can see what you think, Mr
Mockler.

George was small for his age, very wiry, dark-haired, a
darting kind of boy who was always laughing, who had often
to be reprimanded by my father because his teachers said he
was the most mischievous boy in his class. Alice, being two
years older, was just the opposite: demure and silent, but
happy in her quiet way, and beautiful, far more beautiful than
I was. Isabel wasn't beautiful at all. She was all freckles, with
long pale plaits and long legs that sometimes could run as
fast as George's. She and George were as close as two persons
can get, but in a way we were all close: there was a lot of love
in 17 Lorelei Avenue.

I had a cold the day it happened, a Saturday it was. I was
cross because they all kept worrying about leaving me in the
house on my own. They'd bring me back Black Magic chocolates, they said, and my mother said she'd buy a bunch of
daffodils if she saw any. I heard the car crunching over the
gravel outside the garage, and then their voices telling Salmon
not to put his paws on the upholstery. My father blew the

horn, saying goodbye to me, and after that the silence began. I must have known even then, long before it happened, that nothing would be the same again.

When I was twenty-two, Mr Mockler, I married a man called Acland, who helped me to get over the tragedy. George would have been eighteen, and Anna twenty and Isabel fifteen. They would have liked my husband because he was a good-humoured and generous man. He was very plump, many years older than I was, with a fondness for all food. 'You're like a child,' I used to say to him and we'd laugh together. Cheese in particular he liked, and ham and all kinds of root vegetables, parsnips, turnips, celeriac, carrots, leeks, potatoes. He used to come back to the house and take four or five pounds of gammon from the car, and chops, and blocks of ice-cream, and biscuits, and two or even three McVitie's fruitcakes. He was very partial to McVitie's fruitcakes. At night, at nine or ten o'clock, he'd make cocoa for both of us and we'd have it while we were watching the television, with a slice or two of fruitcake. He was such a kind man in those days. I got quite fat myself, which might surprise you, Mr Mockler, because I'm on the thin side now.

My husband was, and still is, both clever and rich. One led to the other: he made a fortune designing metal fasteners for the aeroplane industry. Once, in May 1960, he drove me to a house in Worcestershire. 'I wanted it to be a surprise,' he said, stopping his mustard-coloured Alfa-Romeo in front of this quite extensive Victorian façade. 'There,' he said, embracing me, reminding me that it was my birthday. Two months later we went to live there.

We had no children. In the large Victorian house I made my life with the man I'd married and once again, as in 17 Lorelei Avenue, I was happy. The house was near a village but otherwise remote. My husband went away from it by day, to the place where his aeroplane fasteners were manufactured and tested. There were – and still are – aeroplanes in the air which would have fallen to pieces if they hadn't been securely fastened by the genius of my husband.

The house had many rooms. There was a large square drawing-room with a metal ceiling – beaten tin, I believe it was. It had patterns like wedding-cake icing on it. It was painted white and blue and gave, as well as the impression of a wedding-cake, a Wedgwood effect. People remarked on this ceiling and my husband used to explain that metal ceilings had once been very popular, especially in the large houses of Australia. Well-to-do Australians, apparently, would have them shipped from Birmingham in colonial imitation of an English fashion. My husband and I, arm in arm, would lead people about the house, pointing out the ceiling or the green wallpaper in our bedroom or the portraits that hung on the stairs.

The lighting was bad in the house. The long first-floor landing was a gloomy place by day and lit by a single wall-light at night. At the end of this landing another flight of stairs, less grand than the stairs that led from the hall, wound upwards to the small rooms that had once upon a time been servants' quarters, and another flight continued above them to attics and store-rooms. The bathroom was on the first floor, tiled in green Victorian tiles, and there was a lavatory next door to it, encased in mahogany.

In the small rooms that had once been the servants' quarters lived Mr and Mrs Rachels. My husband had had a kitchen and a bathroom put in for them so that their rooms were quite self-contained. Mr Rachels worked in the garden and his wife cleaned the house. It wasn't really necessary to have them at all: I could have cleaned the house myself and even done the gardening, but my husband insisted in his generous way. At night I could hear the Rachels moving about above me. I didn't like this and my husband asked them to move more quietly.

In 1962 my husband was asked to go to Germany, to explain his aeroplane fasteners to the German aircraft industry. It was to be a prolonged trip, three months at least, and I was naturally unhappy when he told me. He was unhappy himself, but on March 4th he flew to Hamburg, leaving me with the Rachels.

They were a pleasant enough couple, somewhere in their fifties I would think, he rather silent, she inclined to talk. The only thing that worried me about them was the way they used to move about at night above my head. After my husband had gone to Germany I gave Mrs Rachels money to buy slippers, but I don't think she ever did because the sounds continued just as before. I naturally didn't make a fuss about it.

On the night of March 7th I was awakened by a band playing in the house. The tune was an old tune of the fifties called, I believe, 'Looking for Henry Lee'. The noise was very loud in my bedroom and I lay there frightened, not knowing why this noise should be coming to me like this, Victor Silvester in strict dance tempo. Then a voice spoke, a long babble of French, and I realised that I was listening to a radio programme. The wireless was across the room, on a table by the windows. I put on my bedside light and got up and switched it off. I drank some orange juice and went back to sleep. It didn't even occur to me to wonder who had turned the wireless on.

The next day I told Mrs Rachels about it, and it was she, in fact, who made me think that it was all rather stranger than it seemed. I definitely remembered turning the wireless off myself before going to bed, and in any case I was not in the habit of listening to French stations, so that even if the wireless had somehow come on of its own accord it should not have been tuned in to a French station.

Two days later I found the bath half-filled with water and the towels all rumpled and damp, thrown about on the floor. The water in the bath was tepid and dirty: someone, an hour or so ago, had had a bath.

I climbed the stairs to the Rachels' flat and knocked on their door. 'Is your bathroom out of order?' I said when Mr Rachels came to the door, not wearing the slippers I'd given them money for. I said I didn't at all mind their using mine, only I'd be grateful if they'd remember to let the water out and to bring down their own towels. Mr Rachels looked at me in the way people have sometimes, as though you're insane. He called his wife and all three of us went down to look at my bathroom. They denied emphatically that either of them had had a bath.

When I came downstairs the next morning, having slept badly, I found the kitchen table had been laid for four. There was a table-cloth on the table, which was something I never bothered about, and a kettle was boiling on the Aga. Beside it, a large brown teapot, not the one I normally used, was heating. I made some tea and sat down, thinking about the Rachels. Why should they behave like this? Why should they creep into my bedroom in the middle of the night and turn the wireless on? Why should they have a bath in my bathroom and deny it? Why should they lay the breakfast table as though we had overnight guests? I left the table just as it was. Butter had been rolled into pats. Marmalade had been placed in two china dishes. A silver toast-rack that an aunt of my husband had given us as a wedding present was waiting for toast.

'Thank you for laying the table,' I said to Mrs Rachels when she entered the kitchen an hour later.

She shook her head. She began to say that she hadn't laid the table but then she changed her mind. I could see from her face that she and her husband had been discussing the matter of the bath the night before. She could hardly wait to tell him about the breakfast table. I smiled at her.

'A funny thing happened the other night,' I said. 'I woke up to find Victor Silvester playing a tune called "Looking for Henry Lee".'

'Henry Lee?' Mrs Rachels said, turning around from the sink. Her face, usually blotched with pink, like the skin of an apple, was white.

'It's an old song of the fifties.'

It was while saying that that I realised what was happening in the house. I naturally didn't say anything to Mrs Rachels, and I at once began to regret that I'd said anything in the first place. It had frightened me, finding the bathroom like that, and clearly it must have frightened the Rachels. I didn't want them to be frightened because naturally there was nothing to be frightened about. George and Alice and Isabel wouldn't hurt anyone, not unless death had changed them enormously. But even so I knew I couldn't ever explain that to the Rachels.

'Well, I suppose I'm just getting absentminded,' I said. 'People do, so they say, when they live alone.' I laughed to show I wasn't worried or frightened, to make it all seem ordinary.

'You mean, you laid the table yourself?' Mrs Rachels said. 'And had a bath?'

'And didn't turn the wireless off properly. Funny,' I said, 'how these things go in threes. Funny, how there's always an explanation.' I laughed again and Mrs Rachels had to laugh too.

After that it was lovely, just like being back in 17 Lorelei Avenue. I bought Black Magic chocolates and bars of Fry's and Cadbury's Milk, all the things we'd liked. I often found bathwater left in and the towels crumpled, and now and again I came down in the morning to find the breakfast table laid.

On the first-floor landing, on the evening of March 11th, I caught a glimpse of George, and in the garden, three days later, I saw Isabel and Alice.

On March 15th the Rachels left. I hadn't said a word to them about finding the bathroom used again or the breakfast laid or actually seeing the children. I'd been cheerful and smiling whenever I met them. I'd talked about how Brasso wasn't as good as it used to be to Mrs Rachels, and had asked her husband about the best kinds of soil for bulbs.

'We can't stay a minute more,' Mrs Rachels said, her face all white and tight in the hall, and then to my astonishment they attempted to persuade me to go also.

'The house isn't fit to live in,' Mr Rachels said.

'Oh now, that's nonsense,' I began to say, but they both shook their heads.

'There's children here,' Mrs Rachels said. 'There's three children appearing all over the place.'

'Come right up to you,' Mr Rachels said. 'Laugh at you sometimes.'

They were trembling, both of them. They were so terrified I thought they might die, that their hearts would give out there in the hall and they'd just drop down. But they didn't. They walked out of the hall-door with their three suitcases, down the drive to catch a bus. I never saw them again.

I suppose, Mr Mockler, you have to be frightened of ghosts: I suppose that's their way of communicating. I mean, it's no good being like me, delighting in it all, being happy because I wasn't lonely in that house any more. You have to be like the Rachels, terrified half out of your wits. I think I knew that as I watched the Rachels go: I think I knew that George and Isabel and Alice would go with them, that I was only a kind of go-between, that the Rachels were what George and Isabel and Alice could really have fun with. I almost ran after the Rachels, but I knew it would be no good.

Without the Rachels and my brother and my two sisters, I was frightened myself in that big house. I moved everything into the kitchen: the television set and the plants I kept in the drawing-room, and a camp-bed to sleep on. I was there, asleep in the camp-bed, when my husband returned from Germany; he had changed completely. He raved at me, not listening to a word I said. There were cups of tea all over the house, he said, and bits of bread and biscuits and cake and chocolates. There were notes in envelopes, and messages scrawled in my handwriting on the wallpaper in various rooms. Everywhere was dusty. Where, he wanted to know, were the Rachels?

He stood there with a canvas bag in his left hand, an airline bag that had the word *Lufthansa* on it. He'd put on at least a stone, I remember thinking, and his hair was shorter than before.

'Listen,' I said, 'I would like to tell you.' And I tried to tell him, as I've told you, Mr Mockler, about George and Isabel and Alice in 17 Lorelei Avenue and how we all went together for a walk with our dog, every Sunday afternoon in Richmond Park, and how on Christmas Eve my mother always gave a party. I told him about the stained-glass pane in the window, Moses in the bulrushes, and the hide-and-seek we played, and how my father and I always shared the old boot in Monopoly. I told him about the day of the accident, how the tyre on the lorry suddenly exploded and how the lorry went whizzing around on the road and then just tumbled over on top of them. I'd put out cups of tea, I said, and biscuits and cake and the little messages, just in case they came back again – not for them to eat or to read particularly, but just as a sign. They'd given me a sign first, I explained: George had turned on my wireless in the middle of the night and Isabel had had baths and Alice had laid the breakfast table. But then they'd gone because they'd been more interested in annoying the Rachels than in comforting me. I began to weep, telling him how lonely I'd been without them, how lonely I'd been ever since the day of the accident, how the silence had been everywhere. I couldn't control myself: tears came out of my eyes as though they'd never stop. I felt sickness all over my body, paining me in my head and my chest, sour in my stomach. I wanted to die because the loneliness was too much. Loneliness was the worst thing in the world, I said, gasping out words, with spit and tears going cold on my face. People were only shadows, I tried to explain, when you had loneliness and silence like that, like a shroud around you. You couldn't reach out of the shroud sometimes, you couldn't connect because shadows are hard to connect with and it's frightening when you try because everyone is looking at you. But it was lovely, I whispered, when the children came back to annoy the Rachels. My husband replied by telling me I was insane.

The letter finished there, and Mr Mockler was more astonished each time he read it. He had never in his life received such a document before, nor did he in fact very often receive letters of any kind, apart from bills and, if he was fortunate, cheques in settlement. He shook his head over the letter and placed it in the inside pocket of his jacket.

That day, as he stitched and measured, he imagined the place Mrs Acland wrote of, the secluded house with twenty female inmates, and the lawn and the rosebeds. He imagined the other house, 17 Lorelei Avenue in Richmond, and the third house, the Victorian residence in the Worcestershire countryside. He imagined Mrs Acland's obese husband with his short hair and his aeroplane fasteners, and the children who had been killed in a motor-car accident, and Mr and Mrs Rachels whom they had haunted. All day long the faces of these people flitted through Mr Mockler's mind, with old Miss Acheson and Sarah Crookham and Dr Scott-Rowe and

Dr Friendman. In the evening, when he met his friends Mr
Tile and Mr Uprichard in the Charles the First, he showed
them the letter before even ordering them drinks.

'Well, I'm beggared,' remarked Mr Uprichard, a man
known locally for his gentle nature. 'That poor creature.'

Mr Tile, who was not given to expressing himself, shook
his head.

Mr Mockler asked Mr Uprichard if he should visit this Mrs
Acland. 'Poor creature,' Mr Uprichard said again, and added
that without a doubt Mrs Acland had written to a stranger
because of the loneliness she mentioned, the loneliness like
a shroud around her.

Some weeks later Mr Mockler, having given the matter
further thought and continuing to be affected by the contents
of the letter, took a Green Line bus out of London to the
address that Mrs Acland had given him. He made enquiries,
feeling quite adventurous, and was told that the house was
three-quarters of a mile from where the bus had dropped
him, down a side road. He found it without further difficulty.
It was a house surrounded by a high brick wall in which
large, black wrought-iron gates were backed with sheets of
tin so that no one could look through the ornamental scroll-
work. The gates were locked. Mr Mockler rang a bell in the
wall.

'Yes?' a man said, opening the gate that was on Mr Mockler's left.

'Well,' said Mr Mockler and found it difficult to proceed.

'Yes?' the man said.

'Well, I've had a letter. Asking me to come, I think. My
name's Mockler.'

The man opened the gate a little more and Mr Mockler
stepped through.

The man walked ahead of him and Mr Mockler saw the
lawns that had been described, and the rosebeds. The house

he considered most attractive: a high Georgian building with beautiful windows. An old woman was walking slowly by herself with the assistance of a stick: Miss Acheson, Mr Mockler guessed. In the distance he saw other women, walking slowly on leaf-strewn paths.

Autumn was Mr Mockler's favourite season and he was glad to be in the country on this pleasantly autumnal day. He thought of remarking on this to the man who led him towards the house, but since the man did not incline towards conversation he did not do so.

In the yellow waiting-room there were no magazines and no pictures on the walls and no flowers. It was not a room in which Mr Mockler would have cared to wait for long, and in fact he did not have to. A woman dressed as a nurse except that she wore a green cardigan came in. She smiled briskly at him and said that Dr Friendman would see him. She asked Mr Mockler to follow her.

'How very good of you to come,' Dr Friendman said, smiling at Mr Mockler in the way that Mrs Acland had described in her letter. 'How very humane,' said Dr Friendman.

'I had a letter, from a Mrs Acland.'

'Quite so, Mr Mockler. Mr Mockler, could I press you towards a glass of sherry?'

Mr Mockler, surprised at this line of talk, accepted the sherry, saying it was good of Dr Friendman. He drank the sherry while Dr Friendman read the letter. When he'd finished, Dr Friendman crossed to the window of the room and pulled aside a curtain and asked Mr Mockler if he'd mind looking out.

There was a courtyard, small and cobbled, in which a gardener was sweeping leaves into a pile. At the far end of it, sitting on a tapestry-backed dining-chair in the autumn sunshine, was a woman in a blue dress. 'Try these,' said Dr Friendman and handed Mr Mockler a pair of binoculars.

It was a beautiful face, thin and seeming fragile, with large blue eyes and lips that were now slightly parted, smiling in the sunshine. Hair the colour of corn was simply arranged, hanging on either side of the face and curling in around it. The hair shone in the sunlight, as though it was for ever being brushed.

'I find them useful,' Dr Friendman said, taking the binoculars from Mr Mockler's hands. 'You have to keep an eye, you know.'

'That's Mrs Acland?' Mr Mockler asked.

'That's the lady who wrote to you: the letter's a bit inaccurate, Mr Mockler. It wasn't quite like that in 17 Lorelei Avenue.'

'Not quite like it?'

'She cannot forget Lorelei Avenue. I'm afraid she never will. That beautiful woman, Mr Mockler, was a beautiful girl, yet she married the first man who asked her, a widower thirty years older than her, a fat designer of aircraft fasteners. He pays her bills just as she says in her letter, and even when he's dead they'll go on being paid. He used to visit her at first, but he found it too painful. He stood in this very room one day, Mr Mockler, and said to Dr Scott-Rowe that no man had ever been appreciated by a woman as much as he had by her. And all because he'd been kind to her in the most ordinary ways.'

Mr Mockler said he was afraid that he didn't know what Dr Friendman was talking about. As though he hadn't heard this quiet protest, Dr Friendman smiled and said:

'But it was, unfortunately, too late for kindness. 17 Lorelei Avenue had done its damage, like a cancer in her mind: she could not forget her childhood.'

'Yes, she says in her letter. George and Alice and Isabel – '

'All her childhood, Mr Mockler, her parents did not speak to one another. They didn't quarrel, they didn't address each other in any way whatsoever. When she was five they'd come to an agreement: that they should both remain in 17 Lorelei Avenue because neither would ever have agreed to give up an inch of the child they'd between them caused to be born. In the house there was nothing, Mr Mockler, for all her childhood years: nothing except silence.'

'But there was George and Alice and Isabel – '

'No, Mr Mockler. There was no George and no Alice and no Isabel. No hide-and-seek or parties on Christmas Eve, no Monopoly on Sundays by the fire. Can you imagine 17 Lorelei Avenue, Mr Mockler, as she is now incapable of imagining it? Two people so cruel to one another that they knew that either of them could be parted from the child in some divorce court. A woman bitterly hating the man whom once she'd loved, and he returning each evening, hurrying back from an office in case his wife and the child were having a conversation. She would sit, Mr Mockler, in a room with them, with the silence heavy in the air, and their hatred for one another. All three of them would sit down to a meal and no one would speak. No other children came to that house, no other people. She used to hide on the way back from school: she'd go down the area steps of other houses and crouch beside dustbins.'

'Dustbins?' repeated Mr Mockler, more astonished than ever. '*Dustbins?*'

'Other children didn't take to her. She couldn't talk to them. She'd never learned to talk to anyone. He was a patient man, Mr Acland, when he came along, a good and patient man.'

Mr Mockler said that the child's parents must have been monsters, but Dr Friendman shook his head. No one was a monster, Dr Friendman said in a professional manner, and in the circumstances Mr Mockler didn't feel he could argue with him. But the people called Rachels were real, he did point out, as real as the fat designer of aircraft fasteners. Had they left the house, he asked, as it said in the letter? And if they had, what had they been frightened of?

Dr Friendman smiled again. 'I don't believe in ghosts,' he said, and he explained at great length to Mr Mockler that it was Mrs Acland herself who had frightened the Rachels, turning on a wireless in the middle of the night and running baths and laying tables for people who weren't there. Mr Mockler listened and was interested to note that Dr Friendman used words that were not easy to understand, and quoted from experts who were in Dr Friendman's line of business but whose names meant nothing to Mr Mockler.

Mr Mockler, listening to all of it, nodded but was not convinced. The Rachels had left the house, just as the letter said: he knew that, he felt it in his bones and it felt like the truth. The Rachels had been frightened of Mrs Acland's ghosts even though they'd been artificial ghosts. They'd been real to her, and they'd been real to the Rachels because she'd made them so. Shadows had stepped out of her mind because in her loneliness she'd wished them to. They'd laughed and played, and frightened the Rachels half out of their wits.

'There's always an explanation,' said Dr Friendman.

Mr Mockler nodded, profoundly disagreeing.

'She'll think you're Mr Rachels,' said Dr Friendman, 'come to say he saw the ghosts. If you wouldn't mind saying you did, it keeps her happy.'

'But it's the truth,' Mr Mockler cried with passion in his voice. 'Of course it's the truth: there can be ghosts like that, just as there can be in any other way.'

'Oh, come now,' murmured Dr Friendman with his sad, humane smile.

Mr Mockler followed Dr Friendman from the room. They crossed a landing and descended a back staircase, passing near a kitchen in which a chef with a tall chef's hat was beating pieces of meat. 'Ah, Wiener Schnitzel,' said Dr Friendman.

In the cobbled courtyard the gardener had finished sweeping up the leaves and was wheeling them away in a wheelbarrow. The woman was still sitting on the tapestry-backed chair, still smiling in the autumn sunshine.

'Look,' said Dr Friendman, 'a visitor.'

A woman rose and went close to Mr Mockler. 'They didn't mean to frighten you,' she said, 'even though it's the only way ghosts can communicate. They were only having fun, Mr Rachels.'

'I think Mr Rachels realises that now,' Dr Friendman said.

'Yes, of course,' said Mr Mockler.

'No one ever believed me, and I kept on saying, "When the Rachels come back, they'll tell the truth about poor George and Alice and Isabel." You saw them, didn't you, Mr Rachels?'

'Yes,' Mr Mockler said. 'We saw them.'

She turned and walked away, leaving the tapestry-backed chair behind her.

'You're a humane person,' Dr Friendman said, holding out his right hand, which Mr Mockler shook. The same man led him back through the lawns and the rosebeds, to the gates.

It was an experience that Mr Mockler found impossible to forget. He measured and stitched, and talked to his friends Mr Uprichard and Mr Tile in the Charles the First; he went for a walk morning and evening, and no day passed during which he did not think of the woman whom people looked at through binoculars. Somewhere in England, or at least somewhere in the world, the Rachels were probably still alive, and had Mr Mockler been a younger man he might even have set about looking for them. He would have liked to bring them to the secluded house where the woman now lived, to have been there himself when they told the truth to Dr Friendman.

It seemed a sadness, as he once remarked to Mr Uprichard, that on top of everything else a woman's artificial ghosts should not be honoured, since she had brought them into being and given them life, as other women give other children life.